Cat Shining Bright

ALSO BY SHIRLEY ROUSSEAU MURPHY

Cat Shout for Joy

Cat Bearing Gifts

Cat Telling Tales

Cat Coming Home

Cat Striking Back

Cat Playing Cupid

Cat Deck the Halls

Cat Pay the Devil

Cat Breaking Free

Cat Cross Their Graves

Cat Fear No Evil

Cat Seeing Double

Cat Laughing Last

Cat Spitting Mad

Cat to the Dogs

Cat in the Dark

Cat Raise the Dead

Cat Under Fire

Cat on the Edge

The Catsworld Portal

BY SHIRLEY ROUSSEAU MURPHY
AND PAT J.J. MURPHY

The Cat, the Devil, the Last Escape

The Cat, the Devil, and Lee Fontana

Cat Shining Bright

A JOE GREY MYSTERY

Shirley Rousseau Murphy

HARPER LUXE

An Imprint of HarperCollinsPublishers

CAT SHINING BRIGHT. Copyright © 2017 by Shirley Rousseau Murphy. All rights reserved. Printed in the United States of America. No part of this book may be used or reproduced in any manner whatsoever without written permission except in the case of brief quotations embodied in critical articles and reviews. For information address HarperCollins Publishers, 195 Broadway, New York, NY 10007.

HarperCollins books may be purchased for educational, business, or sales promotional use. For information please e-mail the Special Markets Department at SPsales@harpercollins.com.

FIRST HARPERLUXE EDITION

ISBN: 978-0-06-267083-0

HarperLuxe™ is a trademark of HarperCollins Publishers.

Library of Congress Cataloging-in-Publication Data is available upon request.

17 18 19 20 21   ID/LSC   10 9 8 7 6 5 4 3 2 1

For Amanda, Ellie, and Sophie

When a young cat dreams, what far lands and ancient times does he bring alive once more?

Does his wild spirit brighten again the fading road he once traveled, embrace again those he knew upon his endless journey?

Does man's own past, if cherished and observed, tell us where *we* have been, and, perhaps, where our own untrodden road might lead?

—ANONYMOUS

Cat Shining Bright

Prologue

O n this early May evening in Wilma Getz's stone cottage, the tall, older woman kneels by the hearth, the blaze reflecting from her long silver ponytail as she adds another log to the fire. Around her, cat friends and humans sit in the flowered chairs and couch but no one is at ease as they usually are in Wilma's welcoming home. All are rigid, waiting. Wilma's slim, redheaded niece, Charlie, holds Joe Grey securely on her lap, the tomcat struggling to get free and go to Dulcie, so nervous he can hardly be still. Hearing his tabby lady's cries, he has tried twice to claw Charlie, shocking them both. Beside them, blond, beautiful Kate Osborne waits restlessly, as do Lucinda and Pedric Greenlaw. The elderly couple snuggles tortoiseshell Kit between them, stroking her fluffy coat, trying to calm her fidgets as well as their own. But Kit will not be calmed, and she does not want to be petted. Rising irritably, she drops to the floor and settles stoically before the hearth beside red tabby Pan, the tomcat straight and solemn, attempting in his own stern way to show no unease. Kit, beside him, tries hard to hide her own nerves, intently listening.

They hear no more cries of pain—but when, from the bedroom, Dr. Firetti calls Wilma, Joe Grey starts to fight Charlie again trying to break free, trying to go to Dulcie, the vanished echo of his lady's whimpers still striking deep through him.

But John Firetti's voice is cheerful. "Could we have the warm blanket now? While Mary and I clean up?" At the pleasure in his voice, everyone relaxes, worried faces turn to smiles. From the bedroom there is only silence, no more cries of pain from Dulcie. As Wilma rises to get the blanket, soft footsteps come down the hall; the doctor's wife appears, Mary's brown hair mussed, her brown eyes aglow with pleasure. "The last kitten has been born. Oh, so beautiful. Three fine kittens," Mary says, "healthy and strong. And Dulcie is just fine," she says, looking deep into Joe Grey's worried yellow eyes. "Let's give her a little while before we go in. Except you, Joe," she says, reaching to pet the tomcat. "You can go see your new family."

Joe leaps off Charlie's lap and heads for the bedroom, shy suddenly, nearly electrified with uncertainty. He has never seen newborn kittens, *not his own kittens*. He slips up onto the bed where he can look down into the kittening box.

There they are, three tiny, beautiful babies. So little and naked, wriggling weakly against their tabby mother: the two buff-colored kits are boys, he can tell by their scent. And, oh my, the girl is going to be a striking calico, he can already see the faint patterns on her tender skin. Dulcie has cleaned them up; she lies resting. The tiny ones squirm close to her, pressing at her, nursing hungrily against her striped belly.

Dr. John Firetti, kneeling over the box, looks up and nods. "Come, Joe. Come down and see your babies."

Joe Grey eases off the bed, approaching warily. He crouches very still, looking into the birthing box at his new family, breathing in their intriguing kitten scent— but he is fearful. Even now he is afraid of how he might respond, he is too aware of the ancient instinct of some tomcats to ravage their own young. Would this age-old urge surface in *him*? Shivering, he is ready to turn and run before he hurts his helpless kittens—and when Dulcie lifts her eyes to him, he sees for an instant the female's equally primitive response, the inborn ferocity of a mother cat to protect her babies.

But then her look softens, her green-eyed gaze is content, loving their kittens, loving him. Joe Grey purrs extravagantly for her. Watching Dulcie and their three beautiful newborns, he knows only wonder; he knows they have made a fine family. Three infants so tiny and perfect that Joe can't resist reaching his nose in, breathing deeper of their sweet kitten aroma.

"Courtney," Dulcie says, licking the calico and looking up at Joe. "You can hardly see her markings, but she will grow into them." She licks the boys. "What kind of lives will these three make, our three tiny mites?" Powerfully the moment holds them, holds the little family in the hands of gentle grace.

1

Those first weeks were idyllic, Dulcie caring for the kittens, washing and nursing them, Joe Grey with them more often than not, galloping over the rooftops between his house and Dulcie's. If he swung by Molena Point PD for a moment to read police reports as he lay casually on the chief's desk, if he worried about the car-theft ring that was working closer and closer down the coast toward Molena Point—already the cops had readied extra forces—if Joe knew in his wily cat soul that it wouldn't be long before the thieves hit their village, he kept his concerns to himself. Dulcie didn't need to fret over a possible new crime wave, all she and the kittens needed was their cozy, safe home, quiet and secure. Wilma kept the TV and radio off, and the newspaper out of sight; nothing of the outer world intruded to disturb the little family's tranquillity, only soft music on the CD player, or a little easy jazz, or Wilma would read to Dulcie, something bright and happy.

Two weeks after the kittens were born their eyes were open and their tiny ears unfurled. Another week and they could see and hear very well and were toddling about their pen. Courtney's colors were clear now, the bright orange and black markings along her back, her white sides and belly, her little white face with orange ears and a circle of pale orange and darker freckles around her muzzle, the three perfect black bracelets circling her right front leg. Now, when the kittens heard Joe Grey come in through the cat door, they squealed with delight. When Joe jumped into the cat pen that Wilma had set up in the kitchen, the babies climbed all over him, pummeling and mauling him, rolling under the tomcat's gentle paws. The biggest question in both parents' minds, the same question that nudged those few humans who knew that Joe Grey and Dulcie could speak, was *when* would the kittens say their first words?

Would they speak? Would they be speaking cats like their parents and like tortoiseshell Kit and red tabby Pan? Or would Joe and Dulcie's babies grow up without knowing the human language, without the humanlike talents of their parents? Everyone was filled with anxious hope, with nervous waiting. Wilma's niece, Charlie, came often to visit, the kittens climbing from her lap to her shoulder to tangle wildly in her long red hair and to pat with curiosity at the celestial scattering of freckles that spilled across her cheeks, making her laugh. Charlie, as Police Chief Max Harper's wife, knew all the details of the coastal auto thefts. She said nothing in front of Dulcie, though she might exchange a glance with Joe Grey. Charlie talked to the kittens of other things, naming items in the kitchen, asking questions, hoping to draw out a word or two. But the babies only meowed.

June rolled away, and still no kitten said a word. Soon it was July and then August. The kittens at three months old were all claws and teeth, loud and demanding yowls, boundless energy, leaping from chair to table, climbing draperies; but not a word did they say. A cat tree stood by Wilma's desk looking out at the garden, another at the dining room window, a third in the bedroom, their carpeted shelves and climbing posts already shredded by sharp claws where calico Courtney and her buff-colored brothers leaped, flew, battled one another, wildly fierce and happy. And still, Courtney and Buffin and Striker said no word.

Every night Wilma read to them, the book open on her lap with the kittens crowded around. Dulcie read to them, and often fluffy, tortoiseshell Kit came to visit and read to them, too; always the kittens' blue eyes followed the words on the page; though they wanted to wrestle and play with Kit, as well, for she was much like a kitten herself. "Will you ever speak to me?" Kit asked them, her yellow eyes wide. "When we read to you—fairy tales or the old myths—I know you understand. Speak the words, Courtney. Say them back to me."

Courtney meowed happily, pawed Kit's nose playful and sly, and switched her calico tail. Kit turned away irritably, settling on the boy kittens. "Speak to me, Buffin. Read to me, Striker." No one said a word. Kit knew they could read, she could tell by their expressions. None of the three were normal kittens. And if they could read, surely they could speak. *Stubborn*, she thought. Her yellow eyes staring into baby-blue eyes, all she could say was, "You are toying with us. You are stubborn kittens, stubborn and willful."

But a week later, it happened: Buffin was the first.

The sand-colored kitten with the gray patch on his shoulder had sneaked out the cat door when it was accidentally left unlocked. Padding into the garden, where he was not allowed alone—because of hawks and stray dogs—he discovered a fledgling bird perched low among a tangle of bushes. The nestling, having tried to fly, had ended in a crash landing.

Buffin, with a surge of inborn killer instinct, was about to pounce on the youngster with raking claws and sharp teeth when a strange new emotion stopped him. He backed away, puzzled.

He had no notion that Dulcie had slipped out the cat door behind him, that she crouched among the flowers feeling excited that he would make his first kill, but feeling sad for the bird as she often did. Mice and rats didn't stir her sympathy but this little bright creature was as lovely as a jewel. But what was Buffin doing?

Carefully and gently he crept forward again. He reared up and, with soft paws, he lifted the little bird down and laid it on the grass. It was only a tiny thing, yellow and brown. Dulcie could have told him it was a warbler. She watched him stroke the bird softly. She watched him put his ear to the bird, gently listening—and suddenly Buffin spoke.

"There, there," the kitten said softly. "There, you can breathe all right. And I can feel your heart beating. Bird," he said, "little yellow bird." His words were in full sentences, not baby talk at all. He crouched over the bird, hardly touching it but keeping it warm; for a long time it didn't move, and Buffin was still and silent. Only when he felt the bird stir beneath him, felt it shiver and move its wings, did he back away from it, waiting.

The bird shook itself, and gave a little "peep." Poised between Buffin and the bushes, it fluffed its wings and flapped awkwardly, trying to rise. It flapped twice more, clumsily—then suddenly it flew straight up, stumbling on the wind; beating its fledgling wings hard, it climbed straight up the wind and crashed into its nest among the reaching oak branches.

"Oh my," said Buffin.

"Oh my, indeed," said Dulcie behind him. When he spun around, she cuddled him and licked his face and her tears fell on his nose. Buffin had spoken, the first of her children to say a word; and what a strange thing he had done. What kind of kitten had she borne, what kind of little cat was he, so caring and tender that he would save the life of a bird? How could he be her and Joe's son, the son of fierce hunters, when he didn't want to kill a baby bird? (Though Dulcie, too, had had her moments.) But what kind of cat would he grow up to be? Indeed this kitten, Dulcie thought, had inherited something strange and remarkable in his nature.

Buffin looked at his mother, happily purring. He looked up at the bird in the tree, and purred louder. "Little yellow bird," he said again, softly.

Everyone had thought Striker would be the first to speak because he was so bold. He was always first to start a battle, the first to show his rowdy ways and swift claws. He was first to dive into the food bowl, the swiftest up the cat trees, the first to do anything wild and foolish. But not until a week after Buffin's debut, as Wilma called it, did Striker shout out his own first words, and he sounded just like his daddy.

The cats' human housemate stood tying back her bright gray hair into a ponytail, watching Striker's usual crazy race around the house. Even Wilma, a retired parole officer who had seen plenty of mayhem, shivered at the chances the kitten took. She watched him sail to the top of the china cabinet, leap six feet up to the cat tree, foolishly misjudge his balance, lose his footing, and plummet to the buffet, knocking a glass bowl of flowers to the floor, spilling blossoms and water and shattering the vase. Striker's shout filled the house.

"Damn! Damn, damn *it to hell,"* he yowled.

He stared down at the mess he had made and before he could be scolded he fled, diving from the buffet through the dining room, racing down the hall into the guest room and deep under the bed. There he stayed, in the darkest corner, listening to Wilma and Dulcie laughing. Laughing at him! He was far more embarrassed by their amusement than by his own clumsiness.

Only when Dulcie crept deep under the bed herself and hugged Striker and told him it was all right, only when Wilma had swept and vacuumed up the broken glass and sopped up the water and thrown away the flowers did Striker come out from under the bed. He meowed with pleasure when Wilma told him it was all right, when both Wilma and Dulcie hugged him and laughed with joy because he had spoken; because, they said, he was a very special cat. No one scolded him for the mess; and certainly no one scolded him for swearing.

But what of calico Courtney? It was September, the kittens were four months old. Both boys were talking. Courtney had spoken not a word. The calico was keen and observant, she saw everything, she listened to every conversation; Dulcie had thought *she'd* be the first to ask questions. Their human friends, redheaded Charlie Harper; Joe Grey's own housemates, Ryan and Clyde Damen; and Lucinda and Pedric Greenlaw, Kit's lean, elderly couple, all waited expectantly for Courtney's first words. Dr. John Firetti came to visit far more often than was needed, greeting Wilma but then going right to the kittens. John had known about Joe and Dulcie for years, had known the secret of speaking cats since he was a boy. He had waited all his life to see new, speaking kittens born, which was indeed a rare event. He loved these kittens with an amazing rapport and they immediately loved him. The minute he knelt down by their pen the boy kittens were all over him, talking and cuddling and playing, Buffin stroking his face with a soft paw. As Buffin clung to him snuggled under his throat, John would look over at Courtney.

"No words yet?" he would ask Wilma.

"None. She hasn't spoken," Wilma would say sadly, looking down into Courtney's baby-blue eyes.

Courtney would lie in Wilma's lap as Wilma read to her, would lie purring but mute, loving the ancient myths and tales, listening in total silence—until one evening before the fire, as Joe Grey stretched out on the couch, Dulcie and the kittens on Wilma's lap, Courtney suddenly put her paw on the page, on the very words Wilma was speaking.

Wilma hushed, watching her. Courtney sat up straighter and began to read aloud, just where Wilma had left off. She read the tale smoothly and clearly all the way through, she spun the story out as lyrically as Wilma herself had ever done.

When she'd finished, they were all silent. Joe Grey looked so ridiculously proud that Dulcie had to hide a laugh; she licked Courtney, both she and Joe smug with their calico's cleverness—until the morning that the words Courtney read brought not smiles but alarm.

It was a week after Courtney started to read that,

sitting on the kitchen table on the edge of the news-paper, she placed a paw on the front-page article. "'CAR THIEVES MOVING DOWN THE COAST. TO HIT MOLENA POINT AGAIN?'" She looked up at Wilma. "What is this? What are car thieves? What does it mean, to hit Molena Point? Hit *how*?" She kept reading, dragging her paw down the lines of type.

2

J oe Grey still hadn't told Dulcie about the car-
thieving ring, he didn't want her thinking about
village crime. Not because she'd be afraid; Dulcie was
seldom frightened. But because his tabby lady would
be torn with painfully conflicting desires—longing to
prowl the night with him tracking the perps, but too
deep with love for their babies to leave them. Wilma
still kept the morning paper hidden and the TV news
off. Dulcie was so entangled in busy motherhood that
she hardly noticed Wilma's changes in the household.

But the village *had* been struck, the thieves had been
there twice, weeks apart and many weeks after the kittens were born. Both times in the small and darkest
hours, the gang working fast, vanishing into the night
in stolen cars. Then they had doubled back north,

striking small towns that thought they had missed the attacks: Santa Rosa, Bodega Bay, San Anselmo, Ukiah, Mendocino. Molena Point PD remained on alert waiting for their return. Both the cops and Joe Grey found it interesting that in only a few cases were the perps able to steal the cars they broke into. Maybe only one of them carried the latest electronic equipment to unlock the ignition, or maybe the device they used worked only on certain makes. Joe slipped into Max's office every day, leaping to the chief's desk, picking up details that were not in the paper about the heists up the coast.

In the gang's first descent on Molena Point they had stolen only three cars but had broken into twelve more, gleaning a fine array of cameras, clothes, money that some fool had hidden in the lining of a beverage holder, three pairs of binoculars, and a handgun tucked into a briefcase under the driver's seat. The car owner reporting the stolen gun had been cited for not having a permit and for not properly securing his weapon. By the time Joe Grey and Kit and Pan arrived on the rooftops, the streets were black, clouds covered the thin moon, all was silent and the perps had apparently fled.

The second round of thefts was up in the hills beyond Wilma's cottage. A houseguest had awakened hearing glass shatter, had looked out his bedroom window to the drive where two men were breaking into his new Audi. Grabbing the bedside phone, he had dialed 911.

The dispatcher sent out the call and then had called the chief at home. Max had risen, dressing hastily. Behind him, Charlie sat up in bed, pushed back her red hair, and tried to come awake, watching him pull on his boots. "What's happened? Another car heist?"

Max nodded. "Up on Light Street. They broke into an Audi but couldn't get it started, and burglarized five other cars."

"They'll be all over that neighborhood."

"So will we," Max said, belting on his holstered gun. Heading out, he didn't imagine that his call from the dispatcher threw Charlie, too, into high gear. The minute his truck skidded up the drive, throwing gravel, Charlie called the Damen household to alert Joe Grey.

In the Damen master bedroom, Clyde snatched up the ringing phone, listened, then shouted grumbling up at Joe in his rooftop tower. "It's Charlie. Are you there?" Hearing Joe yowl an answer, he laid down the phone and immediately dropped back into sleep. Beside him Ryan lay half awake, her short dark hair tumbled across the pillow. Above them, Joe Grey pushed in through his cat door onto a rafter, leaped down to Clyde's study onto the desk, talked with Charlie on the extension, and was out of there, grabbing a small leather pouch in his teeth, leaping to the rafter, out through his tower, and racing across the rooftops. At the same time, at the Harper ranch, Charlie was calling the Greenlaws. By 2 A.M. tortoiseshell Kit and red tabby Pan had hit the roofs, too, heading for Light Street. Spotting the red lights of two cop cars and following them, they soon saw Joe Grey on a nearby peak, carrying his small cell phone in its leather pouch. Separating, the cats roamed the roofs watching the dark streets just as, below, the law was searching. They could see two cops attending to the Audi, taking prints, their flashlights and strobe cameras flashing off broken glass.

By three o'clock the cats had spotted and called in five other cars with broken windows. They could only imagine what contents might be missing. In the dense night they had barely seen two dark-clad men running, vanishing among the houses; one tall and heavily muscled, the other tall and thin. Not much for the cops to go on but Joe made the call, sliding out the phone, its pouch wet with cat drool. They watched three officers melt into the bushes, searching, but they never found the men. From the roofs, the cats watched patrol cars slide along the streets, spotlights flashing in among the houses, while other officers on foot prowled the tangled yards. Cats and cops found no one. There was no sound but the quiet passing of patrol vehicles.

The next morning Joe hit the station early, slipping under the credenza in Max Harper's office, into the smell of freshly brewed coffee. Max was at his desk, Detective Dallas Garza sitting on the arm of the leather couch blowing on his hot brew. Two missing cars had just been called in, probably hours after the vehicles were taken.

Now, several weeks later, none of the stolen cars had been recovered. The first round of thefts had run for three days, each night in a different neighborhood. Weeks passed before the next assault. Both times, all MPPD got were fingerprints of the cars' owners or passengers, many smeared by the thieves' gloves. That second round began when a man getting home at midnight was knocked down in his driveway. The perp grabbed his keys, took his car, and was gone. The victim's cell phone was in his car. His house key was on the ring with the car key. He dug a spare key from between two strips of wooden siding near the garage door, ran in the house and called the department. Patrols hit the streets. And, at Charlie's call, the cats hit the rooftops. This time the thieves got away with four cars, one an antique Bentley, but they had broken into nine other vehicles.

Now, as Courtney read the article and Wilma explained to her what car theft was, the calico looked up at her, wide-eyed.

"Surely," Wilma said, "they won't return now, the weather page says a big storm is brewing. Slashing rain, high winds." Already the kitchen had grown dim; outside the windows, high, dark clouds lay waiting to descend. "Why would that front-page reporter think car thieves would be out in a downpour?" She pushed back her long, silver hair. "Surely they'll wait for better weather."

"Maybe," Dulcie said, "a storm is the best time. Harder for the cops to see or hear a man jimmy a car window, harder to see them drive away." She was shocked and annoyed that neither Joe nor Wilma had told her about the thefts, that even Kit had been silent. But then, on second thought, she was glad. These last weeks, life had been so peaceful, nesting with her kittens, training them, reading to them, seeing them grow each day to develop his or her own unique habits and interests; no crimes to distract her, no worries about Joe out in the night stalking thieves—until now. Now she began to fret. Life beyond the cottage began to push at her; she longed suddenly to run with Joe across nighttime roofs hunting the bad guys. She was torn sharply between the excitement of the hunt, and the security of snuggling and caring for their bright and riotous kittens, safe in their peaceful cottage.

But she couldn't leave her family, not yet, it wasn't time yet to go off in the night leaving her babies for Wilma to tend.

Though she *had* been right about the weather. By midnight the September storm had hit Molena Point hard. The car thieves hit just as fiercely.

Again they chose the predawn hours, the black night windy and rainy, wind so powerful a cat could hardly cling to the rooftops. That whole late summer had become a grand slam for the meteorologists as they tried to explain storms that arrived months after El Niño should have come and gone.

The first report was a hijacked car. The woman driver, when officers reached her, was crying, badly bruised, and rain soaked. While medics took care of her, Max put out double patrols along the village's hidden lanes where cottages crowded together, invisible in the dark, where all sounds were muffled beneath blowing oaks and pines. Ten cars were robbed between three and four in the morning while the village slept; ten cars robbed, five more stolen.

The next night in the predawn hours patrols were increased, prowling the tangled neighborhoods with their twisting roads among the woods but with expensive cars parked behind houses and in narrow carports; and of course no streetlights, Molena Point did not have streetlights.

But this night, Joe Grey and Kit and Pan didn't follow the cops, they chose the very places where police patrols were thinnest, just in the center of the village. Staying to the most open streets, they separated across the dark rooftops, Joe Grey taking one route while Kit and Pan took another, all three of them straining to hear, over the wind, any sound of a wrench on metal or of breaking glass. The rain increased, the wind fierce as a tornado. Kit thought she heard Joe Grey shout, but couldn't see him, couldn't tell what he was saying. Had he even *seen* the stolen car that she and Pan had been watching, had he seen the man hide it? Or had Joe come from the other direction? And now she'd lost sight of Pan. Clinging to the shingles, she searched the dark for both tomcats and searched for the vanished thief, the wind slamming her face so hard she thought it would tear out her whiskers.

3

Kit clung to the rooftop, wind lashing her black and brown fur, flattening her ears and whipping her fluffy tail. Creeping along on her belly, digging her claws into the shingles, she watched the dark shadow below that she and Pan had followed—but now she followed alone, she'd lost Pan. As she turned to look behind her, the wind slammed her so hard she thought it would throw her to the sidewalk. Joe Grey had *said* the gale would come harder, close to dawn, that it would grow so violent that she and Pan had better be off the roofs early.

But they hadn't listened to Joe.

Right now the gray tomcat was most likely safe at home wondering where they were, ready to come out again looking for them. So far they'd seen only the one break-in, the lone, dark-clad figure jimmying a white car and starting it, driving away so slowly they were able to follow him. Only three blocks away they had watched garage lights come on, the driver getting out to swing the old-style garage door open. He'd driven in, gotten out, they'd had one good glimpse of his back, heavyset, a black jacket. They'd watched the lights go out as he shut the door. Hiding that nice BMW? Or did he live here, was this his house? They didn't think so, the way he was prowling around it now, even if he did have a garage key. And then she'd lost Pan—a minute ago they'd been together. Now, not a sign of the red tabby—when she turned back to look for him the twisting wind hit her face so hard it choked her. *Come on, Pan!* She cringed lower, searching—wishing they *had* listened to Joe Grey. *Did* Pan have to linger, snooping around that house? They knew where the car was, they could report it later, could call the law in a little while.

She dug her claws harder into the crusty shingles as the wind, like great hands, tried to throw her straight down to the sidewalk. Wind made the moonlight race and shift, that's how they'd first seen him walking the street stopping to look at each car, a darkly dressed man caught in moving streaks of light. A broad man, not fat but heavily muscled under his padded jacket. A hard-looking man, dark cap pulled down against the weather or against recognition.

Having ditched the sleek white BMW and locked the garage padlock, he had moved close to the house, pressing his ear to the wall where, from the size of the windows and the drawn shades, there might be a bedroom. He'd stood listening. He looked angry when he turned away and headed for the front door. Taking another key from his pocket, he unlocked it and slipped inside.

He was gone only a few minutes before storming out again and taking off up the street. That's when Kit followed him; she glanced back once to see Pan, too, listening at the bedroom wall. Kit didn't go back, she stayed close to the thief, clinging to the roofs, wondering where he would make his next hit. He was only two blocks from Joe Grey's house and she thought about Clyde's vintage Jaguar in the drive, and Ryan's nice truck with all her tools, Skilsaws, and building equipment secured in the back and in the side lockers, her long ladder chained on top. *Don't let him steal the Damens' vehicles, don't let him hit the Damens' house.*

Instead he headed up the side street, stopping again at each parked car, whether at the curb or in a driveway. He tried each car door to see if it was unlocked, then tried the various tools he carried; moonlight caught at a long slim blade, at several keys that, she guessed, might have been shaved, at other tools that bulged from his pockets. He avoided some of the newest cars with their sophisticated alarm systems. He carried a duffel bag—if he did get a car open but couldn't start it, he rummaged through, stole whatever he wanted, dropped it in the bag, and left.

Strange, though. He seemed to have stolen the BMW with no trouble. He'd had keys to the garage and house, though he didn't act like he lived there, he was too sneaky as he entered and then slipped away. And now, up the side street another man appeared, a tall, slim shadow moving within patches of blowing moonlight; he stood beside a sleek new sports car, looking down at his hands—operating some device. It didn't take long, he had the door open, and slid into the driver's seat. A few more minutes, he started the engine and drove away, cool as you please, turning right at the next corner. They'd seen only two men, but this was a larger gang than that. *Where are the others? And why does this one have more sophisticated equipment than the other?*

All summer Kit and Pan and Joe Grey had prowled the rooftops at two and three in the morning watching for the car thieves. Often they had seen plainclothes officers in the shadows of the streets below, and several arrests were made; but the thieves must have had replacements. They would work Molena Point for several nights, then would move north. A few days in one place, then gone again to another town, their movements so evenly spaced that their operation became a guessing game for local TV and small-town papers: Which town would be next?

Molena Point was only a mile square, the streets so crowded with cottages, the yards so dense with bushes and fences and giant trees—and no streetlights to pick out a prowler—that it was hard for cops, or even cats, to spot a thief. Sometimes, if there was moonlight, the cats got a license number or a make and model. More times clouds covered the moon, or the break-in was accomplished in black alleys between buildings or in the thick shadows of sprawling cypress branches. The first week the cats had worked this gig, they had reported five cars with dark-clothed men prowling around them, but by the time they reached a phone the vehicles were gone.

The next time, Joe Grey carried the small old cell phone with its fake registration, thanks to Clyde, his human housemate. Because of Joe's calls, a number of stolen cars were apprehended, and arrests were made— but still the thefts continued.

Below Kit, the heavy man had stopped and began

working on a car door. Even in the windy dark, she could see it was an older Jeep sedan. Before she knew it he'd popped the lock. He slid right in, and soon, through the sound of the wind, she heard the engine start.

He moved the car ahead slowly, driving without lights, turning left in the direction of Joe Grey's house—maybe meaning to heist the Damens' vehicles? *Had* Joe come home? Was he in his tower out of the worst of the blow, waiting for her and Pan to come bolting in out of the storm? Would he see the Jeep? She had to smile, that Joe had been so much more careful of his own safety since the kittens came. The responsibility of the three babies had made him, not less brave, but far more watchful for his own safety. Now, was he up there watching the Jeep approach? As Kit scrambled down a little pepper tree to cross the street to Joe's house, the wind shook the small tree so hard she thought its limbs would break—the next instant, a tree did break. Not the lacy pepper tree but a tall eucalyptus that spread across the narrow street: there was a giant splintering screech as a reaching branch cracked, the main trunk split, and the tree came crashing down filling the street and covering Joe Grey's roof, its upper branches hiding his tower, its heavy trunk twisted across the Jeep's hood.

The man inside moved fast; killing the engine, he swung the door open. Kit bolted from the pepper tree across the fallen eucalyptus onto Joe's roof. She heard the perp running up the street, the pounding of his shoes soon lost in the roar of wind.

Joe Grey's tower was buried in the top of the fallen tree, covered with leaves and twiggy branches, Joe's beautiful windowed aerie. Praying the gray tomcat had escaped, she yowled and yowled for him—she couldn't shout his name, since the thief might still hear her. Worried for Pan but terrified for Joe, forgetting the vanishing thief as she scrambled across the last of the broken tree limbs and into the tangle of the shattered tower, she heard Clyde's voice from within.

"What the hell! Joe, are you all right?"

"Fine!" Joe yowled. "Get this damn tree off me."

Kit bolted through a jammed-open tower window into Joe's broken aerie, into a mass of leaves and branches, and broken safety glass scattered like small diamonds. She watched the tomcat crawl out from under. "You okay?"

"Fine," he repeated crossly, the white strip down his face narrowed with anger, his gray ears flat to his head. "I never in all hell thought *that* big tree would fall." He began to paw glitters of glass from his face, from his sides and shoulders. "Cops, go call the cops. This stuff sticks like glue."

Kit fought her way past him through the tower and in through Joe's cat door onto the nearest rafter, dropped down to Clyde's desk to report the thief but already Clyde was on the phone—mussed dark hair, rumpled robe—describing the fallen tree to the dispatcher. Apparently he hadn't seen the smashed car, hadn't seen the driver run. Kit could see Ryan through the sliding doors to her studio; she had grabbed the extension before Clyde hung up, her blue robe twisted around her, her green eyes frightened.

"A car," she told the dispatcher. "The tree fell on a car, I can see it from my studio. The driver jumped out and ran. A square, heavy man, dark clothes, dark cap . . ." At the same moment, Kit thought she heard, up the street, another car starting. She leaped to the mantel to see better. "There," Ryan said, "around the corner. He's getting in another car, just the parking lights on. They're moving off, turning north, maybe headed for Highway One?"

Kit didn't hear Rock; the Damens' big Weimaraner should have been barking up a storm from the moment the tree fell. Then she remembered he was off on a fishing trip with Ryan's dad and his wife, Lindsey; they often took Rock with them. On the love seat Snowball, the Damens' little white cat, sat rigid with alarm in her mound of quilt. She usually had the Weimaraner to shelter and protect her. Now, alone, she was shivering at the crash, her eyes huge and afraid, though she was unwilling to race downstairs and leave the comfort of her humans. Snowball didn't speak, she could only meow, and now her cry was pitiful.

Clyde stopped to cuddle and reassure her, then stepped into Ryan's studio, put his arm around her, stood looking down through the window at the wrecked Jeep. He turned to look at Kit. "Where's Pan? He's still out in the storm?"

"Firettis called," Ryan said. "They're worried about him, worried about you cats out in this. And Lucinda . . . she knows I'll call the minute *you* show up, Kit. I can just see her pacing, I know how she fusses over you. But Kit, *where is Pan?*"

Kit didn't answer, she leaped back up to the rafter and pushed out through the tangle of eucalyptus branches. Joe, having freed himself of some of the sparkling glass pellets, shouldered through beside her. "Kit, where is he? Were you together? Watch the glass. *Where the hell is Pan?*"

Kit's heart was pounding so hard it shook her all over. Had other trees fallen? Could Pan be hurt? She raced from the broken tower down the pepper tree to the street, Joe beside her. Across the street and up again to the roofs on the other side, back the way she had come. The wind shifted and twisted, was choking them, pushing against them so they could hardly move. "We *were* together," she shouted in Joe's ear, "we saw that man hide a car then hurry away looking in other cars. I chased him but Pan jumped up to peer in the bedroom window of the house where the car was hidden and he never caught up with me." The full terror of what might have happened to Pan sent her racing hard into the heavy blow.

In the Damen bedroom, Clyde had pulled on a pair of pants and was grabbing a jacket when Ryan stopped him. "We can look for Pan but no good trying to follow that man from the Jeep, by now the car that picked him up is probably on the freeway." She had dressed quickly, she was reaching for her slicker when Clyde shook his head.

"Wait here, Ryan, please. Someone needs to be here, Pan might be hurt, they may need us." He was halfway down the stairs when they heard sirens: Ryan ran to the studio window. Below, headlights were coming from either end of the street, their red flashers bright on the fallen tree and smashed car. The two black-and-whites drew close to the wreck and parked; their loud whooping stopped. Ryan followed Clyde down to meet them, praying that their noise and lights might bring Pan home.

Out in the wind Joe and Kit heard the sirens, heard them stop, heard the squawk of a police radio. The wind had died a little, the rain had stopped, and several blocks down where swaying trees led across from roof to roof, they saw a pale shape among the blowing branches. When they reached it, the ghostly shape was gone.

As they searched, balancing among swinging tree limbs, they heard scrambling, the sound of claws on rough bark. When they looked up, a cypress branch shook hard and Pan leaped down, straight into Kit's and Joe's faces. Kit threw herself at him nuzzling and scolding him; the three hunched together as the wind gusted harder.

"Where were you?" Kit said. "I thought you were behind me and you weren't and that man stole another car and then a tree fell and I thought Joe was killed, it fell right on top of his tower and I couldn't see you anywhere and I went to help him . . . Are you all right?" She stopped talking long enough to lick Pan's ears, to look him over and see he wasn't hurt.

"I'm fine," Pan said. "I'd started to follow you, then

I saw the same man up the side street breaking into cars and when he couldn't get one started he just stole what he wanted. I thought you'd be following but I couldn't find you. There was another, skinny man breaking into cars, taking things, then he broke into a black Audi.

"It didn't take him long, he got the engine started, neat as you please. He took off, turned right at the next block but moving real slow as if looking for someone. I followed him. Behind me, I heard a couple of windows break, heard a car start. I kept following the Audi. He met another car, they stopped and talked, so low I couldn't hear, then they both took off without lights. When I heard a tree fall I went back to look for you to see if you were all right. The street was quiet, the Jeep that had been parked there was gone. I was two blocks past the plaza when I heard sirens, saw red lights. Looked like the cops were at Joe's house and I headed back fast."

"The tree *fell* on Joe's house," Kit said, "on Joe Grey's tower and on the stolen Jeep! The driver squirmed out and ran. Ryan reported it but we need to tell the cops he stole the BMW and locked it in that garage and—"

"No," Joe said.

"But—"

"No way. How do you think that would look? What would the phantom snitch be doing at this hour out in the storm, so close to Clyde's house?"

There had already been too many questions over the years about who the snitch was, the voice that had given the department so many useful leads but who would never identify himself. Even though the cops knew the snitch's voice wasn't Clyde's, they'd have to wonder who *would* be out in this blow, so close to Clyde's, at three in the morning, following the thieves.

"No," Joe said again, his ears back, scowling at Kit.

She hung her head in silence. It wasn't likely the cops would ever guess anything so bizarre as that a cat was their informant—though there had been some strange looks from the chief, and from the officers. "But," she said, "someone has to tell them . . ."

Pan nuzzled Kit and licked her face. "Let it be. We'll think of a way."

"But we need to tell them now."

"Let it be, Kit," Pan said gruffly.

"I guess," she said doubtfully, rubbing her face against his—and wondering how long the stolen BMW would remain in that garage.

Joe, watching the two, wanted suddenly to be close to Dulcie and the kittens, wanted to be tucked up with his own family, listening to the storm's howl only from beyond solid walls.

He knew Dulcie worried about him, out on a wet, windy night. But he worried about her in a different way.

Ever since the kittens were born Dulcie, in the house with them most of the time, had experienced fits of cabin fever, a fierce longing to run the roofs with Joe and Kit and Pan, tracking the car thieves—or just to run the roofs alone, to snatch a few moments of freedom. Even now, when the kittens were four months old, even with Wilma to watch them, Dulcie wanted another cat to be near the youngsters, a cat who would make the unruly kittens behave, a cat more stern with them than Wilma ever was. Those three were so hardheaded, so adept at thinking up new trouble. To Wilma, disobedient kittens were amusing, they were not the same as a human parolee, to be sternly disciplined.

Now, crouched in the wind, the three cats moved quickly back to the safety of Joe's house, dodging the blaze of lights from the two patrol cars and the cops' LED flashlights. Near the wrecked car, Clyde and Officers Crowley and McFarland stood talking. On the roof, Pan paused, intently watching the officers. "Maybe we *do* need to call in and report that white BMW hidden car in the garage."

"No," Joe said again. "It's too close, they don't need to get curious." Backing down a pine tree beside Ryan's studio they beat it to the downstairs cat door. In the living room they were safe from the wind and, hopefully, from falling trees. They were wildly hungry; they were heading for the kitchen when Joe saw three white flecks clinging to the rug behind Pan's hurrying paws.

He sniffed at them, and nudged Pan. "Hold up your paws."

Puzzled, Pan held up one hind paw, then the other. Deep in the creases between his pads Joe found five more flecks. "What are those?" The specks had a faint but unfamiliar smell. Pan frowned, studied his paws and sniffed at them. Kit sniffed, and nosed at a fleck that clung to the rug. It came away sticking to her nose.

"Styrofoam," she said, pawing it off. "Flecks from Styrofoam packing? Like they use to ship china or glassware? How could that stuff stick to your paws when you were running, out in that fierce wind?" She nosed at Pan's front paw. "It *does* stick. Like wool threads stick to your fur. Static electricity, Lucinda says."

"Where did it come from?" Joe said. "From that house?"

"Maybe," Pan said. "Even in the wind and dark, I noticed some specks. I thought they were from the bushes, maybe flower seeds. I was more interested in trying to get the smell of the man."

"Did you?" Joe said.

"A sooty smell," Pan said, "like he could use a bath. I still say we need to report that BMW before . . . the way he acted, he doesn't live there. So why would he leave the car there for very long? You can bet your paws he plans to move it, and maybe pretty quick."

"We can't report it," Joe repeated. "Too close to my house. The cops know all our voices, and of course they know Ryan or Clyde."

"We'll think of a way," Pan said. He said no more as the cats raced for the kitchen where a battery light was burning and the smell of coffee and of the butane camp stove wafted out to them. They could hear someone puttering about, and Joe thought about the leftover roast beef he knew was in the refrigerator. With the camp stove and a minute's wait, they could settle in for a nice warm feast.

4

From the kitchen Ryan heard the cat door flap open. She looked out to the living room as the three cats bolted in, sopping wet. As they fled for the kitchen she grabbed the phone. First she called the Firettis. "Pan's here, and Kit, too. They'd better stay until morning, until the storm dies. Yes, Joe's fine, they all seem fine, just hungry as bears." The cats stared up at her impatiently, dripping puddles on the linoleum. On the phone, John Firetti said something that made her laugh but that made her wipe a tear, too. "I know, John. Well, it keeps the adrenaline flowing."

When she'd hung up, she dialed Kit's house. Normally, Kit might be out anywhere at night getting into all kinds of trouble, Lucinda and Pedric had learned to sleep through their worries; but they didn't often have a storm like this. She had started to tell Lucinda about the fallen tree when Kit hopped to the counter. Ryan held the phone so Kit could talk; she imagined tall, gray-haired Lucinda Greenlaw in her robe and slippers listening patiently as the bedraggled tortoiseshell went on and on in her usual endless narrative. ". . . and there was glass over everything, too, all over *us* like little diamonds, but Clyde and Ryan got it off us and Officers Crowley and McFarland are here lifting prints off the car and . . ."

Ryan put a hand on Kit, and at last Lucinda, at the other end of the line, was able to quiet her. Lucinda gave her strict orders, she was not to come home until morning, until the wind died and branches quit falling, and she was to watch for power lines. Kit, switching her tail, hissed at the phone and stalked away. She did not like to be told what to do.

Ryan, laughing, breaking the connection, called Wilma because Dulcie would be worried about Joe; then she called Kate Osborne. Their beautiful blond friend was staying by herself up in the hills at the cat shelter that Ryan and her construction crew had just completed. The living arrangement was temporary, until Kate could hire acceptable caretakers; she wouldn't leave the shelter cats alone at night, in case of fire or some other emergency. But it was a lonely place, and Ryan worried about her, in this storm. When Joe and Pan leaped to the counter beside Kit, crowding close to listen, Ryan turned on the speaker.

"I'm fine," Kate said. "Scotty's here. He . . . wanted to make sure we didn't have any damage."

Joe and Pan glanced at each other, guessing that Scotty had been there much of the night.

"But then there was an accident," Kate said. "That neighbor who lives alone on the five acres that I wanted to buy? Voletta Nestor? The wind broke the window over her bed, cut her pretty badly. Scotty drove her down to emergency and they patched her up. They just got back, he covered the window with plywood. I had cleaned up the glass, pulled off the bedding, dumped it on the back porch and remade the bed. Scotty told her he'd order a new window.

"You can imagine how grouchy she was," Kate said. "She's bad tempered at best, and the storm and broken window and her cuts and pain didn't help. He was glad to get her home again, see her settled and get out of there. The doctors wanted her to hire a nurse to be with her, but of course she refused." Voletta Nestor, small and wrinkled, with frizzled gray hair sticking out as if she'd stuck her finger in a light plug, and her disposition about the same. Kate said, "She seemed edgy and nervous to have Scotty in her house, even if he was helping her. Taking her home, helping her down the hall, he glimpsed, on the dresser in one of the guest rooms, a stack of cartridge boxes, .38 specials. Voletta didn't see him looking, she was too busy trying to use the walker the hospital rented her."

Ryan laughed. "That little old woman with a firearm? Well, it is lonely up there. I hope she's had some sensible training—she can be pretty cranky."

"Scotty said that in her bedroom she kept glancing nervously out the other window down at that flat half acre of mowed weeds that she calls her lawn. What was she looking at? Or looking for?"

Ryan said, "She *is* strange. Could you put Scotty on the phone? We have a tree down, across the roof. And we'll need new windows for Joe's tower."

"Oh my," Kate said. "Is Joe all right?"

"He's fine," Ryan said as the cats began to wash themselves dry. Scotty came on the line, he said he'd be down in the morning to clear away the tree and start repairs. Ryan said, "I'll have Manuel and Fernando here. It's that big, heavy tree that stood just across the street."

Hanging up, she turned to feed the cats. They sat glaring at her, demanding her full attention, hungrily licking their whiskers. She warmed up a helping of roast beef but saved a nice slab for Officers Crowley and McFarland. If they stayed to watch over the stolen Jeep as she guessed they would, they'd be hungry before morning. Her last words to the cats were, "You three are to stay out of the refrigerator. Paws off. The rest of the roast is for the law."

Joe Grey scowled.

"If you ever want to eat in this house again, Joe, you will leave the rest of it alone. Eat the cold spaghetti." Followed by another angry scowl, she moved out to join the men. She stood with Clyde, his arm around her, looking up at Joe's poor, damaged tower.

Officer Crowley, tall and gangly, and young Officer Jimmie McFarland stood beside the wrecked Jeep. They watched Detective Dallas Garza pull up in his tan Blazer and get out, carrying his camera and strobe light. Garza's dark, short hair was tangled in the wind, his square, Latino face solemn from sleep. He had pulled on a faded sweat suit. His shoes had no laces. "My God, a straight hit. Is Joe Grey all right?"

Clyde laughed. "We thought a bomb had struck. It took Joe a while to untangle himself and shake off some of the glass beads."

"But he wasn't hurt?" Dallas said. The Latino detective had never been much for cats, had been a dog man all his life, but with Joe Grey hanging around the station, Dallas had learned to care for the tomcat. Dallas didn't know Joe's secret, no one in the department knew that the tomcat could have sassed them back as cuttingly as they needled each other.

Dallas put his arm around Ryan. "Did you see the driver before he took off, did you see anything?"

"I saw just what I told the dispatcher," Ryan said. "Darkly dressed, heavy man. Ran around the corner, got in a waiting car, and took off. The car was running dark." One could see the resemblance between uncle and niece; though Ryan's eyes were green, and Dallas's nearly black, their hair was dark, they had the same warm Hispanic coloring, the same fetching smile—and often the same deadpan expression that gave nothing away. Dallas had been her mother's brother. Redheaded Scott Flannery, her building foreman, was her father's brother—Ryan a charming Scots-Irish and Hispanic mix. Her two uncles had moved in with Mike Flannery and the three little girls when their mother died. Raised by three men, two in law enforcement, the girls had grown up obedient, hard workers, and with minds and tempers more keyed to the interests of three sensible men than to frilly dresses and callow high school boys.

"The crash woke us," she told Dallas. "I grabbed the flashlight, I thought the tree would be halfway through the ceiling. But there were only leaves and smaller branches poking through Joe's cat door. Clyde and I pulled the ladder off my truck, he held it while I had a look. In the wind, the whole roof was a mass of blowing leaves. With clouds coming over the moon, I couldn't see much of the shingles, just the damaged tower."

Dallas photographed the Jeep, the damage to its body and interior, as much as could be seen beneath the fallen tree. Working in between the broken branches, wearing gloves and using a flashlight, he found and copied information from the registration so he could notify the car's owner. When he'd finished, he turned to the two officers.

"I'll be back as soon as it's daylight, for more shots. Crowley, McFarland, go ahead and set up sawhorses and reflective lights. You're on watch, leave your cars where they are. And try to stay awake. On my way out I'll check the side streets." None of the three officers, heading for the fallen tree, had seen on the dark side street the vandalized cars that the cats had observed. With the noise of the wind, it was doubtful any of the nearby residents had heard the sound of breaking glass and called the station, unlikely that anyone yet knew that their cars had been broken into or were gone.

Ryan told Crowley, "Give me your thermoses. I have a fresh pot of coffee, and I'll put together some sandwiches."

In the kitchen, the cats heard Dallas's Blazer pull away. They heard Clyde come in, fighting the front door against the wind. He was carrying a roll of plastic from the garage. "I gave Crowley a key to the front door. Make sure the coffeepot's full."

The cats followed him upstairs, watched him cover Joe's broken window and cat door with plastic and duct tape to break the heavy wind. Clyde cleaned the rest of the glass fragments off Joe, removed those that clung in Kit's long, fine fur. Ryan toweled them dry, and they all piled into the big king bed, Ryan and Clyde, the three cats, and little Snowball. As the wind howled harder, the down comforter felt deliciously cozy. Kit, curled up beside Pan, fell at once into deep sleep, worn out and full of supper. But in sleep she dreamed of her own small house, her tree house blowing and shaking, she could feel its oak branches whipping and her pretty pillows sucked away and thrown across the yard; in her dream she thought the wind grabbed her and carried her away, too, she thought the whole world was blowing apart.

5

Voletta Nestor was so drugged with painkillers, with whatever the doctors had given her, she should have slept at once. But she still hurt and some of the bandages felt tight enough to strangle her. Tucked in her bed, trying to drift off, she woke fully and suddenly, remembering the front door. Had that Scott Flannery locked it as he'd promised? Sitting up, reaching painfully for the walker, she made her way unsteadily down the hall.

Yes, the door was locked. But coming back along the hall she could swear she'd left the middle bedroom door closed. Now it was open. She peered in, then shut it, wondering what he, or that woman from the cat shelter, might have seen lying on the dresser. Crawling back into bed, trying to get comfortable, she wondered about that blonde throwing her money away on useless pens for stray cats.

She had never expected a new building to rise so close to the ruins, she didn't like people so near. That's why she'd kept her share of the Pamillon property separate from the family trusts. She'd figured they'd never be able to sell the estate, never do anything with the old place. And then that Kate Osborne buying the mansion and the whole acreage, her and her sharp attorney finding a way to untangle the trusts. That was a nasty shock, and then Kate trying to buy *her* five acres, too.

Well, she and Lena had put a stop to that. Her niece was just as hard-minded as Voletta herself, they weren't selling to anyone. And then that woman contractor shows up, her and her carpenters. And the foreman, this Scott Flannery, who she'd heard was Ryan Flannery's uncle.

At least he had been there to help her tonight. She supposed she should have been polite and thanked him, he might be useful again sometime. Maybe he was Kate Osborne's lover, he was over there a lot. She didn't care what they did but the arrangement complicated things for her. From up at that shelter they could see her whole property, she knew that from when she'd walked up there, looking around at the half-finished building. Who would build a "shelter" for cats? Cats got along fine by themselves.

Well, she'd picked up a good trowel and a hammer. They wouldn't know where they lost them. Scowling, she got as comfortable in bed as she could and drifted off into a mildly drugged sleep. If she dreamed of her own plans, she floated down into them, smiling.

When Lucinda and Ryan had hung up, Pedric turned off the gas log and set the camping coffeepot off the heat. With the power off, the house was freezing. They were both up when Ryan had called, had been looking out into the night, calling Kit. Now, carrying the emergency battery light, they hurried back to their warm bed, Pedric silently giving thanks that Kit was safe and that she would follow Lucinda's instructions—and Lucinda wondering if Kit *would* do as she was told. Wondering if she herself would now be able to sleep.

Lucinda did sleep, but she woke at first light. Maybe it was the silence that woke her: there was no wind beating at the windows.

When she tried the bedside lamp, there was still no power. The tall woman rose, brushed back her gray hair, pulled on her robe again, relit the fire, and put the coffeepot back on the flames. She supposed there would be trees down all over town. Beyond the windows the sky was heavy with clouds. One small streak of red glowed behind the eastern hills. Nearer the house, down in the hollow to the west, lay the torn branches of eucalyptus and acacias, and four fallen pine trees. The coffee started to perk. She heard the cat door flap open and she turned.

Kit sat on the dining table looking smug.

Her tangled fur was a wet mess covered with damp leaves. Lucinda grabbed the tortoiseshell up in her arms hugging her close, pressing her face against Kit's cold little face, stroking litter from her flyaway fur— saying a silent prayer that she was safe. Never had they had such wind, not in the middle of summer. Never had she worried so over Kit as she had last night—well, almost never.

The sweet cat was purring so loud she drowned out the sound of the perking coffeepot. "I dreamed my tree house was all blown apart, but before I ever dreamed, that one tree *did* fall, Lucinda, the one that fell on Joe Grey's tower and the windows are broken and it fell on a car, too, a stolen car and smashed it in the middle, I was following the man and he crawled out and ran but I didn't follow I was so worried for Joe, but then Joe was all right and Ryan and Clyde, too, only

I'd left Pan behind and Joe and I went to look for him and—"

Lucinda placed a soft hand over Kit's mouth. "Slowly, Kit. Slowly, you're making my head spin. You told me most of this last night."

Kit had to tell it again but she tried to go slower. "And Pan was following another man but we found him— Pan—and he came home to Joe Grey's and Ryan made breakfast and she called the Firettis and we called you and it was still dark and we all piled in bed and went to sleep and the police were down on the street at the wrecked car and I dreamed about my tree house blown away and when I woke up the wind was gone but when I slipped out on the roof there were no lights down in the village, no power anywhere, but I *was* careful of loose wires anyway and Pan went home to the Firettis, they need him, they were worried about him."

Lucinda hushed her again, picked up the phone, and dialed the Firettis.

"Did Pan get home?" Pan had been staying with the Firettis much of the time since Pan's father died. The doctor and Mary mourned Misto so, he had been very special to them. Misto passed away shortly before Joe and Dulcie's kittens were born. Now his headstone and little grave graced Mary's flower garden; and Pan had moved in to fill the empty place in their lonely household, to ease their grieving. Though late after midnight he still prowled the rooftops with Kit, or dreamed away the small hours in her tree house.

"Pan just got here," Mary said. "And Kit? Is she all right?"

"She's home, she's telling me all the details. Did you have much damage?"

"John's been over at the clinic most of the night. Everything seems fine." They talked for a few moments as, outside, the dark sky began to bloom with thin red streaks. As Lucinda hung up, Pedric woke, came out to the kitchen and was treated to another long dialogue before Kit devoured a lovely breakfast of pancakes and leftover salmon.

At Dulcie's house, Wilma, too, had been up and down all night, checking the windows with a flashlight as the blow increased, checking the cage in the kitchen making sure the babies weren't upset by the rattling wind. But they, tucked down in the blankets warm against Dulcie, had slept right through; what sturdy kittens they were. Dulcie looked up at her and purred and curled down deeper among them. The house was so cold, with no power, but the kittens' bed was warm.

Taking her cue from them, Wilma went back to her own bed.

Wilma was asleep, her long gray-white hair spilled across the pillow, when the wind ceased; the silence woke her, and the kittens' mewling and hissing in play from the kitchen. They, having slept all night, were wild with energy. Wilma pulled the pillow over her head and closed her eyes, hoping to doze again.

In the kitchen, Dulcie played with them, tussling and wrestling, up over table and chairs and counters, atop the refrigerator and down again, running and leaping until she was worn out, but she hadn't worn them out. She hadn't slept much, the night wind had made her feel trapped, as if she were its prisoner.

Ever since the kittens grew older she had gotten these locked-in feelings every few days, hungering to be out of the house, yearning for a wild run under the open sky unencumbered by demanding youngsters. She loved her babies dearly—but did all mother cats feel this way? The kittens were big enough to be left in their pen, with Wilma to watch over them, but they made such a fuss when Dulcie left them. And now, this morning, her housemate needed sleep.

She wouldn't take the kittens outside with her, they were still too small, with hawks in the sky and an occasional loose dog roaming. She had resumed batting and chasing them across the linoleum, trying to wear them out, when the two-sided bolt of her cat door slid open with an impatient paw, the plastic door flew up, and Joe Grey pushed inside.

The kittens hadn't figured out the latch yet, but it wouldn't be long. Joe Grey nuzzled Dulcie for only a moment then was mobbed by their babies, all three climbing Joe's sleek gray sides, biting his ears and nipping his paws. He pressed Striker down with a big paw, then looked tenderly at Dulcie. "You look battered." He licked her ear. "Go run, the wind's gone. Be careful of the wires and . . ." But Dulcie was already out the cat door and up an oak tree onto the roofs running, running . . .

"Run safe," Joe said to thin air. He pawed open the cage door and settled inside, the kittens following him. With sharp claws he pulled closed the top of the cage to keep them from climbing out and tearing up the house. The kitchen curtains were glowing with the first touch of dawn.

Out on the roofs Dulcie ran, she did flying leaps, she dodged loose wires and broken trees; the village below was dark, not a light burned anywhere. Racing across the tops of the neighbors' houses between thin, rising paths of wood smoke, she watched the dawn come flaming and then fading to peach, the color of her ears and nose. She ran until she was winded, until the last twitches of constricted nerves had eased, until her heart pounded with freedom instead of frustration—until, in her wildness, the world was hers again. She passed a man below walking the neighborhood looking at the damage, the fallen trees, the rubble-strewn gardens, at a lawn chair in the middle of the street—a tall young man, thin face, thin, long nose, wearing a tan golf cap and tan Windbreaker. At last, eased and purring and feeling whole again, she sat down and licked loose bark and wet leaves from her paws. Life was good. Joe Grey was dear and loving to have taken over the kittens after a hard night himself, to offer her a little freedom. Refreshed, she galloped home longing to snuggle down with her big gray tomcat and their youngsters, hoping that Joe had played hard with them and had settled the last of their wildness—for the moment.

Yes, Joe had quieted them. Dulcie arrived home to find the kittens sleepy and docile, willing to stay in the cage as she and Joe played gently with them. Joe gave her a brief picture of last night's thefts, the tree falling, its leafy branches breaking his tower windows and sticking through into the main house, the smashed, stolen Jeep; the thief's escape; their windy race to find Pan. "Ryan and Scotty will be taking down the tree.

Will they break my windows even more, cutting the branches out? Can Ryan fix it, can she make it right again?"

"Of course she can fix it. She *built* the tower!" Dulcie lashed her tail. "It will be as good as new." Seeing how restless he was, that he was beginning to fidget, "Go," she said, "go hit the PD, you'll feel better when you can see some reports, find out what *they* have."

Joe gave her a whisker kiss, nuzzled the kittens, and was gone, out through the cat door.

He was back in less than a minute. He flew into the kitchen, leaped to the table then to the sink to peer out the window.

Wilma was up now, she came into the kitchen, clipping back her pale hair. In the dawn light it shone silver against her blue T-shirt. "What?" she said, frowning at Joe and stepping to the side of the window, out of sight.

"There's a man walking the street," Joe said, "stopping here and there in the shadows. He keeps looking this way as if he's casing the house. He was there when I got here, but then he was just strolling along."

"I saw him, too," Dulcie said. "Walking casually, looking at the rubble, at the broken trees and damage . . ."

"He isn't casual now," Joe said.

Wilma, hidden by the blue curtain, frowned as she

stood looking. Just as Dulcie leaped up beside her, the man backed deeper between the neighbors' houses, but still looking at their windows. Only when light from the rising sun hit his face did he move deeper into the shadows—but not before Wilma got a good look.

Startled, she stepped back farther beyond the curtain. A tall, slim young man, thin but with strangely broad shoulders slightly hunched forward. A thin face but with wide cheekbones, a straight, thin nose and narrow chin. Light brown hair sticking out from beneath his cap. Wilma was very still, her hands gripping the edge of the sink so hard her knuckles were white. Behind them Courtney leaped to the counter, pressing against her.

Wilma stroked the calico idly, her attention on the man. "I saw him near the market yesterday, I got just a glimpse. For an instant I thought I knew him—as if he had stepped right out of time, stepped into *this* time from some twenty years ago."

Courtney's eyes, when Wilma mentioned stepping out of time, blazed with interest. The boy kittens leaped up, too, cocking their heads, intrigued.

Wilma said, "He's a dead ringer for one of my old parolees. Calvin Alderson." She studied the man, his face, his stance. "I had his case for over a year, until the PD picked him up for murder. He was indicted, went to trial, was convicted—some twenty years ago, but this man's a dead ringer for young Calvin just as he looked then."

"And at the market," Dulcie said, jumping up beside Wilma and Courtney, "he was watching you?"

"He seemed to be. Passing a row of shelves twice, glancing in at me, standing in the shadows as I left, turning away when I went to load my car."

Dulcie had never before seen her housemate afraid. Wilma Getz was no shrinking violet, she had been well-trained in her profession.

"Same build," Wilma said, "slim but with those broad, angled shoulders. That day when they led him out of the courtroom he yelled that he'd find me one day, that he'd take care of me good." She said this almost amused. "That wasn't the first time I was ever threatened. It goes with the program. But seeing him now, exactly the way he looked then . . . Seeing someone who looks exactly like him," she corrected herself.

"Alderson was on death row five years before they executed him. He was convicted of killing his wife's lover. The investigating detectives were convinced he killed the wife, too, but her body was never found. They had some shaky evidence, but no body. Not enough to make a second case for murder."

Wilma stood looking into the shadows at the man. "This could well be his son, their little boy, Rickie. He was placed into child care, he was about seven then. He was in trouble later, in his teens. I check his record now and then, except for small local crimes that might not be included. He did a couple of long stretches for assault, and here and there short jail time for theft or breaking and entering. Last I heard, he was in prison in Texas." She stroked Dulcie. "I'll call Max later, see if he can find out where Rick is now. Meanwhile, it's nothing to worry over. That young man isn't *Calvin* Alderson, and why would his son care about me? He hated his father, scared to death of Calvin. He should have been glad we locked him up—at the time, just a little boy, he was furious at me, at the law. Later, when I visited him in child care, he was fine."

Courtney, snuggled between them, looked up at Wilma, intently curious about any new, intriguing human event. But her eyes held a shadow, too. As if the presence of a stalker, of danger to Wilma, stirred some long-ago memory, some ugly dream.

The sun was higher now, pushing back the shadows between their neighbors' houses, and the man across the street moved briskly away, turning at the next corner, out of sight. They heard a car start and drive off. Joe Grey raced out the cat door and scrambled to the rooftops meaning to follow but already the car was gone.

Joe returned to the kitchen feeling concern for Wilma and frightened for Dulcie and the kittens. He didn't want this guy hanging around. *Was* he Calvin Alderson's son? Why would he be here? What did he have in mind? How did Wilma fit into his unfortunate life if, as she said, he had hated his father?

But Wilma wouldn't let anything happen to Dulcie and the kittens, or to herself. A break-in wasn't likely; she had good locks on her windows, and more than one handgun.

Still, restless over the watcher, hastily he licked up the cold custard Wilma set before him. Then using his damaged tower as an excuse, wondering aloud if the carpenters had started on it, if they were taking proper care, if Ryan was there to oversee the work, he headed for the cat door.

Dulcie, watching him, had to smile. "Go," she said. "Go see to your tower, they'll be clearing away the rubble." And Joe Grey hit the roofs, making detours, peering into alleys, watching the streets for the prowler as he headed home.

6

Joe was three blocks from home, coming across the roof of the house where the BMW had been stashed, when he paused looking away along the side street. The department had put up sawhorses and crime tape barriers at either end of a three-block area. Along the curb stood seven cars with broken windows. All other parking places were empty where, before, there had been more than two dozen vehicles, many damaged. How many had the thieves gotten away with? How many had already been towed to the police lot, or their owners had been contacted and allowed to claim them? Two squad cars were parked inside the yellow tape, an officer seated in each, most likely running the license plates to find the last seven owners.

They would want to check for fingerprints on the

cars and their interiors, or maybe wait for Dallas to do that. They would need lists from the owners of what was missing. He thought about the BMW that had been hidden just below him. He hoped it was still there, he still felt guilty that they hadn't reported it. He thought of Pan's words, *Let it lie. It will come right, we'll think of a way.* The padlock was still hanging locked.

But maybe the cops had already jimmied it, and found the car. Was it there or was it gone? That was a nice BMW, one of those sporty models. Joe wondered if the owners even knew, yet, that it was missing, if they had even reported it stolen.

The tomcat still wasn't willing to risk calling in, risk placing the snitch so close to his own home. *Leave it*, he thought, but it wasn't like Joe Grey to do that.

He arrived home on his own roof to find Ryan, her uncle Scotty, and two of their carpenters clearing away the fallen tree. They had cut the heavy trunk into sections, had removed all but the spreading top that was still tangled in Joe's tower windows. Corners of one window stuck out at an alarming angle. Another of the shattered panes had given way, scattering more diamond-bright fragments across the dark shingles. Ryan knelt beside the tower carefully cutting small branches, pulling them free of the structure.

At the curb, Manuel and Fernando were stacking the cut lengths of the tree into a truck bed. Joe stood looking at his beaten-up tower, his belly feeling hollow. He'd never realized how much the destruction of his cozy, private aerie would shake him. Staring at what was left of his private digs, his ears were back, his growl was fierce and yet dismally sad.

Below him, Officers McFarland and Crowley were going over the wrecked car, lifting prints. Dallas Garza was working inside the front seat also taking prints and dusting with a small brush for lint, fabric fragments, human hairs. Just up the street a tow car waited to haul the wreck to the department's impound yard for further inspection. Joe guessed Clyde had gone on to work, concerned about damage to his automotive shop, to the windows and the tile roof. As Joe stood looking at his tower, Ryan tossed an armload of branches down to the lawn below, then came to sit beside him. Her short, dark, windblown hair was full of eucalyptus leaves, her green eyes more angry than sad.

"It's all right," she said, smiling down at him, smoothing her hand down his back the way he liked. "It will be all right, we'll soon have it good as new."

He couldn't talk, couldn't answer her, with the men working so near them. But she could talk to him, holding him, speaking softly without anyone paying attention, women talked to their cats all the time, and even tomcats endured cuddling.

"We'll order the new windows as soon as we've finished clearing out," she said. "I need to see what else is needed. Meantime, with the plastic and duct tape, you'll be as snug as your kittens in their quilt."

Joe wasn't sure he'd ever feel snug again. Life seemed to have gone totally off center: the destruction of his tower, and Dulcie so moody at home, tied down with the kittens—even if she did love them more than life itself; and now, the threat of that man watching Wilma's house.

If that guy came after her and there was a dustup in the house itself, even if Wilma *was* armed, Dulcie and the kittens would be in danger—his family was too vulnerable there, as was Wilma herself. Though she was armed and well trained, still she was alone. Despite the many dangers Joe had known, working behind the scenes snitching for the cops, life seemed now more perilous than he could ever remember—maybe his sudden sense of threat and concern since the kittens arrived had changed the way he viewed the world, maybe he was suddenly not so wild and devil-may-care anymore. From the moment he'd looked down at those tender babies, and had realized his full responsibilities,

Joe Grey's every thought seemed heavier and more serious.

Quietly, he snuggled closer to Ryan.

"It will be all right," she repeated, scratching his ears. And almost as if she could read his thoughts, "The kittens and Dulcie are fine and safe with Wilma, you know that."

Yes, Joe thought. But Ryan didn't know yet, and he couldn't tell her now, about Wilma's prowler; not with an audience busy below them.

"And these car break-ins," she said softly, "are no different from any other village crime—most of which *you've* helped to solve." Tenderly she scratched under his chin. "You and the cops will get to the bottom of these thefts. Your tower will be fixed before you can sneeze, and everything will be fine. The world, Joe, is just making its bumpy rounds, that's all." She kissed him on the forehead, set him down on the shingles, and got back to work.

It was only when Ryan had cleared the last branches from his tower; when Manuel and Fernando had gone to dump the logs and detritus from the cut tree; when Officers McFarland and Crowley had left; when Dallas had finished fingerprinting and photographing the car and had gone in the house to clean up; when the tow truck had hauled the wrecked car off to hold for additional evidence; and Scotty had left in his truck to get shingles and lumber and order Joe's and Voletta's windows, only then could Joe say a word. Before Ryan began to sweep up broken glass, they sat side by side on the roof in a comfortable two-way conversation as they looked out at the village. Most of the power was still off. A strip of shop windows was lit where one power line had been repaired. Joe told her about the man watching Wilma's house.

"Wilma doesn't need this," she said angrily, her green eyes flashing, her Irish-Latino temper blazing. "We'll know more once Max has done some checking. Maybe this *is* the killer's son, but why go after Wilma after all these years, if he hated his father? It was Wilma who helped put the man away, he ought to thank her. Maybe," she said, "he's just curious. Maybe he just wants to learn more about his father?" She sighed. "You don't always know what's in people's heads when they look back at their past.

"Well, I know one thing," she said, scratching his back, "the night's events and the storm have left us all feeling ragged and out of sorts."

"Even that cranky old woman Voletta had to get into the act," Joe said with very little pity, "had to roust Scotty out, drag him out in the storm."

Ryan nodded. "Kate is trying to get hold of her

niece, Lena. She needs someone with her until her wounds start to heal. Lena comes down every few weeks to see her aunt anyway, she lives somewhere up the coast. I think there's a husband and son. Remember, Kate contacted Lena when she was trying to buy that five acres from Voletta, and the old woman refused to sell?" Voletta Nestor's five acres lay just below the mansion and below the land where Ryan had built the new cat shelter. CatFriends had wanted it for parking and for extra space if they needed to expand.

"That was too bad," Ryan said. "But it's her property, she can do what she wants with it."

"She was lucky Scotty was up there in the middle of the night," Joe said innocently, "to take her to the ER."

Ryan gave him a look. He didn't need to get nosy. Kate and Scotty's sudden, low-key romance was none of his business.

"It's lucky Scotty was there," Ryan said. "Kate could have helped her, but there's no way she would have left the shelter cats alone in that storm, she said they were all nervous." She tipped up his chin to look at him. "Kate said Scotty was very good with them. They moved all the feral cats that were in the screened runs out of the wind, into the infirmary and offices. She said they spent hours calming individual cats, talking to them and soothing them."

"I just meant—"

"I know what you meant. Let it be, Joe, and wish them happiness."

She looked into his yellow eyes. "But it *is* worrisome. If they do become a serious twosome, if they were to marry, Kate would have the same problem as Charlie Harper. Keeping the secret of you cats from her husband. It's hard to conceal a lie, even for a good cause, and keep a marriage honest and happy.

"Though Max Harper," Ryan said, "would be more disbelieving than Scotty would, if he came face-to-face with the truth."

"You mean if I spoke to Max?"

"Don't even think it," she said, laughing. "You *are* kidding?"

"Why would I spoil a good thing? Why would I give the chief nightmares? And where would that put Charlie? She'd have to admit she'd lied or she'd have to play stupid, and Charlie Harper is anything but stupid."

She just sat looking at him. "After all these years, the way Max has grown to like you, you *wouldn't* speak to him, you wouldn't give away your secret?"

The tomcat laid a paw on her hand. "I'm not about to do that—my problem is, can we keep the kittens quiet?"

Ryan sighed, and hugged him, and prayed that he

and Dulcie *could* keep those youngsters in line. "I wonder about the clowder cats last night, I wonder how they fared, up at the ruins? Kate told me she'd walk over this morning and try to find them."

"There's plenty of solid shelter," Joe said. "They know every inch of the mansion, they know the cellars, the safe places that won't crack or fall. But what about Dr. Firetti's sun dome? That big kennel space is half the hospital." The solarium had been built to join two small cottages together, to form the large veterinarian complex.

"The dome's fine," Ryan said. "I talked with John again, he said not a crack, nothing damaged, and their patients were all settling down."

But when she stroked Joe, she felt his muscles tense. "You're still wound tight. Go on down to the station. You'll feel better when you look at the reports on the car thefts." She envisioned Joe sitting in Max's bookcase peering over his shoulder at his computer screen as officers logged in information on the stolen cars and on whatever property was missing from the remaining, damaged vehicles.

Thinking of the PD, of the homey atmosphere in Max Harper's office, Joe gave her cheek a nudge, and trotted off. Leaping across the neighbors' roofs, he paused a moment to watch the cordoned-off street below where Dallas and Officers Crowley and McFarland were at work. The owners of three cars had appeared. Two were quietly answering questions as the officers filled in their reports. The one woman, standing beside her black Audi, was making clear to Dallas how disgusting it was that the department had allowed this shocking spree of vandalism and thefts to happen yet again in their quiet village—and to *her* nice new Audi. "Just look at the damage they've done, the side window broken out, glass everywhere, my expensive camera and leather jacket gone." Joe Grey smiled, watching Dallas's blank expression as the detective controlled his temper. Joe could imagine what the Latino detective would like to say. There was always one critic among the victims, vitriolic and rude—it didn't matter that the cops had been up most of the night, or that she shouldn't have left her valuables in plain sight in the car. Heading for Molena Point PD, he wondered if the desk clerk, soft, blond Mabel Farthy, might have brought some homemade cookies to work this morning or maybe a snack of fried chicken. Galloping over the rooftops toward the station, Joe Grey had no notion he would be followed or, more accurately, that his point of destination had already been invaded by unwanted company.

7

Wilma Getz's cottage was cold, the power still off, the morning light through the windows a depressing gray. Buffin and Striker were curled in an afghan near the fire, warm and half asleep. Dulcie and Courtney lay on Wilma's lap as she read to them but soon Wilma was yawning. The boy kittens watched her. When her book slid to the carpet, when she fell asleep reading, Striker woke fully. He looked all around. There was no roar of wind now, no sound but the crackle of the fire, and the drip of water from the eaves—he watched Dulcie and Courtney drift into sleep. He lay thinking about the car thefts, what little their pa had told about them, then with a soft paw he nudged Buffin.

The two kittens watched their mother, watched their

sister and Wilma. When no one stirred or looked up at them the two young cats smiled, slipped out from the folds of the afghan, and padded silently from the living room, through the dining room and kitchen, and into the laundry to the cat door.

Striker tried to slide the bolt, though he had tried many times before. This time, more determined, he made only tiny sounds as he worked metal against metal until at last the shiny lock gave way and the forbidden door swung free.

Slipping out, they stopped the plastic flap with careful paws, easing it quietly down, and they shot out into the garden. Around the house they sped, out of sight of the front windows. Scrambling up a bougainvillea vine to the neighbor's roof, their pale coats blending with the tan shingles, they reared tall, looking down at the village, gray in the cloud-smothered morning. They had never been in the village, the crowd of cottages tangled among tall trees fascinated them.

"There," Buffin said.

"The courthouse tower," said Striker. "That's where MPPD is, that's where Pa goes when there's been a crime."

"If he catches us, he'll kill us," Buffin said.

"Maybe only bat us a little," said Striker.

"And scold. I don't like scolding."

Intently they looked at each other. They could go to MPPD, stay hidden from their father—they hoped. Or they could go to where the crime scene had been, but they weren't sure where that was among the tangle of village streets. The courthouse tower stood tall and clear and was easy to follow. Another conflicted look between them, their blue eyes wide, a twitch of ears, a lashing of tails, and they were off over the roofs heading for the cop shop.

They had no notion, when they arrived, what they would do, how they would get inside, and how they would avoid their dad. They just wanted to know more about what went on last night, to know more about the crimes and what secret clues their pa had found—even if they were heading for trouble.

Joe Grey approached MPPD from the south, from the direction of his own house, galloping atop a row of shops, not over the taller courthouse that rose on the north side. One of the new shops smelled of chocolate. He peered over at the fancy little tearoom that Ryan said had good desserts and salads but that, with its flowery décor and frilly curtains, no cop would ever be caught there. There were no lights on, on this street, though lights shone farther away in the village. Only a dim glow here at the back, from the kitchen, as if the chef were cooking on a gas stove, working by lantern light.

At least MPPD was brightly lit, from their emergency generator. Gaining its roof, Joe watched the glass door swing busily back and forth below him as officers entered. This was change of shift, men coming on duty heading for the conference room, for morning count. Each time the door opened it emitted a strong waft of cinnamon to mix with the chocolate scent from down the street. Licking his whiskers, waiting until the foot traffic had all but ceased, he backed down the oak tree and slid inside behind the heels of Detective Juana Davis. He didn't duck into the holding cell that stood to the right of the door, a small barred room meant for a few minutes' confinement before an arrestee was taken back to the jail and booked. There was no one in the lobby but Davis, heading back for her office, black uniform, black stockings, black regulation shoes. And, at the front counter, clerk Mabel Farthy, grandmotherly blond, soft and round and always with a smile. When Mabel saw Joe her face lit up. She turned to her desk for a familiar baking dish that she often brought from home. Joe leaped to the counter. Mabel gave him a big hug, then broke a warm cinnamon roll into pieces, onto a paper plate. Joe devoured it as if he hadn't eaten in days.

Purring for Mabel, he enjoyed a nice ear scratch as she went on about the kittens. "New babies, Joe Grey. Well, not so new anymore. Four months old already, and Charlie says they're beautiful." Charlie was often in and out of the station, her freckled, red-haired beauty always turning heads. Though Mabel had no notion the cats could answer her, she talked to them in a long and loving ramble as she fed them whatever treat she'd brought for the officers, and for the cats themselves.

"Two boy kittens as sleek as you," Mabel said, "but pale as sand. And the girl kitten . . . a little calico. Charlie says she's a beauty. So, Joe Grey, when do we get to see them? When will you bring your family to the station?"

Not any time soon, Joe thought, feeling a shiver of dismay. He lived in mortal fear of the kittens finding their way to MPPD, slipping in to prowl, all wild energy and curiosity and forgetting they were never to speak to a human or in front of a human, one of them blurting out a question before they realized the blunder they'd made. *They can't come here,* Joe thought nervously. *The department is used to Dulcie and me, and that's fine. We keep our mouths shut. But wild, scatterbrained, half-grown kittens wanting to know everything? They don't need to be anywhere near the station.*

At that very moment two of the kittens peered out at their father and Mabel from deep beneath the bunk that occupied the holding cell, their buff coats blending well into the shadows. They were as motionless and silent as stuffed toys. They were thankful for the strong smell of cinnamon and chocolate and the stink of the holding cell itself that they hoped had hidden their own scent from their father as he'd passed by.

They had not come through the front door as Joe had, padding in behind the skirts of the woman detective.

Up on the department's roof, they had found the open, barred window that looked down into the cell.

"Here we go," Striker had said, slipping in through the bars. Buffin had looked with trepidation at the long leap down to the bunk's thin mattress. Striker had gone first, had waited until Mabel was talking on the phone and then slipped in between the bars, hitting the mattress in a flying leap. Quickly Buffin followed. Now, in the far corner beneath the cot they were out of their father's sight.

All the officers had vanished into the conference room where, even with the door pushed closed, the kittens could smell coffee and hear the mumble of voices. They watched Joe drop from Mabel's counter, approach the door, and casually lie down beside it with his ear to the crack.

Max Harper didn't waste much time at roll call. He went over the details of the stolen Jeep that was wrecked in front of the Damens' house; that bit of news drew angry comments, both because it was the Damens' house and because the perp had gotten away. Joe didn't need to see into the room to know that the officers sat at the big table, papers and electronic notebooks scattered around them, and most with freshly poured coffee. The chief was quickly into the rest of the car thefts, but soon turned the meeting over to Detective Garza, for the numbers, models, and makes of the cars, which young Officer Bonner recorded on his laptop. They went over which cars belonged to tourists, how many were local vehicles. The square-faced Hispanic detective read off a list of what had been stolen from each car that wasn't driven away, how each car was broken into, and the few that were able to be hot-wired and so actually stolen. Dallas hadn't had much sleep, working the street during the predawn hours. He had cleaned up at Joe's house, he was clean shaven, thanks to Clyde's razor. He no longer looked as if he'd just rolled out of bed, as he had when Ryan served him a quick breakfast. Joe had to smile because he was wearing Clyde's newest T-shirt.

"These guys are mostly amateurs," Max was saying, "yet look at the number of cars they've stolen. Looks like three or four have the devices or phone apps, and the know-how to use them on the newer cars. Who knows how many others there are, just to do break-ins or hot-wire older cars. We've got twelve older Jeeps reported missing, those are easy pickings—a few professionals and maybe a dozen or more to do break-ins, and to drive the stolen cars out of the village. Question is, to where?"

Dallas looked over at Max. "An antiques dealer called in half an hour ago about a missing white BMW. Robert Teague?"

Several officers, who knew Teague, nodded.

Brennan said, "Teague was dating Barbara Conley."

A few officers laughed. Dallas said, "Half the town was dating her." He gave them the description and license of the BMW. "I went on over, talked with Teague, he was pretty upset. He lives in the area the thieves were working, said he left a valuable tea set, some kind of very old antique porcelain, in the back of the car."

"Parked outside overnight?" Crowley said. "That was smart."

"No. It was in the garage," Dallas said. "He told me he drove up to the city yesterday to sell a few pieces of china for a friend. He spotted this tea set at the dealer's, which Teague appraised at about thirty thousand but that he picked up for much less. Said he got home late, he was tired. Instead of carrying the box in the house he locked it in the car, locked the car in the garage. He thought it would be as safe there as in the house.

"He gets up in the morning, the car's gone and the box with it. And no sign of a break-in." No one had to say the thief, maybe at some earlier time, had used an electronic device to record the opening mechanism for the garage door.

"Apparently," Dallas said, "the thief opened the car door all right, but his device wouldn't start the car." Dallas shook his head. "Teague, in a hurry last night, forgot about the concierge key he kept hidden on a wire under the seat."

The concierge key, Joe thought, *the key with no electronic signals. So when he pulls into a fancy restaurant he can give the attendant that key without electronic features that can be copied. He must have thought no one ever thinks to look for that. Last night, he goes on to bed, the key right there in his car. Human inventions are a wonder—until something goes wrong. Look at the world of computers . . . is nothing safe anymore?*

But worst of all was the fact that Joe Grey knew where the BMW was and that information needed to reach the department. He still didn't know how to report it without putting the sleuth within seconds of Joe's own house at three in the morning on a stormy night when no human would be out on the streets except the thieves, or some nearby neighbor, like Clyde.

"So far," Max said, "we've picked up three perps. And we have Ryan's rough description of the guy driving the wrecked car. Some departments think there are more than a dozen members; but if they're stashing the cars somewhere close, then moving them later, even three or four men could take down a dozen cars or more in one night. How many home garages have these people rented or made deals for? Given two or three days, as they're doing up the coast, that many cars each night, that's three dozen cars, some broken into and left, maybe a dozen stolen. Those are the numbers we're getting from Watsonville, Santa Cruz, Sonoma."

Max wrapped it up quickly. When Joe heard feet shuffling and chairs pushed back, he beat it down the hall and into Max's office. Leaping to the desk, he didn't see two pale shadows race soundlessly in behind him and under the credenza where Joe had often hidden, long ago, when he was still wary of being seen.

Under the credenza, Buffin and Striker smiled. So far, so good.

They hadn't been able to hear much from the conference room. Leaving the holding cell, they had crouched below Mable's counter where she wouldn't see them without leaning over and looking straight down. They had waited nervously until Joe Grey pulled back from the crack beneath the door and fled down the hall. Like shadows they had followed him.

All in the timing, Striker thought boldly as they slid through Max's door behind Joe and into the shadows. *All with the grace of the great cat god*, thought Buffin with more humility as he crowded close to his brother.

They knew the office layout from listening to Joe's tales; they had only prayed that Joe wouldn't slip under the credenza with them. But he wouldn't; they knew their pa made himself at home in Max's office. Peering out, they watched Joe leap to the bookcase and settle in among stacks of files and manuals behind the chief's desk. When Max Harper and Dallas came in, the kittens pressed deeper still into the shadows.

In the bookcase Joe Grey, licking icing from one white paw, watched the officers casually. He hadn't a clue that the kittens were in the room, all he could smell was cinnamon, and the clean, horsey scent of Harper's boots. Detective Davis came in behind Dallas; she was, as usual, the only one in uniform. She and Dallas sat at either end of the couch, their papers, laptops, and two clipboards spread out between them.

Davis looked at Max. "Who was the friend that Robert Teague sold the china for, when he made that run up to the city?"

"Barbara, the hairstylist he was dating," Max said. "Why, what do you have?"

"Nothing. Just curious. She gets around, doesn't she?"

Max smiled. "Teague said this was china Barbara's mother had left her, said the pieces were rare and expensive, two hundred years old. Said she'd never liked them. He said the market was good now, and she'd rather have the money."

They had pretty well covered, in roll call, the locations and number of cars broken into and robbed, or stolen. That information would now, thanks to Officer Bonner, be on all the officers' computers. They were discussing the gang's mode of operation and waiting for more reports from men still on the street, new reports on other cars vandalized or missing, property damage from the storm itself, and reports on anyone injured. They had Scotty's report on Voletta Nestor, the old woman living below the Pamillon estate.

"He took her to the hospital," Max said, "brought

her home and got her settled. He was . . . up at Kate's. When the wind got bad he went up to check on the cat shelter, he knew she was alone up there."

Dallas smiled. "About time he found someone. Ryan should be pleased." Ryan was always matchmaking for her uncle, but so far no one had come up to Scotty's standards. If more officers had been present, they wouldn't have discussed private matters.

"Voletta Nestor shouldn't be living alone up there, either," Davis said. "She can hardly get around. She's a Pamillon, part of that big family. Even if they are all at odds, have all moved away, you'd think someone would help her."

"None of the Pamillons want anything to do with her," Max said. "You hear a lot of rumors. I don't know what the real story is."

For years the Pamillon estate had stood partially in ruins while heirs squabbled over selling it. None of them, nor even their attorneys, could sort out the tangle of various trusts and wills to a point where the property could legally be sold. It was Kate Osborne's attorney who finally made sense of the bequests, distributions, land descriptions, and overlapping amendments to make a sale possible.

Kate had the money, the Pamillon family was tired of

bickering, and she bought at once. The day she signed the final papers, she signed a trust donating ten acres to CatFriends for their new shelter—to care for starving cats, cats that had been abandoned when the economy took a sharp downturn, when so many folks lost their homes and, too often, simply left their pets behind. Joe Grey couldn't understand people who would abandon a pet. The tomcat might not be much for religion but he knew there was a hell, all fire and brimstone. And that there was a special place in it for people who threw away a member of their family. He was licking the last fleck of cinnamon from his paw when, over that sweet scent, he caught the faintest aroma of cats. Young, male cats. At the same moment, Max's private line rang.

Max picked up, listened, then, "You're sure they're dead? Get out of there, Charlie. Get out *now*!" At this point, he switched on the phone's speaker. "Are you carrying?"

"I'm out, I'm nearly to my car. Yes, I'm carrying."

"Get in the car, lock yourself in. If you see anyone, take off fast."

She didn't need to be told those things. But she wasn't going to go anywhere and miss seeing the killer; she didn't tell Max that. She said, "I'm parked three blocks north," and she clicked off.

Immediately Max put out the alarm and barked out half a dozen names. Joe heard officers racing down the hall for their squad cars, heard the shriek of the ambulance from the fire department only blocks away; Joe was headed for the door behind Max and the two officers when he skidded to a halt.

The shadows beneath the credenza smelled of young tomcats, *his* young tomcats. Four blue eyes peered out at him, frightened but defiant. Joe sat down. He looked at the kittens.

They crept partway out from under the credenza, their heads down, ears and tails down, looking more browbeaten than he'd ever hoped to see.

He had fully intended to scold them, to give them all kinds of hell. But what good would it do? And after that, what? What was he going to do with them? Take them home, and miss the first part of what appeared to be a murder investigation? He wanted to know if Charlie *was* all right. He wanted to see the victims before the coroner got busy on them.

He could send the kittens home. He doubted they'd ever get there, he knew they'd follow him. Neither Buffin nor Striker said a word. Neither kitten would look at him.

"Come on out of there."

The kittens crept out and sat guiltily before their father, their ears still down, their tails tucked under, waiting for their scolding. Joe's heart pounded with anger—while at the same time he tried hard not to laugh.

How could he be mad? Maybe he *had* fathered a couple of bold little cop cats; he'd been wondering how soon they'd take matters into their own paws.

"You will follow me," he said sternly. "You will stick to me like syrup to whiskers." He had to get them out of the station without being seen passing the front desk, prompting Mabel to make a fuss over them. He wanted to get to the crime scene, and these two would sure slow him down.

"Oh, what the hell!" Joe said. "Come on."

Peering out into the hall, he found it empty. He cocked an ear and the kittens drew close to him. He sped out and to the counter, both kittens crowding him, the three hugging the wall of the counter. They could hear Mabel on the phone. "No, sir, Captain Harper is not available. Would you like his voice mail?" They could see, through the glass entry, a civilian woman approaching, wheeling a baby in a stroller. The instant she entered, backing against the door to push the stroller through, the three cats fled past them. Joe still wanted to scold the kittens, but he couldn't, they were already suffering from their own guilty consciences. And he had to admit he was proud of them. They had gone off on their first adventure, they'd had the chutzpah to come right on into the station. He knew he'd regret this, but what else could he do? Buffin and Striker had wanted adventure. Well, they were going to get their first taste.

8

It was earlier that morning when Charlie Harper pulled her Blazer into a tight parking place a block from the beauty salon, a lucky find where a car had just pulled out. The time was eight-thirty, folks coming into the village to go to work or heading for the several popular breakfast restaurants. Areas of the village had their lights back, the windows bright, other shops flat and dim among fallen trees and work crews. She was still trying to decide whether to have her long, red, kinky hair shaped and trimmed as usual, or to get it cut really short, just feathered around her face. That would be easier to take care of, but would Max like it?

The salon was closed on Mondays, though sometimes Barbara took a few early-morning clients. It was a small shop, just the two hairstylists and the owner-beautician,

Langston Prince. She'd always been amused at Langston's fancy name, and by the austere and impeccable manners of the tall, thin, bespectacled gentleman.

Leaving her car on a residential block, she walked along the edge of the street over pine needles and well-packed earth to where lighted shops began. Max hadn't come home this morning after departing the house in the small, dark hours. He had called later from the Damens' to fill her in on the fallen tree and the wrecked car. Would the thieves spend two or three days in Molena Point as they had before, then move on to any number of towns up and down the coast— their agenda as neatly laid out as a preplanned summer vacation? She wondered if they sold the newer cars in the States or overseas. She supposed the older ones were dismantled and sold for parts. Turning into the courtyard that led to the salon, she headed past potted geraniums and flowering bushes to the open stairway, past a little charity shop, a camera shop, a small but exclusive cashmere shop—and two empty stores with FOR RENT signs in the windows, thanks to the downturn in the economy.

The stairs were tiled in a pale blue glaze, and with an intricate wrought-iron rail leading to the second-floor salon that rose above the two, single-storied wings that enclosed the patio. She could hear music from above, an old Glenn Miller instrumental. Her hairdresser, blond, buxom Barbara Conley, liked the forties bands of the last century, and that suited Charlie fine. As she stepped in, the recording began to play a Frank Sinatra number. The soft ceiling lights were on, and in the back, brighter lights shone over Barbara's station.

Moving on back, Charlie stopped abruptly. Her hand slid beneath her open vest to her handgun. She could smell the residue of gunpowder.

The client's big, adjustable chair was empty. Barbara lay sprawled on the floor beside it, her male customer fallen across her, their smocks and clothes soaked with blood, his glasses lying broken, his unfinished haircut shorter on one side. Shop owner Langston Prince, getting a quick haircut before Barbara's appointments arrived.

Had someone already been in here when they opened the salon? Or had the killer slipped in behind them? A chill shivered through her as she eased against the nearest wall, looking around her.

There were two bullet wounds in Barbara's chest, oozing blood. The shot that had killed Langston had torn through his throat. The blood and ripped flesh sickened her. Backing along the wall, she scanned the shop. The doors to the inner office and two storerooms were closed. No footprints marring the freshly waxed floor, no smears of blood. Drawing her Glock, she eased toward the front door, her heart pounding until she was through it again and outside. Her back to the building, she scanned the patio below then headed down the stairs, her gun still drawn.

She fled across the patio into the recessed doorway of the camera shop, stood watching the courtyard and stairs, watching the street as she slipped her phone from her pocket and hit the single digit for Max's private line.

At MPPD, as Max and his officers raced for their cars, Joe Grey slipped out behind them, the kittens pressing against him. Moving south along the sidewalk close to the walls of the small shops, hunching down whenever they passed a low window, Striker and Buffin were his shadows. *They're good kittens,* Joe thought, still half amused and half angry.

At the new little tearoom, he paused.

A line of tan clay pots planted with red geraniums stood against the low window. "In there," Joe said softly, "in the shadow." The two young cats slipped in between the tall containers and the display window, crouching down, their tan color matching the pots so well that they were almost invisible. They watched Joe rear up, push open the door of the tearoom and slip inside. The door had flowered curtains, tied back with bows, and flowery curtains hung at the windows. An elderly brown cat lay curled on a window seat, sleeping so deeply that he didn't even open his eyes when Joe entered.

There were no customers, the shop had just opened. He could hear voices at the back, beyond the counter and kitchen, an echo as if through an open back door, could hear thumps as if boxes were being unloaded. Leaping onto the front counter, he silently slipped the headset from the phone.

The kittens watched Joe Grey punch in a number, but through the glass they could hear only a few words—enough, though, to tell he was talking about them as he kept an eye on the back for anyone approaching.

"He's talking to Mom," Buffin said.

"Maybe not. Maybe she's already looking for us," Striker said. "Maybe he's talking with Wilma." Whatever the case, they were still in trouble, and their mother would be far angrier than their dad.

"I don't care," Striker said. "This is better than staying in the yard, with Mama watching us like leashed puppies." They had seen the neighbors' dogs pulling at their tethers, longing to be free.

The talking at the back of the shop ceased suddenly. Joe pushed the headset back into place and dropped softly to the floor. Racing for the door he pulled it open with raking claws and slid through. Slipping along the wall, he crouched between the pots beside Striker. The kittens were afraid to ask who he had called.

Dulcie *had* been searching, she had covered the neighborhood and the hill behind her house. Angry and worried, she was pushing in through her cat door to tell Wilma she was going to look farther away, was going to look for the kittens in the village, when the phone rang. She slid quickly into the kitchen, her coat covered with grass and the seeds of a dozen weeds. Usually she cleaned herself off rolling on the back-door mat before she entered. Now she just bolted through as she heard her housemate cross to the phone. On the second ring, Wilma answered.

Dulcie already knew where Joe would be. Twenty minutes ago she had heard sirens moving through the village, police cars and a medics' van. By now Joe would be at the scene, whatever had happened. Were the kittens there, too? Wandering the roofs alone, had they heard the emergency vehicles and gone bolting off after them?

Had they already found Joe, were they with him? Lashing her tail, angry that she had fallen asleep and allowed them to slip out, she was filled with guilt, too.

They were too young to be out on their own, they hadn't learned all the dangers of the village, they hadn't learned nearly enough about cars or about strangers, they might be bold but they were still innocent. Cursing her own neglect, she galloped into the living room where Wilma had answered the call.

Courtney sat on the desk, her orange, black, and white softness pressed close to Wilma, her ear to the phone beside Wilma's cheek, listening, her blue eyes wide and innocent. *She* hadn't sneaked out of the house while Wilma and Dulcie slept. Dulcie wondered if the little calico had seen those two leave. Had seen, and had kept her kitty mouth shut?

On the phone, Wilma said, "Hold on," and she turned on the speaker. "It's Joe, he's in a café by the station, he only has a minute. The boys are with him, he said not to worry."

"They're sticking to me like glue," Joe said. "I'll take good care . . . Gotta go, someone's coming," and the phone went dead.

Dulcie knew they were headed for the crime scene. She knew that Joe would keep the kittens out of the way, and safe; he was always careful not to be seen by the law. If cats are conspicuous at a scene, and then within hours or a day an anonymous call comes in, a tip from the snitch, that was not a good combination.

It will be all right, she told herself. *Whatever happened, the danger's over now.* There was no need for her to show up, one more cat who might be seen, making the cops wonder. Instead she wandered the house, repeating to herself, *They're fine, the danger's over, they'll just watch from cover.* But while Wilma made herself a soothing cup of tea over the open fire, and Courtney sat on Wilma's desk clawing at the blotter, her calico body taut and uneasy, Dulcie paced nervously. Even if the police *were* there and Joe and Striker and Buffin would be safe, she felt that something was yet to happen. As if somehow her boy kittens were edging toward trouble.

Kate Osborne, leaving the small caretaker's apartment in the CatFriends shelter, headed down to the vet's to leave three rescue cats, and then to the hairdresser to meet Charlie for breakfast; for a few moments she sat in her car warming it up, tucking a scarf into the throat of her sweatshirt against the morning chill. Her two daytime volunteers had already arrived, were feeding the rescues and cleaning their cages. The petting and grooming sessions would come later, after the kennels were immaculate and the cats all fed. Neither woman's home had had serious wind damage, only a few fallen branches, but they said trees were down all across the village.

Sitting in the Lexus, turning on a soft CD to calm the yowling cats, she could see that Voletta's blinds, in the left-hand bedroom, were drawn. She supposed she should go down the hill, take her some breakfast, but maybe she was still sleeping after last night's injuries. Scotty said she could get around all right in the walker. Voletta was a strong old woman. How many times had Kate seen her wandering the overgrown estate with its tumbled rocks and fallen walls? Kate liked to walk the ruins, too, but Voletta was always surly if they met. "You shouldn't be walking up here, Ms. Osborne, this is Pamillon property."

"It's mine, now," Kate would say. "Had you forgotten?" She couldn't bring herself to be falsely polite to the old lady. Even if Kate were only cutting a few roses from the estate's wild-growing bushes, Voletta would scold her.

Kate's hair appointment was just after Charlie's. Her short trim wouldn't take long, and they'd have a late breakfast at the Swiss Café, if the power was on. Parking at the vet's, she took two carriers to the door and went back for the third. Two of the scrawny rescues had been brought in last night before the winds grew fierce, the third cat early this morning, found by a paper deliveryman, the old cat shivering, ice-cold and very hungry. They had been fed and warmed up, but all three needed to be examined by Dr. Firetti and have their shots before they could join the shelter community.

The clinic wasn't open yet but when she pulled up to the door and rang the bell John Firetti answered. Tanned, with a boyish face despite his years, brown hair cut short above a high hairline, a kind smile, a hug for Kate, and gentle words for the three frightened rescues. A man who would never look old, not with that happy, caring grin. No wonder Dulcie's kittens liked John so much; whenever he visited, the boy kits were all over him roughhousing and clowning, while Courtney, in the background, rolled over and flirted.

When he took the cages in, Kate headed for the hairdresser, thinking about the thefts and the storm. She knew a tree had fallen on the Damens' roof, she had talked with Ryan earlier; she was thankful that Joe was safe, that everyone was all right. She was tempted to stop for a moment, take a look at the damage; but the street would be filled with cops working the wrecked car, or maybe with Ryan's crew already cutting and clearing away the tree. Life, Kate thought, was a poker game: good luck sometimes, and sometimes not so much; all an inexplicable and surprising mix.

She thought of Scotty, of all the years they'd known each other, and not until these last few weeks had a sudden spark of real interest begun; though both were still a bit shy, both still holding back. Where would this lead, this slow, careful, yet for Kate heart-pounding relationship? Neither of them had ever been deeply serious about anyone. Kate, when she married Jimmie Osborne, had thought she was in love; but that was not the real thing, that partnership hadn't lasted long before she knew the real Jimmie. That painful marriage was why, from the time she left him, she had been so wary of getting involved with anyone else. She certainly didn't have Kit's wild, head-over-heels exhilaration, the way the impetuous tortoiseshell had fallen at once, paws over ears, for red tabby Pan. Kit was so joyous, so certain that *this* was the moment, *this* meeting was the spark that would ignite the rest of her life—of both their lives. In Kit's case, it looked like she'd been right.

Kate thought about Scotty, last night, how quick and efficient he had been getting Voletta Nestor down to the hospital, carrying her out to his pickup, the wind blowing so hard it made her frizzled gray hair stand out every which way, wind had rocked the heavy truck so it nearly skidded off the road. Kate had watched them from Voletta's house as they descended the narrow lane toward the village; hastily she had cleaned up the mess in the bedroom then had fought her way back through the wind to the safety of the cat shelter, to calm the frightened and nervous cats.

First thing this morning she had called Voletta's niece, she told Lena that Voletta had been in the hospital, she described the extent of the wounds just as Scotty had described them to her on the phone from the emergency ward. Lena had sounded shocked and distraught. She said she would be down before noon, and that she would stay as long as Voletta needed her. She wanted to know what she could bring. A walker? A wheelchair? Yes, she would be alone, she said nervously. She said she had no one to help her, but something in her voice was hesitant and uncertain.

Lena was about fifty, she was surely responsible enough to take care of Voletta. Kate had met with her several times when she was trying to buy Voletta's five acres. A small, light-boned woman like Voletta herself, but with smooth complexion, brown hair cut in bangs and straight to the shoulders. A quiet, hesitant woman, she seemed so shy, her voice as soft as that of a young girl. Still, Lena had been strong enough in the sales discussions, siding with her aunt. The cranky old lady had no intention of selling and Lena had been bold in backing her up, cool and emphatic suddenly, as forceful as Voletta herself.

Coming down Ocean Avenue into the village, Kate started to turn onto the side street that led to the beauty salon but she halted abruptly.

The street was blocked with police cars. Charlie's red Blazer was parked just beyond where officers were stringing crime scene tape across the wide entry to the courtyard. Her stomach turned when she saw the coroner's van, Dr. Bern's van, parked inside the courtyard at the bottom of the steps that led up to the beauty salon. Two cops stood at the top of the stairs. She caught a glimpse of Dr. Bern inside. She sat in her car shaky and chilled. Charlie had had the only early appointment. Charlie, and Barbara Conley, their hairdresser, would have been in there alone.

Speeding on two blocks to the first parking place she could find, she skidded in at an angle, jumped out, and ran, she was ice-cold deep down inside. As she reached the patio, the coroner was coming down the tiled stairs. Behind him, four stern-faced young medics came carrying two stretchers, one behind the other. Each stretcher sagged with a wrapped body.

Sick and shaken, Kate spun around searching for Charlie, for her wild red hair and vibrant smile. Looking and not finding her she felt more and more hollow. She didn't dare go to Dr. Bern, didn't dare go to his van, didn't want to see what was there. When she couldn't find Charlie, she sought among the officers for Max Harper.

There: his back to her, Levi's, boots, western shirt. He was talking with someone. He was so tall and the way he was standing blocked her view, she couldn't see . . . she ran . . .

She stopped, and started to breathe again.

Charlie stood close to Max, the two deep in serious discussion. Max held a clipboard, taking notes. Charlie was all right, she wasn't one of the bodies on a stretcher. Kate broke in between them, threw her arms around Charlie trying not to cry.

Charlie held her, both of them shivering. "It's . . . Barbara," Charlie said. "Barbara's dead. And Langston Prince. They were . . . I found them shot." Charlie tried to sound steady, to stay steady in front of Max. "I just walked in and—" She stopped, pressed her fist to her mouth. Behind them, the medics were sliding the stretchers into the coroner's van. "I just . . ." Charlie was saying when a yowl like a cat cry came from the roof above, loud enough to draw the attention of every officer present.

Staring up, Kate and Charlie could see no animal, no shadow among the cluster of metal air intakes and protruding vents. But they knew that voice. Charlie looked at Max. "Are we done, can I . . .?"

"Go," Max said, frowning, watching the roof. He got edgy whenever he saw or heard a cat around a crime scene. Charlie and Kate ran up the stairs, swung over the rail, and along the one-story roof to the metal pipes—but now there was only silence. They called softly, "Kitty? Kitty? Come, kitty," in deference to the men below.

They found Joe and the two kittens crouched among the tangle of air ducts, Striker holding his paw up, blood flowing from his pad, the buff youngster looking frightened, and ashamed because he had cried out. The cats were silent now, staring up at Charlie and Kate wanting help, Joe Grey's eyes fierce with the need to hurry.

Kate, pulling off her scarf, wrapped the cut paw. Charlie picked Striker up, cradling him as Kate picked up Buffin and Joe Grey, father and son draping themselves across her shoulders. She knew Joe wouldn't stay here, and they couldn't leave Buffin alone, she didn't want to think of the trouble he could cause.

Coming back over the roof and down the stairs, every officer watching them with their passel of cats, they ran for Charlie's Blazer to head for the veterinary hospital, and to hell with what the cops thought. Passing Max, he looked at the blood-soaked scarf. "How bad is it? You need help?" And he gave Charlie a deeply puzzled look. Why were Joe Grey and his kittens there, what were they doing there? One was hurt, but why take all three to the vet?

"Not too bad," Charlie said coolly. "Just a lot of blood."

Max studied Charlie again, an unsettling gaze. "Call me on my cell if you need anything, we'll be securing the two victims' houses," and he turned away, frowning.

9

Dulcie paced the living room trying to ignore Wilma's glances. Joe had said Striker and Buffin were fine, but that didn't keep her from worrying nor did it ease her anger that they had sneaked off and that he hadn't brought them straight home. She thought of hawks, of stray dogs, of skidding cars.

"They're growing up quickly," Wilma said. "Wanting adventure just as you did at that age—just as you still do," she said softly. Having encouraged Dulcie to wait, not go chasing after the boy kittens, Wilma sat in a chair before the fire, Courtney in her lap, a book open before them, reading aloud one of James Herriot's stories, about a lone little cat who had no home.

The house was dim, her electricity still off, the only brightness this morning was where the fire's blaze lit the pages of the book and warmed the living room. Wilma had gotten to a part of the story that brought tears to Dulcie's eyes and that made Courtney shiver when suddenly the lights came on. In a moment they heard the soft rumble of the furnace. At the same time, the phone rang. Dulcie leaped to the desk and pressed a paw to the speaker, making sure the volume was turned up. It was Lucinda.

"Is your power on yet? Did you weather the storm all right?"

"Power just came on," Wilma said. "Yours is still out? Is Kit there, is she all right?"

"She's fine," Lucinda said, "but I worried all night. Yes, our power's still out."

"The neighbors have two pines down across the street," Wilma said. "A real tangle. Lucky they hit the garage and not the house. The young couple was out looking at it, I expect they've called a tree service—if they can get one in this mess. Do you want to come down to breakfast? I'll make pancakes . . . There's no one else here," she added, for Kit's benefit.

"We'd love it," Kit and Lucinda said together, Kit's cry almost drowning Lucinda.

Wilma rose as Dulcie clicked off the phone. She put aside the book, tucked Courtney down again in the warm chair, and headed for the kitchen. In moments the two cats could hear the sound of cracking eggs and then the beater going, then soon the sound of Wilma setting the table—but suddenly Courtney was no longer in the chair. She was on Wilma's desk looking out the window. She was not waiting for Kit and the Greenlaws, but peering across the street where the two pines had fallen.

"That man," she said as Dulcie leaped up. "That same man again, watching our house." She crouched lower, just her eyes and ears visible above the window frame. "*Why* is he watching? *What* is he watching?" The cloud-dulled sun rising behind Wilma's house put the cats in shadow. Across the street, the fallen trees and broken branches made their own shadows among the damaged walls of the garage so little of the darkly dressed figure was visible. Dulcie was about to trot out to the kitchen and tell Wilma he was there when, again, the phone rang.

Wilma picked up the kitchen extension. On the desk, Dulcie hit the speaker. What she heard made her hiss and lift a paw as if to strike the tomcat at the other end of the line. "*Oh, Joe!* How could you take them *there* and not keep them safe?"

"I didn't *mean* to bring them! If you'll remember, I left them with you," he said sharply. "The little brats followed me. I didn't see them slip into the station.

When a call came in for the medics and coroner, then I *did* see them. But what was I going to do? It was Charlie on the line, she'd walked into a murder. What else could we do but . . . ?"

"Oh," Dulcie said more meekly.

Wilma said tensely, "Is Charlie all right?" Charlie Harper was Wilma's niece, she was Wilma's only family.

"Fine, Charlie's fine," Joe said.

"But," Wilma said, "I thought she was going to the hairdresser . . ."

"It was the hairdresser," Joe said. "Barbara Conley was shot, and the owner of the salon. Just the two of them in the shop."

Wilma was silent. There was talk around the village about Barbara, and Langston Prince—but then, there was talk about Barbara and any number of men, some who lived in Molena Point and others whom no one seemed to know.

"She . . . Barbara had been giving Langston a haircut," Joe said. "But right now we're . . ." Joe's voice went low, as if he saw another scolding coming. "Striker cut his paw. It isn't bad but Charlie and Kate brought him to Dr. Firetti, he's putting a little bandage on it. I'm in Charlie's Blazer, on her cell phone . . . Dulcie, don't be mad. He's fine, he's enjoying the attention."

Dulcie was silent. Joe, at the other end of the line, heard only a hollow emptiness. She said, finally, "How did he hurt himself? He wasn't in the middle of the murder scene? What was he doing? How bad *is* he? What does Dr. Firetti say?" She knew she sounded tightly wound. And all the while that she was trying not to scold, she and Wilma and Courtney watched the man across the street. She said, "I hope Buffin wasn't hurt, too?"

"Buffin's fine," he said stiffly. She needn't be so judgmental. "He's having the time of his life looking in at all the other cats. Kate's giving him a tour."

Dulcie sighed. "Bring them straight home when you're done." She knew how bossy she sounded. And what good was it to scold? She could hear in Joe's voice his dismay that this had happened. She'd get the details later. The man across the street hadn't moved, blending into the shadows of the fallen trees. As the clouds thinned and the sun lifted higher they could see more of his face: wide cheekbones, straight, thin nose, and narrow chin. He wore a cap, with pale hair sticking out. When the Greenlaws' car pulled up, he slipped back among the branches, there was a ripple of shadow around the side of the shattered garage and he was gone.

Dulcie and Courtney watched the street in both directions but he did not reappear. Dulcie started for the cat door, wanting to follow from the roofs. Wilma picked her up and held her firmly. "Not this time. Let him go, Dulcie."

Dulcie obeyed, startled at the unease in Wilma's voice. They heard the back door open. Kit bolted into the kitchen ahead of Lucinda and Pedric; it seemed strange to see her without Pan, but the Firettis did need him just now, since Misto died. Wilma went to put the bacon in the microwave and pour pancake batter on the grill. Soon the smell of both filled the house, joining the scent of coffee.

But Dulcie's mind wasn't on breakfast. It was partly on the vanished man and, most of all, on her injured kitten. How soon would they be home? Kate and Charlie were with them, and Dr. Firetti would take good care of Striker, yet still she wanted to race over the roofs to her child.

Joe is there, she thought. *And so is Pan. Striker doesn't need his mama racing to comfort him after every little mishap.* Yet even as she lapped up her pancakes, her mind was at the veterinary hospital, imagining needles and blood and the big metal examining table. She watched Wilma, who was nervous, too. About Striker? Or about the man casing their house? Did Wilma know more about him than she had yet told them?

Shortly after breakfast, while Lucinda cleared the table and did the dishes, Wilma turned on the phone's speaker and called the clinic. An aide switched the line to John Firetti.

"Striker's fine," John said. "He had a local sedative so I could put three stitches in his paw. They'll pick him up in a few hours, when that wears off so he can walk steadier."

"*Can* he walk, on the wound?" Wilma said, glancing at Pedric who sat before the fire, intently listening.

"If he's careful," John said. "It isn't bad, but it will take a few weeks to heal fully." When they'd hung up, Wilma and Dulcie looked at each other.

"He's a youngster," Wilma said, "he's going to get a scratch now and then."

"It's more than a scratch!" Dulcie snapped. "Three stitches!" But then she jumped to the desk beside Wilma and rubbed her face against her housemate, apologizing, loving her. Wilma picked her up, cuddling her. Dulcie knew she shouldn't be mad. Striker would be all right, she was just edgy. And now, before the fire, Pedric began a tale—to comfort Dulcie and Courtney, to keep them all from worrying. But the tale was for his own Kit in a very special way. Kit loved Pedric's stories, the tortoiseshell was all about stories, she had been ever since she was a tiny orphan following the wild band of talking cats, trying to cadge enough to eat from their leavings and shyly listening to the ancient tales they told. None of the big, wild cats had wanted Kit, but traveling at the edge of their clowder, she felt protected from larger predators. When they gathered at night, she crouched close in the shadows, hidden but safe, listening to their tales and memorizing every one.

Now, Pedric's story of long-ago Ireland brought a keen brightness to Courtney's eyes, too. There was a band of wild speaking cats in that legend, living among the Irish downs. It was a long tale, and two others about speaking cats followed. When Pedric finished with the classic "they lived happy forevermore," Courtney put a paw on his hand. "Now tell about *our* wild feral band, about the speaking cats that live up in the ruins." She looked at Kit. "Were those the ones you lived with when you were a kitten? Can we go to see them?"

"Who told you about the Pamillon cats?" Dulcie asked gently.

"Striker did. He heard you and Pa talking."

Dulcie wished the kittens didn't catch every casual remark, every whisper. She'd hoped they wouldn't want to make that journey to the wild, feral band until they were older; she had started to explain about the clowder cats when a car pulled up the drive.

In a moment the plastic cat door banged open and

Buffin came bounding through, then Joe Grey. The kitchen door opened behind them and Charlie came in carrying Striker tucked against her shoulder, his bandaged paw tangled in her red hair. Kate was last, carrying a little box of bandages, medicine, and instructions. Dulcie leaped up on the table to greet her child. When she sniffed at Striker's bandage and the strange medicine smells, and then nuzzled him, Striker looked happier. But it was the expression on Joe Grey's face that startled her.

Joe did not look guilty for letting Striker get hurt. He looked keenly excited.

"What?" she said.

"Coming back down Ocean," he told her, "we turned on my street to see how Ryan and Scotty were doing with the tree removal. The tree's all down, and cut up. They were loading it in the truck. Ryan has plastic sheeting over the broken roof. The side street is still blocked, officers still going over the broken-in cars and talking to the residents. But the house on the corner?" Joe said, looking at Kit. "The house where you and Pan saw the BMW hidden? They've got crime tape around it, too. Harper's truck is there and two squad cars. The swinging doors to the garage are open and the car is gone."

"Oh my!" Kit said. "Did the officers break the lock

and *find* the garage empty? Did the thief come back and drive it off before they ever got there? Or have the cops already returned the car to its owner or had it towed to the compound?"

"Maybe," Wilma said, "the car thefts aren't why Harper and Dallas are there."

"Why, then?" Joe said. "They had to get a warrant to search the house, had to get the judge out of bed early . . ." He watched Charlie untangle her long hair from Striker's bandaged paw.

"That house," Charlie said, "is part of the murder scene."

They all looked at her.

"Barbara Conley lived there, she rented it two or three months ago. Didn't you know that? Her rent, where she'd been living, had nearly doubled."

This embarrassed Joe. He lived only two blocks away, he thought he and Ryan and Clyde knew everything that went on in the neighborhood. They did know that someone had moved in, late one evening—a small rental truck, a few boxes, minimal furniture. A curvy blonde, a couple of guys helping her. Joe had watched idly from his tower, and thought little of it. What was there to think? The house was a rental. He didn't know Barbara Conley—sweet-scented beauty salons were not his hangout of choice. And Ryan might not have known

Barbara at all, Ryan cut her own dark, blow-away hair, cut it after she'd washed the sawdust out.

"You sure, last night, there *was* a car?" Joe asked Kit. "Maybe we *should* have called Harper. But it was so damned risky."

"Maybe," Kit said, "we should call him now."

"He knows your voice," Joe said. "He knows Dulcie's voice, and he sure as hell knows mine."

"I can disguise my voice," Kit said. "I can . . ."

But Courtney had already leaped to the desk. "Captain Harper doesn't know my voice." Courtney's voice was quite different from Kit's and Dulcie's, her higher tones were still that of a youngster, a tender human teenager.

"You've never done this," Joe said. "You don't—"

"She's listened to you make a call or two," Dulcie said, lashing her tail. "Take her in the bedroom, Joe, show her how to use Wilma's cell phone, help her with what to say."

But Courtney scowled and lashed her own tail, she didn't need to be told what to say, she knew what to tell Captain Harper.

Wilma's "safe" cell phone lay on the nightstand, the old phone with no GPS, that Clyde had doctored, like Joe Grey's phone, with a false identification. Courtney, hopping on the bed, and with very little instruction from her father, pawed in the single dial for Max Harper.

She told Harper, in her little-girl voice, that she'd seen the police "investigating that house on Dolores Street. I saw something there last night that you might want to know about. In the wind, around four in the morning, a car pulled in that driveway. A man got out, unlocked the garage, pulled the car in, and padlocked the doors again.

"He stood by the house, where the bedroom is, then he went in the front door, he had a key for that, too. He was in there about five minutes then came out again, locked the door and went away. I thought maybe he was visiting, that lady has a lot of company, but then when I saw the police there . . ."

"Do you want to give me your name?" Max said. "Want to tell me where you live?"

"I'd rather not," Courtney said. "My mother would say I was spying."

Max was silent; he'd started to speak when Joe Grey reached out a paw and punched the disconnect.

"You did great," he said, purring and licking Courtney's ear. "You're my big girl. My big, grown-up girl." And that thought, while it made Courtney smile, sent a sinking feeling right to the middle of Joe's belly. She *was* growing up. It seemed like the kittens had just gotten there, tiny little blind things, then soon little balls of fluff. And now look at them, look at his smart, beautiful daughter. All three kittens were growing up too fast, racing toward the time when they would leave home to make their own lives. And Joe Grey followed Courtney back to the living room feeling painfully sad—until he caught Kate's glance and Charlie's, and knew that their minds were on Buffin, on the amazement that had happened at Dr. Firetti's.

Joe wasn't yet ready to talk about that. Nor, it seemed, did Kate and Charlie want to discuss Buffin's behavior this morning while Striker was having his paw tended. Maybe because none of them, maybe not even Buffin himself, knew quite what to make of his keen and peculiar interest in Dr. Firetti's caged patients.

10

It had been just after Charlie walked in on the double murder and then Striker cut his paw, that Buffin discovered a new wonder. An amazement that filled his mind right up.

Charlie had parked her Blazer in front of Dr. Firetti's clinic, its two older cottages joined into a large complex by the sun dome between. She got out carrying Striker with his bloody, wrapped paw. Kate carried Buffin snug across her shoulder but Joe Grey galloped ahead, a frown of worry in his yellow eyes.

The minute the tech behind the desk saw them and rang for Dr. Firetti, John appeared and took Striker from Charlie. Carrying the wounded kitten gently in his arms, he led them back into one of the examining rooms. The space had cages all around three walls, two long metal tables in the middle, and a counter and sink on the fourth wall beneath bright windows.

On the counter was a shallow round basket lined with a clean towel. Curled up comfortably was red tabby Pan; he looked up at his friends, frowned down at the look on Joe Grey's face, and watched John Firetti unwrap Striker's wounded paw. Since Pan's father died, he spent considerable time in the clinic, he could not abandon the Firettis yet, he could only try to fill the empty place in their lonely household—except when the car thieves were at work, when, in the predawn hours while John and Mary slept, Pan and Kit and Joe Grey stalked the rooftops. Now, seeing the bloody scarf around Striker's paw, Pan watched intently, his amber eyes filled with questions.

He didn't leave his basket and approach. He remained where he was, watching as Joe Grey leaped to the metal table where John had unwrapped Striker's paw. A cart stood beside the table, laid out with alcohol, swabs, bandages, local anesthetic, syringes, and more, an array that, Pan could see, made Joe Grey go queasy, made the gray tomcat's ears drop and his pupils darken with alarm.

Joe had had his blood drawn once, maybe on this very table, to help save the life of one of the feral cats. He'd almost fainted at the sight of his own blood flowing into the glass tube. Now, he began to feel the same.

A tech had come in to help, a small, dark-haired girl, but John sent her away and told her to shut the door. He asked Charlie to scrub up, at the sink before the windows. Charlie often doctored her own dogs and cats and horses, sometimes under his telephone directions. Once the tech had gone, and humans and cats could talk freely, John wanted to know how Striker had cut his two pads so badly, and on what.

"A metal roof vent," Joe Grey said, ashamed he'd let that happen.

"You'll need a tetanus shot," John told Striker. "You're lucky not to have cut a tendon." As he prepared the needle, Joe shut his eyes. For a tough, street-battling tomcat, his fear of a hospital was quite another matter. Joe Grey could whip the biggest German shepherd he'd ever met, but that sharp needle undid him. Young Striker, on the other hand, seemed quite in charge of himself. He hadn't let out a sound since that one cry, on the rooftop, when he'd cut his paw.

But it was Buffin who was the most interested in the clinic. He gave John a loving look. John winked at him and then for a moment stood watching him as Buffin looked all around the hospital room, his eyes wide, studying with keen interest each cat or small dog in its cage. Some looked sick, some were bandaged, several were asleep.

"You kittens have had all your shots," John said. "The few cats who are infectious are in a separate ward." He glanced up at Kate. "You and Buffin want to look around?"

"Yes," Buffin said immediately. "They *are* sick and hurt. But you can cure them."

"I do my best," John said. "I mean to heal your brother's paw, if he will follow my instructions." Kate, leaving Charlie to assist at the operating table, took the buff kitten on a little tour, carrying him slowly from cage to cage, pausing at each. Behind them John Firetti was softly asking Striker questions as he worked cleaning and disinfecting the paw's two cut pads.

"How did this happen? This was a roof vent?"

"Something sticking up from the roof. A *bunch* of somethings where we were hiding, watching the cops." Striker was very calm, the sight of his own blood didn't seem to bother him. Joe watched his son with envy.

"There was a murder," Striker said. "At the place where Charlie gets her hair cut. They were bringing two bodies out, all wrapped up. We ducked down behind those metal boxes and pipes on the roof and that's when I hit my paw on a raw edge." He watched without flinching, Charlie's hands holding him gently as John began to put in the stitches. John was telling Charlie all the while where and how to stanch the blood, what to do to assist him. John had helped deliver the three kittens, they were special to him.

John Firetti had spent all his life, as had his father before him, keeping the secret of talking cats—and searching for a speaking cat or kitten among the band of ferals they fed, down at the seashore. They had never found such a wonder there—but John had discovered, early on, the talents of Joe, Dulcie, Kit, Pan, and at last Misto. Never had he and Mary thought they would have such a housemate as the elderly, golden cat, and the end of Misto's life had come far too soon.

Now as John and Charlie worked on Striker's paw, across the room Kate's attention was on Buffin; the kitten knew these were not speaking cats, he didn't try to talk to them. But, "This tabby," he told Kate, "he's healing, but his middle still hurts. Tell Dr. Firetti that his middle hurts, he will want to know that." Buffin didn't know yet what one's insides were called, but he could sense the hurt. He looked in at a Siamese with a splint and a long white bandage on his broken leg. The cat was lying patiently, but in his eyes Buffin saw how tense he was.

"He wants out, he wants to run and he can't. But *his*

leg is healing," he said softly, looking up at Kate. Resting easy in Kate's arms, he said, "What would cats do, if they didn't have humans to help them?"

"Some would die," Kate said, trying not to show her amazement at the young cat's observations. This kitten was sensing what human doctors might not be able to see. He looked in at a little fluffy dog who raised its eyes to him. "He's lonely, Kate. I could stay in there with him while Striker is coming awake."

Kate looked up at the doctor. John nodded, and she opened the cage. As Buffin settled in, the little dog grew brighter and snuggled up to him, licking Buffin and wagging his tail.

When Kate looked up, Pan was watching Buffin. He sat very alert on the hospital counter, she could almost read what he was thinking: *What is this kitten, who seems to possess even more than our own special talent?*

Now, as Dr. Firetti wrapped Striker's paw in fresh bandages, Pan joined Joe Grey on the table. Joe, having tremulously watched the surgery, looked determined to regain his dignity. Pan, having lived with the Firettis for over three months, was used to the blood, the cutting and stitching. What the red tom was wondering was, *What about Buffin and his strange observations?*

What skill does *this kitten have, that is beyond even his gift of speech?* He wondered if Buffin would speak to Dr. Firetti about the caged cats, about what he sensed. He wondered what this son of Joe Grey *would* be capable of, in his amazing life.

11

It was early that evening, just below the Pamillon estate, when Lena Borden arrived to take care of her aunt Voletta until her wounds healed. The sun had sunk behind the woods, night reaching down to quench the last glow across Voletta's five acres that ran from the house down through the trees and on into land that might once have been pasture; land that was now rough with short-nibbled weeds, thanks to Voletta's donkey and three goats. Kate watched from up the hill at the shelter. She had just finished feeding the rescue cats and had sent a young couple on their way with a pair of spotted kittens to replace their elderly Siamese whom they had lost to illness a month ago. All the paperwork was done, Kate had talked with their veterinarian, had visited their home, which turned out to have a delightful garden inside a large, catproof enclosure. She had even done a background check, which she knew would be clean. She was pleased with the match, the couple truly loved those kittens.

Now, standing at an open window, pushing her short blond hair back from her cheek, she saw Lena's old white Ford station wagon making its way up the narrow road that branched off to Voletta's cottage, the little lane narrowing as it ran on up into the woods behind the Pamillon mansion. Kate wasn't thrilled to see Lena; the three times she had talked with her, while offering to buy Voletta's place for enough so the old woman might move into a nice retirement home, Lena had at first been surly, then had gotten an almost frightened look in her blue eyes. Kate still wondered what that was about.

She watched Lena pull around the house on the gravel drive, to Voletta's front door, though that entry was seldom used. Voletta Nestor and any occasional visitor parked at the back near the kitchen door. Lena stepped out, opened the trunk, hauled out a suitcase and a large duffel bag and set them on the porch. She was a pretty woman, her creamy complexion and straight-cut hair gave her the look of a young girl. Most of the time, she had the voice and the ways of a young girl, shy and uncertain.

This morning, after Scotty brought Voletta home from the hospital, Kate had taken her down some breakfast, had checked on her twice during the day, and had taken her a hot lunch. For this reason alone, she was glad to see Lena. Her visits to the old lady weren't pleasant—Voletta was crankier than the donkey and goats that roamed her yard and tore up the neighbors' gardens for miles around. Kate wondered how long Lena could tolerate them, as well as tolerate Voletta.

When Kate had offered to have Ryan Flannery's carpenters fix Voletta's falling-down fence to keep her animals in, Voletta's response had been rude and hateful—the wandering goats and donkey still came up to push and nose at CatFriends' outdoor shelters, upsetting the cats. They would keep coming, pushing at the heavy wire mesh until they tore up the shelter or until Ryan had built her own heavier fence to keep them out.

Lena dragged her luggage inside the front door and Kate saw a light go on in the right corner bedroom. Returning to her car she pulled it around the cottage to the back. From the shelter, you couldn't see much on that side of the house, couldn't see who came and went. If Lena had stopped for groceries she would unload them there, directly into the kitchen. Before Kate turned away, glancing up toward the ruins with its exposed living room and nursery where the two-story wall had long ago fallen, she saw three of the wild, clowder cats crouched at the broken-away edge of the nursery floor, looking down watching Lena.

The wall of those two front rooms had, years ago, been shattered by falling trees during a storm far worse than this year's blow. The rotted trees still lay among the rubble, with green saplings growing up through them. Ryan's crew was building supports in preparation for tearing apart and rebuilding that part of the mansion. As the three cats watched Lena, Kate thought they were whispering to one another.

Why would the ferals have any interest in Lena or Voletta—except to stay clear of the cranky old woman and the motley animals she tried to keep corralled within her rickety fence? Kate wondered if the ferals, in the storm, had heard Voletta's window shatter and had come down from their new hiding place, curious, as Scotty took Voletta away in his car. Wondered if they had watched them return this morning, Scotty helping her inside in a walker. Ever since Ryan's engineers had begun tramping the ruins, photographing and measuring, and then when the construction work started, the cats had stayed away. They had chosen for their new lair a northerly hillside above the estate, dense with boulders and cypress trees—one of their favorite early-morning hunting grounds and now a new temporary home.

"We don't mind moving up there," Willow had told Kate. "The carpenters *are* noisy, and when the machines are here we don't want to be anywhere near them. When we do come down, to see what the men are doing, we stay here in the back away from the machinery."

"It won't be for long," Kate told Willow, "and you'll have your favorite places in the mansion back, only better."

Cotton said, "We used to watch Voletta Nestor take her morning walks up among the ruins. Now she's been hurt, I guess she won't be doing that for a while."

"Wandering," Willow said, "as if she's searching for something."

"And other times," Cotton said, "going right to where she keeps her special box."

"Safe," Willow said. "It's a safe. When she goes there she puts in packages wrapped in brown paper. She keeps it locked—in a niche under the back kitchen stairs, and boards pulled over. But now, since you bought the property, she's been taking packages out instead of putting them in."

"How often did she do that, put packages in?"

"Every few weeks," Willow said. "You weren't around much then, we never thought to tell you. She'd go to town, bring home groceries. Later she'd walk up there, the little packages in her pockets."

The ferals had watched Kate, earlier, as she went down to tend to the elderly lady. She had looked up at them and smiled, and they had switched their tails in greeting. It had surprised her that they would return to the mansion when Scotty, Manuel, and Fernando were working there; but this morning it was quiet work, no tractor or heavy equipment, just shovels and hand tools.

Ryan's crew would make this part of the house whole again. It, like some of the other added-on wings, had not been as solidly constructed as the core interior—that main, old house was a ruggedly sturdy, four-bedroom retreat that even now needed only cleaning up, minor repairs, and new wiring and plumbing. None of the later additions, the front rooms and outbuildings, had been so strongly built, and these would be replaced. The basements and cellars were solid enough, Ryan had had an engineer examine them. "A fine foundation," he had told her. Some of those underground spaces would be used for storage, but many would be left for the feral band, just as, outdoors, Ryan and Kate would leave the piles of old stone and rubble, and a number of strength-ened storage sheds to afford shelter and hiding places.

Kate wasn't sure what she would do with the reno-vated mansion. She had in mind a cat museum like the one she so loved in San Francisco. Paintings, sculpture, tapestries; that museum had originals by many famous artists. And she wanted rooms for art classes, too. The cellars and tunnels left for the ferals would be blocked from the public. Parking could be a problem, which was why she had wanted Voletta's land. As dusk gathered, at the back of Voletta's cottage the trees turned bright when the kitchen lights blazed on. Then lights in the living room, too, shining out on the rear yard. At the front of the house, the windows in the right corner bedroom were now dark.

She watched Scotty and their two carpenters, higher up the hill, putting their tools away, wrapping it up for the night. Scotty's red hair and beard caught a last streak of vanishing sun. His big square hands were quick and capable as he loaded the tools in his truck. Watching him, a warmth touched her, a sense of his arms around her. The memory of her head on his shoulder; Scotty holding her as she'd cried against him, the day the old yellow tomcat died.

But a shiver chilled her, too. As much as she knew she loved him, this could never be permanent.

She wanted to stay with Scotty, she wanted them to be married, and she was certain that he did, too. But that could never happen. Not when she must lie to him, when she could never share her knowledge about the speaking cats. That confidence was ironclad among the few humans who did know the cats' secret. And, with Kate, there was even more to keep hidden.

In the Harper marriage, Charlie knew the cats could speak, but Max didn't. Charlie had to swallow back every accidental hint, every incriminating remark that might want to slip out. And Kate would have to do the same. She would have, too often, to lie to Scotty, and she would hate each deception. A solid marriage wasn't meant to harbor secrets, marriage was meant for openness, the only secrets being those shared by both.

But, she thought, *the lies have worked for Charlie, she has made them work.* Though it was never easy. Too many times she had seen Charlie turn away from Max's observing look, cross the room to refill their coffee cups, straighten the kitchen chairs, hunt in her pocket for a tissue, anything to distract from what might have been a misstep. Kate wondered if she could live like that with Scott Flannery, who seemed to conceal nothing, who held back no secret.

But thinking of living without Scotty was even more painful. Now, as Manuel and Fernando climbed in their truck and took off down the hill, and Scotty's truck headed for the shelter, Kate turned away and went to start dinner in the kitchen of the little apartment. Two small filets, scalloped potatoes in the microwave, a salad. While she set the table, hearing Scotty's truck pull up, her heart was pounding with conflicted thoughts, with the sight of him, tall and muscled, his flaming hair and neatly trimmed red beard. She could feel his hand in hers as they walked through the woods, or as he helped her install walkways and bridges in the big enclosures for the shelter cats.

These cats were not meant to be confined for long, they were meant to have homes. Or, if they were feral and had roamed wild and free, they would be returned to their own territory and looked after, from a polite distance, by the CatFriends volunteers. They would have had shots and been spayed, they would have water, and food besides the rats and mice they hunted, and would have secure outdoor shelters. Scotty understood that these wild cats that CatFriends had trapped were wary and frightened, and he was gentle with them.

She had watched Scotty around the ruins, how he would glance at the ferals, knowing they were wild. She could see his smile when they peered out at him, could see his interest in their shy ways. He always paid attention, as the men got to work with loud equipment, to how the cats would disappear, avoiding the very places the men meant to break and dig.

Now, as she watched Scotty come up the steps, moving on into the bathroom to wash up, she put the potatoes in the microwave, the steaks on the hot skillet, and the salads on the little apartment table.

"Those feral cats," Scotty said, sitting down, "that band around the ruins. Will they stay at all, when we bring in more heavy equipment, bigger tractors and backhoes? Or will they leave for good, frightened and displaced? Where will they go?"

"There's a lot of land," she said. "Rocky places up in those trees, caves to hide and to den in. Places so far back in the woods, you can hardly see the mansion. I'm guessing they hunt there, in the early hours."

"You know a lot about them," he said, watching her.

"I've read a lot about ferals. And I know one thing, no cat wants to hunt down there at Voletta's, intently stalking a rabbit hole, when that bad-tempered donkey and those three billy goats might come charging down on them." She was interested that he cared, that he had thought about the cats' fear of the workmen and heavy equipment—but then he startled her sharply:

"Wilma says there are pictures in the library of feral cats centuries ago. Pictures that look just like Dulcie's calico kitten. I told her, that seems pretty strange. Wilma said it must be some special breed of that time, that the kitten is some kind of throwback."

"Could be," she said. "Genetics is a complicated science, I don't begin to understand it all."

"Pedric has seen the pictures. *He* thinks that kitten has been reincarnated," Scotty said, smiling. "That's his Scots-Irish blood, Pedric loves the old, mythic tales—we Scots are all storytellers."

"Are you a storyteller?"

"I can't make up the wild tales that Pedric does," he said easily. But Kate wished, oh how she wished, that Scotty could believe those ancient stories—that he *could* believe all the wonders that surrounded him right here and right now, miracles that she knew to be true.

12

The stalker returned to Wilma's the next night. This time he didn't just watch her house, nor had he followed her as she shopped. He had waited out in the night until he was sure she slept, waited long after the reading light went out in her bedroom, until the house was dark.

Wilma and Dulcie and the kittens were sound asleep, tangled together in the double bed, Courtney's paws in Wilma's hair, Dulcie's head on Wilma's shoulder. Buffin was snuggled close to Striker, who was curled around his bandaged paw to protect it. Striker was the first to wake, raising his head, softly hissing. "There's a noise. Someone . . ."

Wilma sat up, listening. Dulcie reared up beside her. "Someone's out there," the tabby whispered. They all could hear scraping noises at the front window. Dulcie slipped off the bed, stood tall on her hind paws, her tail twitching, her ears sharp. The kittens slid stealthily down beside her, everyone listening.

But now there was no sound. Only silence.

Then the sudden sharp clink of shattering glass.

In a moment they heard the front window slide open, then another sliding noise as if someone was climbing in over the sill.

Quietly Wilma rose, pulled on her robe, lifted her revolver from the nightstand, unholstered it, and slipped it in her pocket. The kittens watched her wide-eyed. Without a sound she opened the bedroom window and silently slid back the screen. She motioned the four cats through—but Dulcie didn't want to leave her.

"Go," Wilma said softly. "Go now. Up to the neighbor's roof, out of the way in case of gunfire."

Dulcie just looked at her. Wilma picked her up forcefully and dropped her out the window, down among the waiting kittens. Thin light from a quarter moon followed the cats as they climbed the neighbor's honeysuckle vine. When they were gone, safe on the roof, Wilma crouched by the bed, her voice muffled by its bulk and covers, and softly called 911. Then she moved to the bedroom door listening.

The invader was in the living room, trying to open

desk drawers. She heard him try the large, locked file drawers first, then pull the small drawers open, heard him rummaging as if he might be looking for the file-drawer key. But why, what did he think she had? She had nothing of real value that she'd ever kept in the house—well, except the Thomas Bewick book, the rare collector's volume that she had at one time hidden in the secret compartment behind the files in the locked drawer. The book that she and Charlie had dug from among the Pamillon ruins.

But how would a burglar know about that? Or know its value? No one knew about the Bewick book except her closest friends. If that *was* Calvin Alderson's son out there, the young man who had been watching her, how could he know about the handmade, one-of-a-kind volume that they'd found on the estate? What connection could Rick Alderson, or his father, have had to the Pamillons?

How could he know about that one volume printed differently from the rest of the edition, the one book that because of what the author had added to it, held a secret that must never be told? A book that, despite its considerable value, she had at last destroyed? How would he know any of the Pamillon secrets?

Quietly she slid the bedroom door open and moved down the hall toward the living room. Across the room he was still rummaging at the desk, his back to her. She watched him trying to jimmy the file lock on her nice cherry desk and that made her mad. "Stand up," she said, cocking the revolver. "Turn around, hands laced on top of your head."

He spun around, staring at the gun. A slim man. In the dark, backlighted by faint moonlight, she couldn't see his face but it was the same man, the same wide, slanted shoulders, exactly like Calvin Alderson twenty years ago. Seeing the cocked gun in her steady grip he was still for only a second then spun around grabbing at the front door, turning the lock, jerking it open, and was gone. In that second she could have fired, could easily have killed him.

She let the hammer down slowly. She heard his footsteps pounding down the walk, then heard a car take off. Quickly she found a tissue, put it over her hand to open the door. She ran, chasing the car . . . a pale SUV. What make? She couldn't tell. Nor, in the faint moonlight, could she see the license number. She was shocked to see Dulcie chasing it, too, running down the street. *Oh, Dulcie!* She was half angry, half filled with love to see Dulcie's dangerous, insane effort. When the brown tabby at last lost the car and returned, Wilma grabbed her up, hugging her.

"It was a Subaru," Dulcie said, "but I only got the

first three numbers." Wilma grabbed the desk phone and called back to the dispatcher. Then, carrying her gun cocked once more, she cleared the house, though she felt certain he'd been alone. When at last she let down the hammer and pocketed the weapon she picked Dulcie up again, hugging and loving her. "The kittens are still on the roof?"

"Yes," Dulcie said. "What was he after? Why didn't you shoot him?"

"He didn't come at me or I would have. Think of all the legal fuss that would bring down on us, when he didn't actually attack me."

They waited sitting together until Officer McFarland arrived. A second squad car stopped briefly. From the driver's seat, Officer Brennan asked her a few questions. He double-checked on the license, on the car's description, then took off fast in the direction Wilma had seen the SUV disappear.

In the house, young Jimmie McFarland, clean-cut, short brown hair, looked the damage over carefully. He took a dozen photos, then began to scan for prints on the window casing, on the front door and knob, on the broken glass, the desk. Most were Wilma's prints, some smeared as if with gloves. He did find a few additional prints where the invader had apparently taken off his gloves to manipulate the locks on the desk. It was the half-dozen white flecks on the oriental rug near the desk that interested him most. "What are these?"

Kneeling to look, Wilma shook her head. McFarland picked them up with a needle, searched the rest of the room for more. He found one speck caught on the concrete step where it joined the doorsill, he put them all in a small plastic bottle and dropped it in his pocket.

"They look," Wilma said, "like bits of Styrofoam packing. Could they have been caught in his shoes?"

Jimmie gave her an interested look but was silent. A look that said, *I'd like to tell you, but I can't,* a look she knew well. These specks were connected to something else, to some other case they were working. Maybe, in the morning, Max would tell her. She sat in her favorite chair holding Dulcie in her lap, stroking her, while McFarland called Dallas.

He told the detective what he'd found, what he'd collected, including the Styrofoam flecks. He answered several questions with a simple yes or no. During their conversation, the kittens were not to be seen. Obeying their mother, they were still on the roof. They were probably freezing, but they had minded Dulcie.

Was the burglar Rick Alderson? That little seven-year-old boy she had known so long ago? Was he not still in prison in Texas, but out on parole? She knew nothing at all to put him together with the Pamillons and the Bewick book. But what other interest would he have here, except a valuable item he meant to sell?

Or was his interest in her, instead, in retribution for his father's death? But that didn't make sense, little Rickie had hated Calvin Alderson.

Once McFarland had every bit of evidence he wanted, Wilma found a cardboard box in her garage, they took it apart and taped it over the window, closing off most of the broken area. It wouldn't keep people out, but it would block the wind and keep more glass from falling.

She knew there were few civilians who would get this much attention from the police, particularly since break-ins had become a misdemeanor in California instead of a felony. *Was* there more to this break and enter that she didn't know, that McFarland wasn't telling her? *Could* the attempted theft be connected to something more than a rare and vanished book?

McFarland said they were sending someone to cruise the neighborhood, and asked what she knew about the man.

"Not much, Jimmie. He looks exactly like an old parolee from twenty years back, Calvin Alderson. Such a startling likeness that I feel sure this must be Alderson's boy, Rick. He's been in and out of jail—but you and Max and Dallas know all that.

"I check on him every few years, out of curiosity. Or maybe a feeling of unease. Even at seven years old, that little boy . . . screaming that it was my fault his daddy went to prison even though the child hated Calvin. But then later he seemed to change his mind, and he was friendly enough. Now, for the past couple of weeks, he's been hanging around watching me. Yes, I talked with Max, he's checking to see if Rick *is* still in jail in Texas, or if there's a warrant out for him."

"Do you have a lock on your bedroom door?"

"That's first on my list in the morning—and *double* bolts on the outer doors. It was the cats who heard him, they got frightened and woke me. For the rest of the night I'll prop the dresser against the door. If he tries to get in, that will wake me."

"And the bedroom windows?"

"I'll turn the outside lights on. And balance some little bottles on the sill so if the window moves, they'll fall."

"You might be smart to move out for a couple of weeks."

Wilma laughed, pushed back her long gray hair. "That's exactly what Max will tell me, to move out." Though what she meant to do was quite different.

"Or have someone stay with you," Jimmie said diffidently. "Though I know you've handled a lot worse than this guy. But even though you're well trained, it's nice to have a backup."

"I'll be careful, Jimmie."

Jimmie gave her a hug, and glanced with confidence at the weight of the gun in her robe pocket. "Take care," he said softly. "There'll be a patrol." He turned, and was gone. Wilma locked the door behind him.

While Dulcie went to get the kittens, Wilma swept and vacuumed up every shard of glass on the floor and rug and in the window casing. She had vacuumed the rug three times, wiped down every surface with a damp cloth to catch the tiniest splinters, and put the vacuum away. She was in the bedroom straightening the covers when the kittens came slipping in through the window, silent and wide-eyed.

Pushing the dresser against the bedroom door, Wilma watched them settle among the covers, then she arranged the bottles along the sill. From the expressions on the kittens' faces she could almost tell what each was thinking. Buffin wasn't sure he liked this disturbance so much. Striker was still all hisses and fight, as if he had wanted to chase the man right along with Dulcie; Wilma suspected only Dulcie's scolding, and his hurt foot, had stopped him.

But it was Courtney who looked amazed and excited, her ears sharp forward, her baby-blue eyes gleaming, one paw lifted, reaching out; her black and orange face wildly alight, she looked as if her head were swimming not just with this crime, tonight, but with remembered scenes, with visions exploding as if from dreams of a time long past.

Gently Wilma took the calico in her arms. "What are you remembering?"

Courtney, her black and orange blotches and three black bracelets bright in the lamplight, only looked at Wilma. At last she said, "Swords. Men on horseback with swords. I was on the roof—but a thatched roof. I was huddled down in the thatch and they didn't see me." She frowned up at Wilma. "That's all I remember, a fuzzy dream, but I can smell the horses and the blood, I can smell the blood. They broke into the house, three men . . ." She closed her eyes. "Later, when they'd gone, when I came down from the roof . . . In the house the smell of fear and blood, two people dead, the old farm couple dead."

"What did you do?" Wilma asked softly, only glancing at the silent boy kittens and Dulcie.

"I . . . The king's soldiers came. I was there in the house, grieving over the old couple, mewing at them, grieving. The soldiers burst in and I didn't know what they would do to me. They swung their swords and

I ran between them, ran between their legs and kep running and . . . and . . .

"That's all I remember," she said softly. She looked up at Wilma, looked at Dulcie and her brothers. "Another life? Not just a dream?" she whispered. "Why do I remember? That man . . . That man, tonight, breaking in. That man, he lusted for something. That man made me remember."

Wilma settled Courtney down under the covers, and slipped in beside her. The boy kittens and Dulcie, quiet and solemn, crawled in beside them.

Easing into sleep, her gun ready on the nightstand, Wilma knew Max would be there at first light. He would come to investigate the scene himself and he would tell her to move out, to take Dulcie and the kittens and go to stay at Clyde and Ryan's house, and Max could be hard to deal with.

What she meant to do was take the cats there, while *she* stayed at home. Next time, she intended to catch the prowler. Next time she would corner him, would shoot close enough to make him talk. She wanted to know if this *was* Rick Alderson, and to know what this was about.

13

Wilma begrudgingly agreed to move in with the Damens after a heated discussion with Max Harper—an argument she knew she wouldn't win. Max arrived early, just as she'd gotten out of the shower. She could hear him knocking, and Buffin ran to get her, the kitten looking very serious. "It's the chief," he whispered. "It's Captain Harper, I looked out the cat door."

Hastily she slipped on her robe. She answered the door barefoot. They sat in the living room for a few minutes before she went to get dressed, to pull on jeans and a sweatshirt. When she returned, Max was wearing cotton gloves, checking out the window and desk, even though he had the trace evidence and prints that Jimmie had collected last night.

He had started a pot of coffee, they sat at the kitchen

table, she knew what was coming. "I want you to move in with Clyde and Ryan until we get this sorted out."

"I don't want to do that, Max. I'll take the cats to the Damens', to keep them safe, but I'm staying here. I want to know what he wants, what he was looking for."

"That," Max said unnecessarily, "is our job. *That* is why I want you out of here. With the evidence we picked up on your carpet, this guy could be Barbara's and Langston's killer. Do you still think this was Rick Alderson?"

Max was quiet, watching her.

"I can only say he looks exactly like Calvin Alderson. Even when he was a little boy, Rick had the same wide, slanting shoulders, slim, long face, thin nose . . ."

Max shook his head. "This man isn't Rick."

She just looked at him.

"Dallas put a rush on the fingerprints. There is no record at all on this man. None. No charges, no arrests, no convictions. Not even a driver's license—which implies he's using a fake."

"But Rick is bound to have prints on record, he's spent half his life in prison."

"We have Rick Alderson's prints, from AFIS. This man who broke in is not Rick Alderson—but whoever this is, we have enough to hold him on the two murders, we have a BOL out on him.

"If—when—we pick him, have him behind bars, you can come down to the station, watch the interview on closed circuit. Meantime, I don't want him back here while you're in the house. I don't want you cornering him in here thinking you can handle him alone, that you can force information from him, by yourself. That's not even good police procedure."

She didn't answer. She wanted to say, *Have you forgotten that I've interrogated hundreds of felons?* She wanted to say, *I think I might* know *what this is about. I'd like a chance to soft-talk him, see if I can ease it out of him.* But she couldn't tell Max about the book, not all of it, the core of the story was too close to the truth about Joe Grey and the rest of the cats.

They argued while they shared coffee and a plate of lemon bars she'd had in the refrigerator. No matter what excuse she made, Max outbullied her. Wilma might be stubborn, but the tall, lean chief—her own niece's husband—was far more hardheaded.

She'd been thrilled when Max and Charlie married. Max's combination of a cop's tough single-mindedness and his kind gentleness was just what Charlie needed. And now, though she and Max disagreed, neither was really angry. But, knowing that the burglar could be the killer that Charlie narrowly missed this morning, she told herself Max was right. She would go to the

Damens'. Scowling at the tall, lean chief, she knew she didn't have a choice.

"We'll move one of the officers into your house for a few days," Max said. "Same lights in the bedroom, same routine of lighted rooms behind the drawn curtains, showers and meals at the same time, and maybe our thief will try again. My hunch is, he wants you here, that he's looking for something you've hidden and, thwarted once, he intends to make you give it to him. That means he'll come well armed. What might he be after? You don't keep stocks and bonds or cash in the house?"

She shook her head. "Nor valuable jewelry or coins," she said, laughing. She couldn't tell Max the whole story, but she could tell him part of it.

The regular copies of the Bewick book were valuable enough, in their own right, to interest a small-time thief maybe intending to auction it to collectors. She told him about the ancient, hand-printed volume with its wood engravings, that for some time she'd kept in the house; she put its value at maybe eight thousand. She left out that this one volume had been a singular and very special copy. If it still existed, which it didn't, the information it revealed would have brought maybe a hundred times that much. She just said, "A break-in, for an old book," and shook her head.

"We'll leave your car in the drive," Max said, "so it looks like you're here. I'd get on over to the Damens' as soon as Ryan or Clyde can pick you up. We'll have patrols on the streets. While you're gone, Ryan's men can replace your window—after the lab has a closer look at the evidence McFarland collected around the desk and your front door."

When Max had left she put fresh sheets on her bed for Officer McFarland. He would keep the shades drawn, lights would go on and off on her usual schedule of supper, reading for a while before the fire, then off to bed to read there for an hour or so—her own habits would become McFarland's habits, except for the company of the cats. Whatever the break-in might involve, she thought as she ran a load of laundry, she was lucky to have Max and MPPD at her back.

Joe Grey woke in his newly repaired tower, new glass in the damaged window, brand-new pillows, the old pillows thrown in the trash to be sure all the broken glass was gone. He yawned and stretched, wondering what had awakened him. Had he heard the phone, had Charlie called? Had the car thieves returned, after all that went on the night before? But then he smelled coffee.

He slid out from under the pillows, stretched again, pushed in through his cat door onto the rafter, and dropped to Clyde's desk. Glancing into the bedroom, he saw Clyde's side of the bed empty and that Ryan still slept. He beat it downstairs to see why Clyde was up at this hour.

Clyde sat at the kitchen table devouring cold, leftover lasagna. Joe leaped up beside him. "That's disgusting. Cold lasagna and coffee in the middle of the night. The combination makes me retch."

"No kind of food makes you retch. You love lasagna. I couldn't sleep, waiting for the phone to ring."

"My guess is, the crooks are gone. Maybe, with the cops all over that house on the corner, they got spooked." Joe looked at Clyde, frowning. "Did one of that scruffy gang kill Barbara Conley? Is that why her house is cordoned off, is that the connection?" Joe intended as soon as Max got to work, to hit the station. Police reports scattered on Max's desk were what he needed now.

"Speaking of Barbara Conley," Clyde said, "why the hell did you bring the kittens to a murder scene? You need to be more careful, Joe! They're too young to drag all the way across town and straight into a murder. What did Dulcie say? And what do you think the cops thought? It's bad enough if you accidentally let *yourself* be seen snooping around—but to bring the kittens! What the hell were you thinking!"

"I didn't drag them across town. I didn't know they were there in Max's office. They beat me to the station. They were hiding under the console when I got there. I didn't see them until Charlie called in, and Max was out of there, me right behind him—and there were the damned kittens! What was I supposed to do?"

"Take them home," Clyde said reasonably.

"There was a murder! Charlie called in a murder! Don't you think I was scared for her? How could I . . . I just took them with me, what else *could* I do? They promised to behave. I didn't know Striker was going to cut his stupid little paw and make a scene."

"The way I heard it," Clyde said, "Striker didn't make a scene. Kate and Charlie made a scene getting you cats out of there. The whole department was watching. Wondering what *you and your kittens* were doing there. You're always hanging around the station. Don't you think they wonder, when you show up at a crime scene, too? Don't you think some of those guys, particularly Max and the detectives, wonder why the hell you're so interested? And *now* you're bringing kittens . . ."

"Everyone knows cats are weird. Some cats steal their

neighbor's laundry and drag it home. Some cats . . . There was a clip on TV, some cat in England rides the train every day. Gets on in the morning, spends the day at the zoo, takes the train home again at suppertime. And James Herriot wrote about a cat that attended all the town meetings. Don't you think Max and Dallas, if they do wonder, would do a little research? That they would look up that stuff on the web and understand that many cats do strange things, that some cats have weird interests like stealing clothes and shoes. Look at Dulcie. Stealing silk teddies from the neighbors. She started that when she was a kitten. There's nothing strange for the cops to wonder about—or for you to get worked up about."

"I'd say you're the one who's worked up."

Joe sighed. In fact he worried a lot about what Max and the detectives thought. But right now it was really too early to argue. Night, beyond the kitchen window above the half curtain, was still as black as a rat hole.

"*And*," Clyde said, "what about Buffin at the vet's? When Kate and Charlie took Striker in to stitch up his paw and Buffin was so interested in the patients. What was that about?"

Joe just looked at him. Who had told Clyde about Buffin's unusual concern over the hospitalized animals? Either Kate or Charlie. Couldn't human females keep their mouths shut? The two were as bad as Kit, with her excited rambling.

Though the fact was, the buff kitten's perceptive remarks had frightened Joe, as did Courtney's inexplicable dreams or memories or whatever the hell they were. Couldn't he and Dulcie have had normal kittens—except for the talking part? He wouldn't want them to lose that talent, but did they have to add to the strangeness?

Royally irritated, Joe cleaned the rest of the cold lasagna from Clyde's plate, turned tail, and went back up to his tower, to calm himself before he hit the station.

When he passed the love seat in Clyde's study, Snowball looked up at him sleepily. She was so lonely with Rock away, on the fishing trip with Ryan's dad. Joe gave her an ear lick, a nose rub, then curled up and snuggled with her for a little while before he jumped to the desk then to the rafter, pushed through his cat door, and burrowed down among his pillows.

His early-dawn nap didn't last long. He was up again before the sun rose, ready to hit the rooftops, to slip into Max's office before the chief arrived. Ready to scan any reports that might have come in, try to figure out the relationship between Barbara Conley and the car thieves.

The sun was barely up when Max Harper called Clyde, who had gone back to bed after Joe left. Answering, Clyde tried to shake off the dark dream that had harassed him. "Of course they can come," he said sleepily. He didn't bother to ask why. "They can stay as long as Wilma likes," and he turned over and went back to sleep.

Wilma called twenty minutes later. She got Ryan, who was fully awake, dressed, and downstairs in the kitchen. Wilma told her about the break-in.

"That bastard," Ryan said. "What does he want? Of course you'll stay here."

"Dulcie will make the kittens behave. Max says—"

"It's a treat to have all of you. The kittens will be a blast. Have you had breakfast? Can I help you move?"

"In fact, you can pick me up. Max wants me to leave my car in the drive. So it won't look like I *have* moved out. This is so . . . unnecessary. If anyone else told me to leave, I'd . . ." Wilma sighed. "Max is so stubborn."

Ryan laughed. "That's why he's a good chief. You're all packed?"

"What little I'm bringing. An overnight bag, and kitten food."

"I'll be right over. Clyde can get breakfast."

While Wilma stood at the kitchen window waiting

for Ryan's king cab, Joe Grey, headed across the rooftops toward the station, had no notion that his family was moving in with the Damens', that his home would be wild with his own mischievous kittens. He slipped into MPPD behind two arriving officers, shortly before Max got to work. Easing down the hall into Max's office, he leaped to the desk where he could read quite handily the reports neatly arranged on the blotter, watching the door and listening for footsteps as he flipped each page with a practiced paw.

One stack was printouts regarding the car gang working up the coast in Cupertino. One stack was copies of Max's officers' reports about Molena Point's break-ins and thefts. Joe was stretching out for a better look at Max's handwritten notes on Barbara Conley's rental when he heard the chief coming down the hall, talking with Detectives Garza and Davis. Immediately he slipped into the in-box, curled up, and closed his eyes in deep sleep.

He heard Juana Davis pause by the credenza to start a fresh pot of coffee. Luckily the maintenance crew cleaned the pot every night, or they'd be brewing road tar. He barely slit his eyes open as Max settled into his desk chair, hardly glancing at Joe.

Dallas, carrying a printout, tossed his tweed blazer

on the back of the couch and sat down. His jeans were freshly creased; he wore a white T-shirt, bright against his fresh Latino coloring; his short black hair was neatly trimmed. Davis, at the other end of the couch, was as usual in uniform, Joe seldom saw her in anything but black skirt and jacket, black hose, black shoes. Her square build, square face, and short dark hair seemed right for the regulation attire—but Joe preferred Juana in something less formal, the jeans and sweatshirt she wore on a hasty night call.

Max reached underneath Joe, into the in-box, to retrieve a sheaf of papers. It had been years since he'd been careful handling Joe, wondering if he'd get scratched; now he glanced down, amused. "Looks like you have houseguests, tomcat. Looks like your family's moving in with you."

His words shocked Joe. Had Wilma kicked Dulcie and the kittens out? What could they have done that she would evict them? He was unsettled, too, that Harper talked directly to him. He seldom did that, sounding as if he expected an answer. But why not? Max talked to his dogs that way, and to his buckskin gelding. What pet owner didn't carry on a conversation with his animals?

But what was this eviction about?

Max looked at the two detectives. "A common break-in is one thing. But the trace evidence in Wilma's living room—same as that from the salon and from Barbara Conley's house."

Joe Grey kept his eyes closed, trying to hide his alarm. Someone had broken into Wilma's? Were Dulcie and the kittens all right? He'd seldom burned so fiercely to speak up and ask Max for the details.

"I want foot patrol, all three shifts," Max said. "Wilma's taking her cats and moving in with the Damens until we corral this guy.

"He broke the living room window around 3 A.M., was going through her desk when Wilma came out. When she drew on him he took one look at the gun, bolted out the door, and was gone. She chased him—a pale Subaru SUV, but she only got the first three numbers."

Davis said, "And you found the same trace evidence as from the murder scene?"

"McFarland did. Apparently the same flecks of Styrofoam, same as from Barbara's house."

Davis sat frowning, Joe could feel her eagerness to compare the evidence from the three sources.

"Ryan's picking Wilma up," Max said. "They'll leave Wilma's car in the drive. I'm sending McFarland to stay there, turn the lights on and off, the TV, the fireplace, let this guy think she's home. Either he's looking for something special or, after he tosses the place, he means to harm Wilma." Max looked at the papers Dallas held. "Is that from the lab?"

Dallas nodded. "Just came in—on some of the trace evidence from the Conley house." The detective smiled. "Looks like Langston Prince was in Barbara Conley's bed, maybe that same night."

Dallas took a sip of coffee. "And also in bed with her, fairly recently, was the man who killed them. The same dark hairs, other than Langston's, that we bagged near the bodies at the salon. Looks like all the Styrofoam flecks are the same, too. The lab is comparing them. And," he said, "they're comparing the blond hairs we found in both houses. Not all were Barbara's. Hers were dyed, long and everywhere in the house. The others were shorter, like a man's hair. But none of those were in her bed," he said, grinning.

Two men in her bed the same night, Joe thought, *isn't that enough? Maybe the car thief was there earlier that same evening. And,* he thought smiling, *she didn't even bother to change the sheets?* Tomcats weren't that fastidious, but Joe Grey found this particular situation disgusting.

"Strange about that neighbor's call," Max said. "Just a young girl, but she was as secretive as our snitches."

"Maybe some teenager," Dallas said. "Sneaked out with her boyfriend, didn't want her folks to know."

Davis said, "What about the fingerprints at Wilma's? Did they come up a match for those at Barbara Conley's? When do we get the word back on Rick Alderson, see if we have a match?"

Max leaned back in his chair. "We have Alderson's prints, from his records. The prints we got from Barbara Conley's match those we picked up at Wilma's—we got a quick answer on that. AFIS says there's no record on them. Nothing. This guy is not Rick Alderson."

"They're sure?" Dallas said. "Wilma says he's a dead ringer."

Max shrugged. "They're sure. No record. The prints from Wilma's match those at the Conley house and no record on them. AFIS ran both, to be certain—but there were smears, too, as with rubber gloves. A few partials where a glove was torn, but not much to go on."

This was all news to Joe. Pretending sleep, he tried to put it together. The trouble was he couldn't be in two places at once, he'd missed too much.

"I picked up a call when I came in," Davis said. "Jerry, the bartender over at Binnie's." Binnie's Italian was one of Davis's favorites, she and the bartender sometimes dated casually.

"He said Barbara Conley had been in the bar a number of times with a guy who looked like a muscle builder. Dark hair, black leather jacket. They'd come in late, stay sometimes until closing. But this was some weeks back, he hasn't seen the guy recently. He said she'd been in for an early dinner with Langston Prince a couple of times."

I guess, Joe thought, *there's nothing wrong with Barbara dating her boss—until the wrong guy sees him in her bed.*

Joe Grey didn't linger long over thoughts of human digression; he was soon out of Max's office, dropping quietly down behind the chief, slipping out then racing down the hall and out on the heels of a pair of attorneys, then up to the roofs and home. He wanted to be there when his kittens arrived, he wanted to be sure they were all right, after the break-in. Wanted to be sure they behaved. And, maybe he'd like to see his family happily settled, in *his* home.

14

Ryan pulled her red king cab into her aunt's drive between Wilma's car and the back door and quickly they loaded up—a small overnight bag for Wilma, a box of food and toys and quilts for the kittens. Leaving the house watched by three plainclothes officers wandering the neighborhood door to door handing out religious pamphlets, and by one of Ryan's carpenters measuring for the window, they hoped this much activity would keep the burglar away from the area until the house was quiet again. Wilma's car had sat in the same spot all night and would remain there.

Quickly the kittens leaped into the backseat, keeping their little mouths shut in case a cop, moving down the sidewalk, might hear them. All three were wide-eyed at this new delight, not only the exciting escape from the burglar, but the adventure of visiting a new house *and* taking over Clyde and Ryan's downstairs guest room all to themselves.

So far in their short lives they had been inside only two other houses besides their own: Kit's hilltop home with Lucida and Pedric Greenlaw, the cats all sitting before the fire listening to Pedric's tales; and Max and Charlie Harper's ranch house with its pastures and stable and hay barn where they could climb the tall bales, and chase mice. Now here was another new place to explore, and the first thing they saw as Ryan approached the Damens' house was Joe Grey's tower rising above the second-floor roof. It didn't look damaged at all, it looked brand-new.

"A tree really fell on it?" Courtney asked, switching her tail.

"It did," Ryan said. "It was all torn branches and broken glass. It doesn't take my crew long to fix a problem." As she pulled into the drive, Wilma, Dulcie, and the kittens all piled out, moving quickly into the shadows of the porch. Ryan took the big box from her, as the kittens fled up the walk, hit the cat door at a run, and bolted inside nearly crashing into the big silver Weimaraner. He stood shocked at the onslaught, but smiling and wagging his short tail.

Joe Grey leaped to the couch watching his unruly

kittens. "This is Rock," he said as the kittens warily backed off from the Weimaraner. They had too often been warned about dogs, especially big dogs. "Rock's all right," Joe told them, "he won't hurt you. He's an exception."

"Exception," Courtney said, not sure what that meant, but liking the new word. Was "exception" a kind of dog? Or did it mean different than others? Rock stepped gently among them to lick their faces. Reassured, the kittens rubbed against his legs. Ryan's dad had brought the sleek gray dog back early that morning from their vacation trip; he had brought, as well, a dozen fresh, cleaned trout that were now in the refrigerator. The kittens, following the delicious scent to the kitchen, searched the counters and table but found no fish at all. Disappointed, they bolted away again through the rest of the house. Dulcie started after them—until she caught Joe's look, and stopped.

"Let them go," Joe said. "Let them investigate."

Ryan agreed. "They can't get into trouble here as they might have up at the Harpers' ranch. No horses to step on them, no territorial barn cats to attack them."

"They have to learn about new places," Wilma said as the Weimaraner poked his nose at her, begging for a pet. "Even a new house is an adventure, they can't stay babies forever."

The kittens raced in again, pounding down the hall to explore the living room more fully, investigating the flowered couch and chairs, the three tall green plants growing in pots against the soft yellow walls, the fresh white draperies that begged to be climbed. But when they eyed the draperies then looked from Dulcie to Joe Grey, they backed off.

As Ryan and Wilma headed for the kitchen, they paused a moment to watch the kittens looking above the couch and the mantel at the framed drawings of Joe Grey and Dulcie, of Kit, of a little white cat and the big silver dog. They looked and looked; and Courtney said, in a whisper, "Charlie Harper did these. Oh my. One day, will she draw portraits of us?"

"I expect she will," Wilma said, wondering at the kitten's use of the word "portrait." A word perhaps from memory? From some long-ago dream?

But Striker and Buffin were most fascinated with Joe Grey's comfortable chair, frayed, clawed, fur matted; Courtney joined them there, they all had to roll in the deep cushions, in their father's scent, flipping their tails and purring.

Joe and Dulcie watched them investigate behind the furniture, picking up new smells; they followed the kittens as they prowled again through the big family kitchen with its round table, the flowered chair at the far end that also smelled of Joe and of Rock and of another cat.

"You smell Snowball," Joe said, leaping to the kitchen table. He looked at his three curious children. "When you discover Snowball, be gentle with her. She's not used to new visitors. She's a shy, tender little cat—but she doesn't speak. Be kind with her, you three."

The kittens looked back, very serious, then raced away to find Snowball; but pausing to investigate the downstairs guest room, rubbing their faces against its wicker and oak furniture, they quickly made it their own room. It was already scented with Wilma's overnight bag and with their own sacks of kibble, their own toys and blankets.

Best of all were the softly-carpeted stairs leading from the hall to the rooms above: they raced madly up and down, leaping over one another, flipping around in midair, dashing between Rock's legs as he ran up the stairs gently playing with them. Dulcie followed to keep them out of trouble. Joe Grey remained in the kitchen watching Wilma slice cranberry bread and Ryan brew coffee; Ryan wore a flowered apron over her worn jeans and khaki work shirt, the ruffled hem brushing the top of her leather work boots. They could hear, upstairs, the thunder of Rock's paws, and the kittens' softer thumps as they leaped from desk to rafter and down again; they had strict instructions not to go out on the roof.

Ryan said, as Wilma sat down at the table and poured the coffee, "I'm still nervous about the break-in. That was no casual burglary, not after his following and watching you. You have nothing of huge value, not like the mansions up in the hills or along the shore."

"Janet Jeannot's painting," Joe Grey said, leaping to the table. "Janet's landscape hanging right there over Wilma's fireplace."

Ryan nodded. "That painting of the village is worth a nice sum. But it isn't as if you own a whole collection of expensive art, or a houseful of priceless silver and antiques. Besides Janet's landscape there are only the few pieces of jewelry Kate has given you. They're worth a lot. But even if he'd seen you wearing them, how would he know they were real? And," she said, putting sugar and cream on the table, "if he was looking for jewelry, why would he look in your desk? He—*Oh*," she said, looking at Wilma, then at Joe Grey. The tomcat's yellow eyes were smugly slanted, waiting for Ryan to catch up.

"*Oh*," she said again, "*the Bewick book?* But how could he know about that? Anyway, it's gone now," she said sadly. "There's nothing but ashes."

It was the feral cats who had first discovered an old

and sturdy, handmade wooden box buried among the ruins beneath a tilted foundation. They had led Wilma and Charlie Harper there to find, within, an ancient and valuable volume, hand printed on thick parchment pages. Old, handmade type, hand set, and printed by some early, manual process. The illustrations were woodcuts, hand carved, hand printed. The volume had been produced by artist and writer Thomas Bewick in 1862.

Of the few original copies that remained, most were owned by collectors, each worth at least several thousand dollars. But this one single copy had an added chapter at the back, where Bewick had written about the cats he had encountered in his travels. Wilma and Charlie had been so excited to find such a treasure; but they were shocked when they read that chapter. Why had Bewick written this?

Later when Wilma researched through all the collectors' and libraries' lists of ancient books, through all the sources she could find, there was no hint of this unique, single volume. She didn't understand why Bewick had produced that copy. He had to know how dangerous any printed word was for the safety of the cats he had so admired—someone who loved the speaking cats should be committed to keeping their secret. Had Bewick let his urge to tell such a wondrous tale, to produce just the one volume with its beautiful woodcuts, override his concern for the cats themselves?

The book, she thought, hidden there in the Pamillon estate, had to have belonged to someone in the Pamillon family. Had they all known the secret, or had only a few? If the wrong person read those words, they might well go searching for the rare cats, meaning to exhibit them, to show them on TV, make fortunes from the innocent creatures.

Fortunately, that seemed not the case with this family—the Pamillons might have been strange in many ways, but the person who had hidden the book had apparently remained silent. One old aunt, who had died recently, had known all her life the truth about the feral band that lived in the ruins but she had said no word, Wilma was certain of that.

There were a few men in prison who knew; no one could say how they found out, but they had cruelly trapped several of the feral band. Charlie had freed the leader of the clowder, and Clyde had helped to release the others from their crowded cage.

The day that Wilma and Charlie found the book and brought it home, Wilma had locked it in her desk; but soon she had moved it to her safe-deposit box, adding Charlie's and Ryan's names and giving them keys. Then, not long afterward, for the future safety of the cats, but their hearts nearly breaking, the three women had burned the rare volume. They had felt sickened, standing around Wilma's fireplace watching the flames devour a treasure singular and precious.

Now, in the kitchen, Ryan said, "How could this Rick Alderson, who is *not* Rick Alderson, how could he know about the book—*if* that's what he was after?" She looked at Joe Grey. "Do *you* know something we don't, tomcat, with that sly look? Or are you only guessing that's what he's looking for?"

Joe lifted his paw, snagging a slice of cranberry bread. "I *wish* I knew more, I wish I could put it together—but that's the only thing Wilma did have of great value," he said, licking crumbs from his whiskers.

"And who is this guy," Joe said, "if not Rick Alderson? He's apparently part of the car thieves, and he could be the beauty salon killer. How does Wilma fit in, how does the book fit in? Could he know about it from someone who'd been in Soledad Prison?" Nothing Joe had picked up, snooping on Max's desk and listening among the officers, had touched on rare books or the theft of books. But, he thought, if the Bewick book *was* what this guy was after, even if it had been destroyed, could it be used to trap him? Quietly enjoying his snack, Joe began to put together a plan. "Maybe . . ." he said. "Maybe if—"

A sound from above silenced him, a rocking and sliding noise, a rhythmic thumping from Ryan's studio. They all looked up, listening—until a crash directly overhead sent Joe and Wilma and Ryan flying away from the table. A thunder so loud they thought the ceiling would fall sent them racing for the stairs. Between their feet the little white cat bolted down headed for the kitchen and safety. From above, Rock's thundering bark filled the master bedroom and studio, an angry, puzzled challenge.

Then, as suddenly, silence.

An empty, guilty silence.

Racing upstairs they found, at the top of the steps in Clyde's study, nothing at all amiss. Ryan moved to her right into the big master bedroom. The doors to the dressing room and bath were closed. She looked in both but everything was in order; the entire room was undisturbed, even the space under the bed.

They headed for her studio.

Sunlight blazed in through the glass walls that framed the oak and pine trees. Sun shone on Ryan's beautiful, hand-carved drafting table, picking out the ornate curves of its metal stand and its sleek oak top. The table lay on its side, the big, movable drafting surface wrenched away from the intricate metal stand, the floor dented where the table had crashed and broken.

Three pairs of blue eyes peered out from among the wreckage, two innocent buff faces and Courtney's calico face serious with guilt. The kittens were too chagrined to even run away.

Dulcie, her ears back, her striped tail lashing, hauled Buffin out from beneath the curved metal legs, her teeth in the nape of his neck. Holding him down with one paw, she nosed at him, looking him over. "Where are you hurt?"

Buffin shook his head. "Not hurt."

"Get up, then. Walk quietly over to the daybed, get up on it and stay there." She watched him walk, saw he wasn't limping. Turning, she bore down on Striker. "Are *you* hurt? Oh, Striker! Your paw is bleeding through the bandage."

Ryan grabbed some scrap paper from the wastebasket, laid it on the floor. Dulcie said, "Come out from under there and sit right here, put your paw on that. Now, Courtney. Are you all right?"

Courtney nodded, her ears and tail down. She wouldn't look at her mother.

"Then you can tell me what happened," Ryan said as she grabbed a roll of paper towels for Striker.

"Rocking," Courtney said guiltily, her eyes still cast down. "We were rocking. We . . . we loosened those bolts just a little . . ." She indicated the handles that held the drafting table at whatever angle Ryan chose. "And we jumped on it and it rocked and rocked and it was such fun that we rocked harder . . ." Now she looked up, her eyes bright. "Rocked harder still, all three of us back and forth, and . . ." She looked down again with shame.

"And the table fell," Dulcie said furiously.

So far Joe Grey had stayed out of it. He was too mad to let loose with what he wanted to say. He watched Ryan wrap the paw in the paper towels, then retrieve rolls of gauze and tape from the master bath; then he turned his fierce scowl on Dulcie. "And where," he said, "where were you when this happened? I thought you were watching them."

Now Dulcie's own look was guilty. "I was on the roof. I heard a car come down the street real slow, heard it stop then creep on again. I got that funny feeling—you know the feeling . . . I thought it might be the burglar, that he'd seen Ryan pick us up this morning, and I raced up for a quick look. The kittens were quiet, nosing at the cabinet drawers and at the mantel, smelling everything. I thought I could leave them for a minute. They loosened the bolts and started this rocking after I left," she said quietly.

"I thought at first it *was* Wilma's stalker, I'm still not sure, you can't see much inside a car from the house roof. I could see the driver's arm, part of a thin face. He was wearing a cap and I think his passenger was, too, a heavy man. They moved on slowly and then paused, moving and pausing, looking at all the houses. There was someone in the back, someone smaller, maybe a woman or child. I was about to race down to the street for a better look when I heard the crash." She looked at Ryan and at Joe. "I'm sorry I left them. Your lovely antique drafting table, Ryan. Can it be mended?"

"It can be mended just fine, Scotty can mend anything," Ryan said, stroking Dulcie, giving her a little kiss between the ears.

"And the kittens are sorry, too," Dulcie said, looking pointedly at Courtney who had seemed to have been the instigator of their game: *Rocked and rocked, she'd said, rocked harder still . . .* her blue eyes bright with the fun.

Joe Grey remained quiet, his ears flat, his yellow eyes blazing. The kittens had never seen their father so angry—though, in fact, Joe wasn't nearly as mad as he looked. Half his mind was further away than broken drafting tables as he put together a plan that he thought might trap Wilma's stalker.

He watched Ryan call Clyde at the shop. "Could you come home for a little while? Wilma's here, and Rock's here, but . . . I have to run an errand and . . . we think the burglar could be watching the house. I'll explain later."

She picked up Striker, as Dulcie ran for the king cab; Buffin followed, refusing to stay behind. Not so much because he was worried about his brother but because the hospital fascinated him—and because he wanted to be near Dr. Firetti, wanted to watch him work. John was like family, his touch, at their birth, had been Buffin's first contact with the human world. His presence had honed deeper into Buffin's emotions even than the love the doctor generated in Striker and Courtney.

Wilma was saying, "I'm fine, Joe, with you and Rock here. Clyde doesn't need . . ."

"Let him come," Joe said. "He needs to keep his mechanics busy." Wilma sat down on Clyde's love seat, holding Courtney, who was still quiet and ashamed. Rock soon joined them, herding Snowball up the stairs, the little white cat calm once more, under the Weimaraner's care. Joe sat on Clyde's desk secretly smiling, thinking about his project, then joining the dog and Courtney and Snowball stretched out across Wilma's lap.

"What?" Wilma said, watching Joe. "What are you hatching?" She knew that devious look.

"Just thinking," he said, hoping to con her into his plan. Wilma might not believe the would-be thief knew about the Bewick book, but Joe wasn't so sure. Why would he search her desk but not take her checkbook or even the little stack of petty cash she kept there with a rubber band around it? If he was looking for that particular volume, he knew it was worth a fortune. If this man—who might be connected to the man who shot Barbara Conley and Langston Prince, connected to the suspect in a bloody double murder—if this man knew what was printed in the added chapter, all their clan of speaking cats was in danger.

But, Joe thought again, even though the book was gone, it might still trap the prowler. He looked at Wilma, considering. "You *do* still get upset over having burned the Bewick book. Even a few weeks ago when Dulcie mentioned it, you looked sad, still full of regret."

"It was a lovely book. The work that went into it, the wood engravings, the hand-set type. I only wish I had one of the other copies, one from the regular edition."

"You've already tried to find one," Joe said. "But when you did, it was too expensive, enough to keep Dulcie and me and the kittens in caviar for years." And, taking the direct approach, his pitch went on from there. Wilma listened, stern and silent, as the tomcat laid out his plan.

15

Ryan, with Dulcie on her shoulder and Buffin rearing up beside her, watched John Firetti tuck Striker into a cat kennel on a soft blanket. Immediately Buffin leaped in, too, refusing to leave his brother. John had resewn the wound where Striker had ripped out two stitches. Same routine, but this time the cats were silent as a technician assisted him. Only when she'd left did John speak to Striker, petting him, but stern, too. "You are to rest. You are to stay off the bandaged foot and behave yourself. No running, no jumping. In fact, to keep you quiet, to let the healing begin, I think I'll keep you for a day or two."

Striker looked chastised and obedient. Buffin looked delighted, hoping he could stay, too. He looked around for his little dog friend.

"Lolly's so much better," John said, "thanks to you, that I've tried sending her home." They looked up as Mary Firetti slipped into the hospital room. She gave Ryan and Dulcie a hug and stood with them beside the cage door. She wore pale tan jeans and a cream sweater that flattered her sleek brown hair. Neither woman liked to see the kittens in a kennel. "They'll sleep with us tonight," Mary said, "if Striker will promise to be good."

"No jumping off the bed," tabby Dulcie said, "or off anything else. You think that paw will heal with you pounding on it and knocking over furniture?"

Ryan, pushing back her dark hair, reached in to stroke and love the two kittens; and Dulcie padded inside to lick their faces; but soon they left the hospital, Dulcie draped over Ryan's shoulder. Crossing the garden, walking Ryan to the truck, Mary said, "It will be nice to have those two beautiful boys for a few days. John does love them. And Pan can go home to Kit for a while; he's refused to leave us since his father died. I've told him he should be with Kit, that Misto would want him there, but talk about stubborn." She looked at Ryan, her eyes tearing. "Pan's been so dear. It's been hard, learning to live without Misto. If Pan hadn't stayed with us, the emptiness in this house would have been intolerable. Even when, sometimes, we sense Misto's spirit nearby, we can't touch him or hold him, we can't snuggle him the way we snuggle Pan—and now will snuggle the kittens."

"He'll never leave you for good," Ryan said. "His spirit will never leave any of us. He might be gone for a while, but he told us all, more than once, that time is different where he is. Misto has families through the centuries to be with when he's needed, other people he loves, but never more than he loves you and John."

"Early that morning," Mary said, "when he passed—the glow rising above us, the echo of his voice as he moved into that next life. We know he isn't gone."

Ryan hugged Mary, nearly squashing Dulcie between them. She swung Dulcie into her king cab, and they headed home, Dulcie curled on the seat beside her, already missing her kittens, her chin and paw draped across Ryan's leg. "They're growing up fast," she said sadly, looking up at Ryan. "They'll want their own lives one day, and they'll choose their own work," she said thinking of Buffin there in the hospital and how happy he had seemed.

When they pulled into the drive, Clyde's vintage Jaguar was there, leaving room for Ryan's pickup. Rock, still nervous from the crashed drafting table, greeted them at the front door as if he had been standing guard. Ryan, heading for the kitchen, glanced up the stairs where Clyde sat at his desk. "Home," she called up to him. In the kitchen, Wilma sat at the table with fresh coffee, reading the morning paper; it was so neatly folded that Wilma wondered if Joe Grey had even touched it; she was amused that she didn't have to read around syrupy pawprints.

Clyde left his desk and came down. "Striker's all right? And where's Buffin?"

"Striker's fine, and Buffin wanted to stay with him," Ryan said, releasing Dulcie to hop down to the table. "The Firettis were pleased, they love those kittens," she said softly.

Dulcie lay down on the table close beside Wilma. Joe Grey leaped up beside her, fixing his yellow gaze on Wilma, giving her an urgent, *let's get on with it* look.

Dulcie watched him, suddenly wary and alert. From the kitchen counter Courtney watched with bright intensity. While she had napped with Snowball, her father and Wilma had had a long, whispering conversation. What wondrous thing they were planning.

But Clyde glared hard at Joe. Not for a minute did he trust that look, nor did he trust the excited amusement in Wilma's eyes. "What?" he said. "What's with you two?"

Wilma shrugged, and looked at Joe. Joe had started to lay out his plan when they heard the front cat door flap open, and Kit and Pan came galloping into the kitchen; smelling cranberry bread, they leaped to the table. As Ryan cut a slice for them, Clyde remained staring at Joe and Wilma, waiting for the bomb to drop. Whatever they were hatching, this was going to mean trouble.

Quietly Joe, under the gaze of his two human house-mates and surrounded by the questioning cats, shared his plan.

"Charlie's the best prospect," he said. "The stalker might not even know her." He looked at Ryan and Clyde. "The prowler, if he's been watching this house, too, he knows both of you. He might have seen Charlie here, but maybe not. And she fits right in, she's in and out of the art shop all the time, and in and out of the PD."

"I don't like this," Clyde said. "It could get someone hurt, probably Officer McFarland."

"But McFarland will be there anyway." Joe reached a paw for another slice of cranberry bread.

"And," Clyde added, "Charlie isn't a good choice, she's Wilma's *niece*. He could have seen her there any time—no one could forget that bright red hair."

"She can wear a cap," Ryan said. "Tuck her hair under." There was a long silence, then Wilma rose, heading for the guest room. Clyde and Ryan followed, the cats dashing past their feet.

Within minutes they were all gathered on or beside the desk as Wilma, comfortable in the wicker desk chair, called Tay's Rare Bookstore, in the village. Yes, they still had the copy she had inquired about several weeks ago, one of the original editions of Bewick's memoir. Despite the cost she put it on her credit card and asked them to wrap it in plain brown paper. When she'd hung up, she called Charlie.

An hour later, Charlie had cut her long red hair nearly a foot shorter. Feeling naked and regretful she left the house, cranked up the old green pickup they used around the ranch. Heading for the village, she parked in front of the art supply as a minivan moved out. She entered the store wearing a cap, not one curl of red hair showing, her dark glasses propped across the crown.

She spent perhaps fifteen minutes choosing her purchases. Leaving them there to be wrapped, she slipped out through the storeroom's back door to the narrow alley that ran through from the art store past the backs of a deli and an upscale camera shop, to the rear of Russell Tay's bookstore; passing trash cans lined along one wall, she slipped in through the unlocked back door.

She moved from the storeroom into the shop, into the smell of old books. She found Russell at the counter, slim, white haired, the lines in his face solemn and patient. He had set the book aside, concealed in brown paper as Wilma had requested. She tucked it into her oversized purse; they talked for only a few minutes, about the weather, the windstorm, and El Niño, then she hurried out the back again.

She knew she was being watched.

Coming down the alley she had glimpsed Dulcie peering over directly above her; and on the roof across the narrow side street she could barely see Joe Grey in a mass of overhanging pine branches, could see only the narrow white strip down his nose, his white chest and paws—and the gleam of his yellow eyes as he watched the street below him.

At the far end of the group of shops, Pan and Courtney crouched at separate corners, Pan above the alley, Courtney above the street looking very full of herself because of this important mission. The calico was as much the drama queen as Kit, giddily proud to be performing a glamorous job while her two brothers lounged in a cage in John Firetti's hospital, even if they were being spoiled.

Charlie caught sight of Kit last of all, up in the pine tree that hung out over the street where, from its branches, she could see both ways down the sidewalk, could see every passing shopper.

Hurrying back down the alley, her package in her

carryall, Charlie was startled when a heavily muscled man turned the corner, coming straight toward
her—he fit too closely Kit and Pan's rough description
of the man they'd seen at Barbara Conley's house on
that windy night.

But no, this was not the same man. This fellow was
lame, limping along. He passed her paying no attention
as she slipped back into the artist's supply.

Above her, the cats, having watched her progress,
crouched together now on the roof of the art supply watching her load her packages in the passenger
seat of the old pickup and set her big carryall on the
floor. That's where the book would be, a book like the
one Wilma had burned—or almost like it, Courtney
thought. How strange and complicated was human life.
As Charlie drove away, Courtney snuggled up to her
daddy, and knew that his anger about the drafting table
was gone. She thought about Charlie going on with Joe's
plans and hoped . . . No, she *knew* his scheme would
work just fine—as sure as hiding cheese to lure a mouse.

From the art shop Charlie drove to the bank. Taking
off her cap, shaking out her red hair, she found a clerk
free and went straight to Wilma's safe-deposit box. She
signed their card, used her own key, removed the metal
drawer and carried it into a small, locked cubicle.

Removing the book-sized package from the metal box she unwrapped the age-stained white paper, then the disintegrating piece of ancient leather wrap, revealing a small and empty, carved chest. Opening this, smelling the lingering scent of the old book that was no longer there, she unwrapped the brown paper from the book she had just picked up. Same title, same binding, same dated first edition. Placing this in the chest she wrapped it up again in the frail leather and then the brown paper.

This she put in her carryall. She took the metal drawer back where the clerk followed her into the vault, slid the safe-deposit box into its slot, saw that it was properly locked then headed for MPPD. There was nothing unusual about her going into the station, the chief's wife was in and out frequently, to have lunch with Max, sometimes to pick up their young ward, Billy, after school was out. This morning she skipped Max's office, found Jimmie McFarland in the conference room typing a report. She gave him the box, and gave him instructions.

"This," Jimmie said, his brown eyes amused, "you know this is entrapment, Charlie."

They looked at each other for a long moment. "It really isn't entrapment," Charlie said, "that's more complicated. And it sure isn't if you don't arrest him for stealing. If all you cite him for is break and enter, that's only a misdemeanor."

McFarland grinned at her. She said, "All Wilma wants is to know if the book *is* what he's after. If he finds it and heads out with it, that will be her answer."

Jimmie still had that stern, cop look that he tried so hard to maintain. The young officer's natural expression was friendly and warm, and didn't always suit his profession. Charlie said, "You're there to protect Wilma's house. She reported a break-in, she's afraid he'll come back and trash the whole place. You're there not only as a cop, but as a friend."

"But the book," he said doubtfully. "How can a book be worth . . . ?"

"It's old, Jimmie. Nearly two centuries. Handmade, hand printed on leather parchment. The type is all hand set, every picture is an original engraving done by the author."

Jimmie shrugged; Charlie knew about these things. The art world wasn't his thing—counterfeit bills, false driver's licenses, fake IDs, fingerprints, and electronic images he understood. But ancient hand-set type and engravings were something yet to learn about.

Charlie said no more. She was hoping their thief would know so little about that one particular Bewick book that he would think he had found the real thing, had found the one incriminating volume.

She thought, too, that it wasn't likely he was alone in his search. Her guess was that several people knew about the book, knew more about the Pamillon history than the stalker might know. Could he have some connection to the Pamillons? Or was that only coincidence? Charlie just prayed that, in the process of planting the book and finding out what this *was* about, they could keep Wilma safe, and Jimmie, too. It seemed a long time, now, until night would fall and deepen and, hopefully, Wilma's stalker would return.

16

Jimmie McFarland went through Wilma's usual evening routine, making sure the lights were on and off at their normal times, the hearth fire burning, the curtains securely drawn. Settling down before the fire to read a batch of reports, he waited for their thief—their possible murder suspect—to make an appearance; and wondering if Wilma's bait, judiciously hidden, was what the guy was really after. Ordinarily, one rare book alone would not be of such interest to a common thief. An entire library of valuable collector's books, yes. As he mulled over the thought that the burglar had more complicated motives, the evening darkened and the wind sprang up sending shadows racing across the draperies.

Turning on an old CD of Dean Martin, settling before the fire thinking about making a sandwich, he rose when a car pulled up the drive. Quietly he moved into the shadowed kitchen.

The knock on the back door was light and hasty. A woman's voice called out, "Wilma?" He smiled at Ryan's voice, she knew Wilma wasn't there but didn't want anyone out in the dark to know it. Hand on his holstered gun he stepped into the laundry.

"It's Ryan," she called out. "I brought you a steak. We grilled, and . . ."

He turned on the outside light. Gun cocked in case she was followed, he opened the door, stepping aside nearly behind it.

She was alone. If Wilma *were* here, and *had* answered, the music would have covered her voice. "Did you get my call?" she said softly. "I left you a message." Ryan handed him a plate covered with foil, it smelled like heaven. He set it on the laundry counter and looked at his phone.

He'd left it off; he felt his face color with embarrassment. She grinned at him. "Have a good evening, my steak's getting cold," and she was gone, backing out in her king cab.

He locked the door, turned his phone on, uncovered the warm plate with its thick, rare filet, fries, and a salad. He knew there was an apricot pie in the kitchen.

This, Jimmie thought, wasn't a bad gig, for overtime work.

Up the hills evening darkened with the same cloud-shifting wind, but not a gale wind like the night of the car thefts. Kate's mind was on McFarland at Wilma's house waiting for the stalker, as was Scotty's as they sat at the little kitchen table, eating a supper of bean soup and corn bread. Wind fingered at the windows, and across the way at Voletta's, wind made shadows dance across the dark bedroom glass. The whole front of the house was dark, and there was only a faint light at the back. Had Lena gone out, leaving her aunt alone? She was here to take care of Voletta, not go chasing around. Kate couldn't see Lena's car, though if she'd parked up close to the back porch it wouldn't be visible. Voletta's old muddy pickup stood farther from the house. As she reached to slice more cornbread, a pair of dimmed car lights came up the back road from the direction of the village and freeway.

The car pulled out of sight close behind the house. They couldn't see Lena get out but they heard her voice as the driver's door slammed. Two more doors closed and they heard men's voices.

"Lena has a boyfriend?" Scotty said. "Or maybe two?"

"She arrived alone, I didn't see anyone. Voletta didn't mention anyone." Soon the living room lights came on, then the lights of all three bedrooms.

"You can see more of the house from the mansion," Scotty said. "From where we're working. I saw the shadow of a man down there today, he was careful to keep out of sight."

"I guess," Kate said, "we shouldn't be judgmental, when we're living . . ."—she flushed—"conjugally."

"Only until you agree to marry me," he said softly. "What is it, Kate? What's the secret? You divorced your husband years ago. You told me there's been no one else. Why can't you tell me what's wrong? Am I not the right man, am I a one-night stand?" He looked at her deeply. "I don't think so. And Kate, nothing can be so bad that I couldn't overlook it. I'm a very forgiving guy."

Leaning over, he lightly kissed her forehead. The wind rustled harder against the windows. Their supper was getting cold. Across the little hill, the lights soon went off in all three bedrooms and the living room. The kitchen lights had been turned up brightly, lighting the trees beyond; and as the clouds moved on, freeing the moonlight, Scotty looked up at the mansion. In the open-walled upstairs nursery, a movement drew their attention.

"The ferals," Kate said softly. Three pale shapes

were crouched at the edge of the floor where the wall had fallen away. Willow, Sage, and Tansy? They, too, were looking down watching Voletta Nestor's house.

"I've seen them watching before," Kate said. "At night when the moon's bright it's not hard to see their pale coloring. Since you've started work, they don't come down here much, only early in the evening or maybe late at night. I don't think they hunt down below Voletta's, her goats and that donkey chase them."

"Why do the cats watch her?" Scotty said. "What are they curious about?"

"Maybe the kitchen lights, watching the movement behind the curtains. Cats are fascinated by movement."

"They're strange little cats," Scotty said lightly. "Sometimes they watch us at work. Always shy, half hidden, but not as if they're afraid." He put his arm around her. "What will happen tonight, at Wilma's? Will the stalker try again, and take her bait? Or go after Wilma herself, thinking that she's there? What *is* the connection between them? I hope McFarland nails him and hauls him off to jail." Beyond the windows, the clouds scattered southwest, opening up the moon-struck night over the village, over the Damens' house.

In the Damen patio, warm in sweaters and jackets, their table pulled up close to the hot barbecue, Wilma,

Ryan, and Clyde, and slim, elderly Lucinda and Pedric Greenlaw, were wondering the same. Would McFarland trap Rick Alderson or whoever the prowler was, land him in jail and keep Wilma safe? *Was* this young man connected to the murder scene, and maybe to the car thefts? Joe Grey and Dulcie, Kit and Pan and young Courtney crowded on one end of the table enjoying their share of steak and fries. Only Dulcie ate a little salad. Courtney, having never had filet mignon, gobbled the sliced steak with greedy delight. Never could she remember, in her dreams of other lives, a meal like this, the meat crisp on the outside, rare within, and more flavorful and tender than any scraps of boiled pork or Irish mutton. She knew she had enjoyed grand feasts as well as leavings, somewhere and sometime; but she had enjoyed nothing like this steak dinner right here and right now. She caught Kit laughing at her, the tortoiseshell's yellow eyes teasing her for her greed. She didn't care, she hissed smartly back, and returned to her supper.

Clyde was saying, "Last time they hit Sonoma, five cars stolen, twenty more left on the streets robbed or trashed or both." He looked at Joe Grey. "Max said the Sonoma sheriff has found the five cars, and has two drivers locked up."

"So?" Joe said. "Sonoma is working car heists. MPPD

is also working two murders and now a break and enter. Give our guys a little credit."

Ryan said, "What about the Styrofoam? How can something as innocuous as scraps of Styrofoam offer a link the police can prove? Seems to me that's circumstantial."

"It's a good start," Clyde said. "If those flecks did come from a stolen car, and then were in Wilma's house, and in Barbara Conley's house . . . If Max can find that car . . ." He looked at Kit and Pan. "The car you saw in the garage that night."

Kit said, "The wind blew away the dust on the drive so clean it blew away the tire marks. But there *were* tiny pieces of packing, wind blew those so hard into the bushes it was like someone pressed them there, stuck tight."

Joe said, "Pretty strong coincidence."

"And you don't even believe in coincidence," Wilma said, scratching Joe's ears. "I hope," she said, "if the thieves come back to work this area, I hope Scotty will stay on at the shelter. I don't like to think of Kate up there alone."

Ryan pushed back her short, dark hair, her green eyes watching Wilma. "With Scotty restoring the mansion, working there all day, it's easy enough for him to stay." She smiled. "Kate says he's grown really interested that the ferals sneak down sometimes to hide and watch them work."

"The wild, speaking cats?" Courtney said. "But Wilma, *you* said they're afraid of humans."

Ryan said, "They like Kate and Wilma. And Charlie and I used to ride up there a lot. But still they're shy of most humans, and that's a good thing."

Courtney drew herself up tall, lifting her front paw with the three black bracelets, the orange and black markings on her back bright even in the soft patio lights. "I want to go there. I want to talk with the ferals, I want to see the ruins, I want . . ."

Joe Grey looked hard at her. "If you go there, Courtney, Dulcie and I will take you. Or Kit and Pan will. You are not to go alone."

"Why not? Kit goes alone."

"It's too far. Kit is not a half-grown kitten. You can't run and dodge and disappear as fast, yet, as she can. You can't climb as high and fast, yet. Do you remember Kit's story of the mountain lion?"

"I remember."

"Sometimes there *are* mountain lions there in the ruins. And bobcats, and always coyotes. You will not go alone, Courtney, until you are a grown-up fighter. And even then, alone isn't safe."

"But if you go with me . . . ?"

"We'll think about it," Joe and Dulcie said together.

"At least there's no gang of thieves up there," Pedric said. "What's to steal at the ruins? Not a car in sight except Kate's. And Lena's car, down at her aunt's. Those crooks want a crowded neighborhood, lots of cars to hit all at once." The older man, tall and regal looking, took Lucinda's hand. "I'm glad I got my gun permit."

"I feel safer, too," Lucinda said. "And I feel easier with Kit home safe at night, and now Pan, too. We missed you," she said, stroking the red tabby's back.

Pan said, "I do love John and Mary, but . . ."

"But," Lucinda said, "you didn't plan to stay forever. Now the kittens have taken over for a few days, and that's good for all of them."

Dulcie and Joe looked at each other, thinking about their boys going off into the world. Only a few days seemed to them like the prologue to forever. Did all parents feel this way?

But Courtney's look was . . . What kind of look *was* that? Regret that her brothers might move away? Or a sly smugness at having Wilma and Dulcie to herself, having their house to herself? And at having their daddy all her own, at least some of the time.

When, even in the walled patio, the wind quickened and the clouds drew down, the party picked up their plates and leftovers, Clyde put out the fire in the grill, and they moved inside; the conversation turning again to Jimmie McFarland, tucked up in Wilma's house, waiting for a window to break, a door to wrench open. But soon the Greenlaws headed home, Kit and Pan trotting close beside them as they unlocked their Lincoln, the car that had once nearly been the scene of Lucinda's and Pedric's own murders.

Well, that adventure came out all right, Kit thought, shivering, *that night on the narrow mountain road when we nearly went over and I ran from the wrecked Lincoln and called for help for Pedric and Lucinda and the coyotes nearly had me.*

When Clyde and Ryan came racing up the highway together with Rock and the cats, they saved me, Ryan shot the coyote and saved me. Life, Kit thought, *life is good when you have strong and loving friends to help you. That night,* she thought, trembling, *they sure saved my little cat skin.*

17

The Damen house was dark except for ghosts of moonlight shifting beyond the shades. Joe Grey woke feeling off center. What had woken him? He was not in his tower, nor was he in Clyde and Ryan's bed. He was downstairs in the guest room stretched out on the quilt between Dulcie and Courtney, the three of them crowded against Wilma. He could just see Rock over by the door, lying on the throw rug, Snowball snuggled warm between his front legs. But where were Striker and Buffin, where were the boys?

When he remembered they were cuddled up with the Firettis, Joe scowled with jealousy. Their kittens were cozy in another household, with new friends. And again Joe felt abandoned.

But the two boy kittens *were* getting big, their

blue eyes showing the first glints of yellow and gold in their pale buff faces. At their age, Joe had been on his own, making his own living—such as it was—evading bigger, vicious alley cats, hiding from stray dogs among the street rubble, rummaging for his supper in San Francisco's garbage cans. Now, it was nearing the time when his own growing kittens would venture into the world for good, choosing the paths of their separate lives—choosing better than the homeless world where *he'd* first landed.

It hurt, deep down, to think of Buffin and Striker leaving the nest, it hurt Dulcie, and it upset Wilma. Wilma's house *was* their nest, Dulcie had birthed the kittens there, had nursed and trained them, had watched them claw the furniture and climb the draperies and duck their heads in shame when they were scolded. Dulcie and Wilma had told the little ones myths, and Joe had told them stories about the real human world that amazed them. He recalled their heart-pounding delirium when each kitten spoke its first words, proved indeed that he or she was a speaking cat, was as rare and talented as everyone had hoped they would be.

Yawning, knowing that Striker and Buffin were safe, he wondered again what had awakened him—then he was sharply alert thinking of the stakeout, of Wilma's house empty but not empty, police moving unseen through the shadows of Wilma's neighborhood, Jimmie McFarland dozing fully dressed atop Wilma's bed with the light on as if Wilma were reading. Jimmie in dark sweats, soft shoes, gun, holster, radio . . .

Carefully Joe eased out from beside Dulcie and slid to the floor. When Rock raised his head, bumping against the closed door, Joe gave him that *be quiet* look. But Rock didn't need it, he was as silent and alert as if he, too, were off to track a felon.

Joe shook his head. "You need to stay here." He nudged Rock gently until the Weimaraner slid over a few inches, easing Snowball with him. Joe pulled the door open with his claws, gave Rock another look that told him to stay, and slipped through.

He trotted softly up the stairs, hopped up quietly on Clyde's desk, leaped noiselessly to the rafter and out his cat door. Nudging open a window he hit the roof and took off running. He didn't hear a sound behind him, heard no stir of soft paws in the fitful breeze as Courtney followed her daddy—and as Dulcie, angry at them both, raced to catch up, both females staying to the shadows, silent as velvet.

Jimmie McFarland woke as disoriented as Joe Grey— but only for a second. He sat up wide awake, swinging his feet noiselessly to the floor, hand on his holstered gun, listening.

He could hear a thief rummaging the house, moving the couch out from the wall, the hush of books being shuffled back and forth in the bookshelves, of the desk drawers opening. He listened to the prowler search the dining room, the buffet and china cabinet. The kitchen and refrigerator took a long time as he tried not to rattle the dishes and pots and pans. He went through the laundry, Jimmie heard him open the freezer, after a few minutes closing it again. Heard him move the washer and dryer as if to look behind them. Heard him come down the hall, check out the guest bath, then open the linen closet, listened to the soft hush as he shuffled towels and sheets. Then the thief was in the guest room.

The faint sounds of drawers opening, of bedding being tossed aside, of the bed being moved, perhaps so he could look at the back of the headboard. When Jimmie heard the closet door slide open he silently turned the lock on his own door, the heavy bolt that had been installed and oiled the night before.

Moving soundlessly down the hall, he heard the boxes on the shelves being shoved aside—then, a second too late, heard the guest room window slide open, heard the guy hit the ground running. Jimmie was down the hall, through the window after him, racing between the line of neighbors' garages and the rising hill, moving south, half his thoughts on the two officers working the street, wondering where they were. Tall, big-handed Crowley, six feet four, could pick the thief up like a rag doll if he caught him. Portly Brennan was slower, but tough, and reliable with a gun.

He hadn't stopped to see if the book was missing, he knew it would be. The guy running between the hill and the garages stopped sometimes as if to listen. Yes, as he fled again, a gleam of moonlight caught the corner of the package. Same size, same pale color like brown wrapping paper. Strange he didn't climb the hill—except he'd make a perfect target against the moon-pale grass. The moon hung low in the west, hitting the hill, leaving the yards dark. Beyond Wilma's, the houses were close together. The runner paused at each narrow, dark side yard then went on, dodging bushes and trees. Suddenly he vanished. No sound, no movement in the shadows.

Jimmie used his flashlight, shining it into the narrow yards, into the crowded shrubbery. He was about to double back when he heard someone running again, and then two men . . .

He knew Crowley's footfall. He heard the faintest hush of a door closing. Crowley stopped, they both stood still, one at each end of a narrow yard, listening, the faintest streak of moonlight touching Crowley's cap where he stood by the corner of the garage; the walk-in door was halfway between them.

When there was no more sound, when they shone their lights around the door and into the shrubbery there were only empty shadows. Jimmie flashed his light once, then covered his tall partner while Crowley, wearing gloves, tried the door.

It was locked.

Moments earlier when Wilma's stalker had slipped out the guest room window carrying the box, he heard McFarland come out behind him. He knew there'd be other cops. Earlier, he had jimmied the lock of one of the garages down the row—when he heard McFarland drawing too near then heard a second man running, he eased open the door, slipped in, locked it from inside. He heard them try the door, fiddle with the lock, then soon they moved on down the row of houses, one at each end of the side yards.

The garage was neat and uncluttered. Low moonlight shone through the narrow, obscure glass in the big double door. There were two cars, both of them unlocked. Silently rummaging, he found little of value in the Ford Taurus.

In the black Mercedes he found, shoved back under a tangle of pamphlets in the glove compartment, the concierge key on a big ring. People were so stupid. They hid, or thought they had hidden, the nonelectronic model so when they went out to dinner or to a hotel they could give the attendant only the car key, no opening codes, no handy house key attached. He was thinking about starting the engine, opening the garage fast and taking off, when he heard a car start up the street, heard it move away south. A quiet, heavy vehicle that could be a cop car.

Quickly he left the garage, he couldn't lock the side door behind him but the cops had already checked it. Slipping away, keeping to the shadows, he was lucky this time, the patrol car had gone on.

Moving fast and silently along the dirt path, he hustled down the last four blocks to the little corner grocery. He stepped behind it into the narrow strip of woods that separated it from the motel above and from Ocean Avenue. There were two homeless men asleep between the pines. They didn't wake. The grocery's little parking lot, which opened to the cross street, was empty. Staying beneath the bordering trees, he watched for the dark SUV that would pick him up. He had no notion that he was stalked by more than cops. When he heard a car coming he was prepared to race to it—

until he saw the cop car behind it, and backed deeper into the woods. It wasn't his ride anyway, but a white minivan.

Dulcie, running shoulder to shoulder with Courtney, didn't say a word to her. She couldn't talk, with cops down there on the street, and if she did speak, she didn't know what would come out; she didn't want this to end in a spitting match—she was so mad at Courtney for following Joe that she wanted to smack the headstrong kitten.

But Courtney had only meant to help her daddy. The calico's busy paws tore across the shingles, her determined little face so coldly serious that Dulcie couldn't scold her. They had crossed Ocean Avenue under dark trees, well behind Joe. There was no traffic. They climbed a vine silently and hit the roofs again. They were on the shop next to the little corner grocery when suddenly ahead of them Joe stopped. Dulcie and Courtney froze.

But he hadn't seen them, he was peering over the roof's edge where trees lined the market's parking lot, intent on a man hidden in the trees' shadows. When the figure heard a car coming he moved out among the row of trees that led to the street. Dulcie could barely make out his long thin face. He carried the box, wrapped in paper. He stepped back when a minivan passed below, moving slowly. A cop car followed it.

The officers pulled the driver over with flashing lights. They got out, ordered the driver out. He stood facing his van, hands on the roof. They frisked him and questioned him. They searched the van, looked at his driver's license, then sent him on his way.

At first sight of the patrol car, the burglar had slid deeper in the pines and shrubbery. Now, when the cops had gone, he slipped his phone from his pocket. He spoke softly. Dulcie watched Joe listen from the roof then quickly choose a pine and back down, she watched him warily. If someone was picking this guy up, she knew what Joe meant to do.

"You stay here," she told Courtney; but already the young cat was wired to move. *"Right here!"* Dulcie repeated. "Don't you dare go down off this roof, not for anything. If I . . . if you are left alone, you are to go to your pa's house. Do you know how to get to the Damens'?"

"Of course I know," Courtney said, bristling. "Down that street four blocks, and to the left past Barbara Conley's with the yellow tape." And she turned her face away, sulking.

As Dulcie slid into a bougainvillea vine and down among its thorny branches a car pulled into the lot, a dark, older SUV. At once the thief fled from the bushes and opened the driver's side back door. He folded half of the backseat down so it matched the platform of the rear storage space. Leaning in, he rummaged among the jumble at the back, tucking the box he carried under some duffel bags and bundles.

Behind him, Joe Grey sped for the open door, leaped in and slipped over behind the passenger's seat. He could say nothing as Dulcie flew in and pressed against him; he glared at her, furious, ears back, yellow eyes narrow. He watched her claw a dark blanket down from the seat above them. As they slid under, Courtney flew in behind them.

They couldn't scold, they daren't even whack her lightly for fear she'd hiss and fight. This calico was getting too big for her britches.

Quietly the thief shut the door, went around and opened the front passenger door and slipped in. The driver took off, skidding as he turned.

Headed where? Where was he taking them?

Dulcie pushed the blanket aside for a little light. Courtney was wide-eyed and shivering. She hadn't thought, she had only meant to help her pa. She hadn't helped him at all, and now she was filled with fear. Dulcie thought of the time Joe had gotten in a car headed who-knew-where, and ended up in the parking garage of the San Jose airport, some eighty miles north. Lost, alone, surrounded by cars driving in and pulling away, a regular riot of moving wheels, he'd seen a woman he knew shot to death. He had, at last, stolen a cell phone from an open truck, had called Clyde and Ryan to rescue him.

Now, sliding around where she could see between the two front seats, Dulcie got a look at the driver: a heavy fellow, dark, short hair, heavy shoulders. He was built like Pan's description of the car thief that windy night, the man whose trail bore the same white, flaky evidence as that from the beauty salon murders. Looking closely, she could see the same white specks stuck in the crepe soles of his dark shoes.

Kit and Pan hit the roof of the village market at the moment that Joe Grey, Dulcie, and Courtney dove into the dark SUV, saw them flash into the car and disappear. "Oh my," Kit said and crouched to leap after them but Pan jerked her back, teeth and claws in her shoulder.

The two cats had, shortly after they'd returned home from dinner at the Damens', slipped away again after giving Lucinda and Pedric face rubs, and loving them. They beat it out the cat door, headed for the stakeout at Wilma's house where they knew Joe would be. There they had waited on the roofs across the street for a long time, they had watched Wilma's living room light go out, then the reflection of the bedroom light come on, glancing off the pale back hill—and Wilma's stalker appeared from the shadows near the front door.

This time he must have had a lock pick; it didn't take long and he was inside. They came down from the neighbor's roof and up onto Wilma's shingles. They listened to him toss the house, the living room, the kitchen, they moved across the roof just above him the way they might follow the underground sounds from a squirrel tunnel. They heard, after some time, the stealthy sliding of a closet door in the guest room, the dry sound of shuffled boxes. Where was Jimmie? They scrambled down from the roof, they were racing for Dulcie's cat door when they heard a back window slide open, heard the soft sound of running on the dirt path behind the house. From that moment, everything was confusion; climbing to the roofs again, leaping across the side yards scrambling from tree to tree chasing running footsteps. More than one man running but, in the dark below them, in the windblown night, all was uncertain. What they thought was the perp turned out to be a cop. What they thought were two perps, they saw suddenly were McFarland and Crowley. Where was Joe Grey? The running was louder, then it stopped; a door opened and closed softly. Silence, then a cop approached the door, found it locked, and moved on, looking back. The cops were gone when the door eased open and a tall, thin man came out, closing it behind him. He ran, almost soundlessly, racing along the edge of the hill and behind the village market. When he hid among the trees they crouched on the roof, listening.

They could smell Joe Grey's scent on the shingles, could smell Dulcie and Courtney. Below, the black, windy, moonlit scene held them, the white van and the cops' car, then the dark SUV, the perp leaping in, the three cats behind him. Kit crouched at the edge, ready to leap down. Pan grabbed her, stopping her—and the car skidded away, turning onto Ocean.

They followed up Ocean, over cottages and shops. When they couldn't see up the hill any farther they scaled a tall pine to the top. *"There!"* Kit hissed. The SUV was climbing the last hump to the stop signal. They waited, panting, to see which way it would turn.

It turned north where Highway One would lead to a cluster of freeways. Kit couldn't stop shaking. *Oh, how did Joe let this happen?* And the road was empty behind, no patrol car was tailing them. How did the cops, scouring the neighborhood, how could they miss such a blatant escape? Kit wanted to yowl.

"A phone," Pan hissed, and they spun around, heading down the tree, dropping from branch to branch.

Joe's house was the nearest; but as they dropped to the sidewalk Kit said, "Wait . . . Wait one minute." She raced across the parking lot to where the SUV had stopped. She sniffed where its tires had stood, smelling at the paving; she looked up at Pan making a flehmen scowl. The pavement smelled of . . . *what?*

"Garlic," she said, inhaling again. "Garlic, geranium, eucalyptus, and . . . goats." It was a sickening combination. "And here's a eucalyptus leaf bent and crunched as if it fell out of a tire tread."

"There are eucalyptus trees all over the village."

"But that's exactly what grows at the edge of Voletta Nestor's weedy yard. I notice it every time we hunt on the Pamillon land, the eucalyptus, that ornamental garlic, its long silver grass. Red geraniums. And the damned goats," she added. She looked at him, her eyes bright.

"Come on," he said, and they raced through the dark for Joe's house.

"If we can slip into the kitchen," Pan said, "make the 911 call without waking anyone . . ."

"But we'll have to wake Clyde, we need wheels. We can tell the cops about the car the prowler got into, and which way it went. I couldn't see the license, only the first part, 6F . . . couldn't see the rest. But how do we tell them that three cats are trapped in there, that the department's Joe Grey is shut inside with those crooks?" She shivered, approaching the Damens' cat door. The night was moving toward dawn, and where were Joe and Dulcie and Courtney headed? Slipping inside through the little plastic door, hurrying to the kitchen and a phone, Kit imagined the car turning onto the freeway, its three stowaways crouched out of sight, unable to see much out the windows above them, no idea where they were going or what would happen to them, and again she thought, *Why did Joe do this? Dulcie and his own kitten? How could he let this happen?*

18

Joe and Dulcie knew they were on Highway One, they had felt the car turn north. Soon they felt the echoing rumble as they went through the long tunnel where, above the highway, the grass grew tall, the land rolling away into the hills so one often forgot that the freeway snaked underneath. They sometimes hunted that lush verge, so dense with ground squirrels, snakes, and mice. Often they caught the scent of coyotes there or a cougar or bobcat that had come down into the village canyons. Now, the cats were more tense at their present situation than at the smell of a four-legged predator. Dulcie and Courtney wished they hadn't jumped in the car so rashly but they couldn't have left Joe to be carried away alone. What had he been thinking, to trap himself in here with two killers? Courtney wished her daddy hadn't come out tonight, wished they were all safe at the Damens', snuggled among the quilts with Wilma. When they felt the car change lanes, felt it speed tilting down an exit ramp, they dug their claws into the floor mat. Then they were on level road again, moving fast to the northeast.

"For crissake, Randall, slow down."

"Let it rest, Egan."

The cats looked at each other. *Egan?* Then the AFIS records hadn't missed anything, this man really wasn't Rick Alderson—unless he was using a fake name.

"We don't need the CHP on our tail," Egan said, "after that beauty parlor mess. Maybe, Randall, you need to be more careful."

"What I need," Randall said, "is a hamburger, before we load up and take off." Wide shouldered, muscled, and broad, *was* this the man who had been in Barbara Conley's house that windy night?

"We're already past anywhere to eat," Egan said. "Why don't you think of these things sooner?"

"I wanted to get out of there. Them cops . . ."

"It was you said you'd drive. Ma would have done it, if you hadn't argued."

"She's all over the damned road. I love your ma but I wish we didn't have to use her for transport."

"We need every driver we can get. You love her all

right. And every other woman who gives you the come-on." Egan turned, looking dourly at Randall. "You can cheat on them—cheat on Ma—but they better not double-cross you."

Randall jerked his hand up as if to smack Egan's face.

"Watch the road, for crissake."

"I'm watching the damn road." Randall glanced up at the sky above them. "Hope they're ready. It'll be getting light soon, we don't have that much time."

Dulcie looked again at the driver's short black hair, dense and wiry, and thought of the black hair in the trace evidence that the cops had bagged from the murder victims. Slipping over behind the driver's seat, she peered around to get a good look at Egan, his long thin face, thin nose, and light blond hair. That color hair hadn't been among the evidence at the murders, but his blond hairs had been collected in Wilma's house, and Barbara's, along with the bits of Styrofoam packing that stuck to everything. They could smell the men's sweat. And could smell the mud on Egan's shoes—mud from behind Wilma's house, the scent of mint that grew at the foot of the hill.

Courtney, clinging to her mother, trying not to panic at what might lie ahead and trying not to feel car sick, closed her eyes and ducked her face under her paws.

Willing her memory-dreams to take her, carry her away from whatever was going to happen.

Closing her eyes, slipping into another time, another place away from her terror, she eased down among sod houses with thatched roofs, a woman she had loved, milking a small, cranky cow, her long hair tied back, her rough-spun skirts muddy along the hem.

But fear was *there*, too. When the woman's sour husband came out and started sharpening a sword, the calico had fled. The scene was so clear. Soon there were more men, in steel armor and helmets, tall men on horseback. She felt the woman pick her up and carry her into the cottage, then the dream twisted into a haze of tall mountains, then broke apart into a meaningless jumble, the woman holding her softly; and she slept.

Dulcie, snuggling her kitten, knew she was off in another time. She felt both curiosity at what Courtney was seeing, and envy that she could bring back those ancient days—just as their friend Misto had remembered his past. As sometimes Kit while dreaming reached out a paw as if to touch someone or something that, in sleep, must seem very real.

Randall had slowed and was looking around almost desperately as if seeking a way past something ahead. The cats could see nothing from their angled view up through the windows, could see only night and the flash from moving car lights. Randall slowed even more, pulled over abruptly onto the bumpy shoulder, speeded up as if to go around some impediment—but suddenly slammed on the brakes. "Hell! Damn it to hell!" His maneuver woke Courtney, startled at his shout and at the lights all around them glaring through the windows, blazes of flashing red, now, that could only be the demanding signals of emergency vehicles.

Earlier that night, when Kit and Pan had raced to the Damens' to call 911, they'd thought the house would be dark, that everyone would be asleep. But a light burned in the living room, glowing through the plastic cat door as they slipped through.

Three scowls met them: Ryan and Clyde and Wilma, in their nightclothes, solemn with anger. Kit and Pan could smell their fear.

"Where are Dulcie and Joe and Courtney?" Wilma said. "Oh, they didn't go home to my house? Not in the middle of a stakeout? Oh, Kit! Why do you think I brought Dulcie and Courtney over here, but to keep them safe!"

"But I . . . we didn't," Kit began.

"Where are they?" Clyde said, his frown fierce. He wore a Windbreaker over his sweats and was jingling his car keys. Kit had never seen him so angry, she didn't know what to say, she didn't know how to tell them.

"The phone," she whispered. "We need . . . They're in the getaway car . . ."

Ryan fled for the kitchen, Kit in her arms. Within seconds she had dialed 911; she held the headset for Kit, her own face pressed close to listen. Behind them Clyde and Wilma crowded against them.

"The stakeout at Wilma Getz's house," Kit told the dispatcher. "Two men took off from the market parking lot, maybe ten minutes ago. Dark older SUV, maybe a Toyota. First two numbers of the license are 6F, that's all I could see. They're heading north . . . Heavy man like a body builder, dark hair. Thin young guy, blond, long thin face . . ." She paused a moment, thinking how lame was her little whiff of scent-evidence, wondering if it meant anything.

"They might," she told the dispatcher, "be headed up toward the ruins, toward Voletta Nestor's house, the house with that old barn behind, but that's only a guess." As the dispatcher put out the call, Kit pressed the disconnect.

Clyde had left the kitchen, they heard the Jaguar start. Ryan shouted and ran, raced out the front door. They heard the Jaguar idling, heard the car door open, heard them arguing, Clyde's voice quick and angry. "You can't leave Wilma alone."

"Her stalker's gone, Clyde. You heard what Kit said. *You're* not going off alone after those men!"

"Shut the door, Ryan. The cops don't know about the cats. If they catch that car, there's no one to help the cats. Shut the damn door. Stay with Wilma, she . . . Oh hell . . ."

Wilma flung the back door open and slid in, Kit and Pan clinging to her. "I locked the front door," she said as Rock bolted over her to the other side of the seat. She handed Ryan a jacket, and pulled on her own short coat.

Clyde, looking back at her, swore again briefly before he headed for the freeway. Wilma had been his best friend since he was a small boy when she was his neighbor, a glamorous college student living next door. They'd never abandoned that friendship; she was family—but right now he could have gladly strangled her. He scowled in the rearview mirror. "You carrying?"

"Of course," Wilma said coolly, pushing back her gray-white ponytail, frowning back at him as he turned onto the freeway.

"Ryan?" he said.

"Yes," she told him, slipping an automatic and a shoulder holster from her handbag, buckling on the holster then pulling on her jacket.

Kit crowded onto Wilma's shoulder, looking out the window, prayed the cops were ahead of them, already cornering the SUV. What if the dark car had turned off and somehow evaded the patrol cars? "Oh hurry, Clyde. Please hurry."

"Driving as fast as I dare," he snapped; he seldom snapped at Kit. The speedometer said eighty-five. "If we get a cop on our tail, it'll only slow us down, trying to explain."

When Kit looked at Pan, he was as nervous as she. She thought of the SUV's tires that smelled of Voletta's place. *Could* they be headed there?

Did they mean to take the book there to Voletta? Who else would know about a hidden book removed from the Pamillon mansion, who else but a Pamillon? Who else would have sent someone to steal it back? None of the family lived anywhere near nor seemed interested in anything about the old place, even Voletta's niece, and she hadn't been there often before her aunt got hurt. And if Voletta had hired those men, what was the relationship between them, that she would trust them to bring her the book?

Could Kit's wild guess about the smells be right?

Garlic, eucalyptus, and geranium, growing thick around the old barn. She prayed to the great cat god that her hunch was on target, that the crooks were headed there with their unknown captives, prayed as hard as a little cat can that Joe and Dulcie and Courtney would escape safely.

19

Something woke Kate. She glanced through the bedroom door to the shelter office and caught her breath. A dark figure stood at the window silhouetted by bright lights. Then she saw it was Scotty.

The bedside clock said 3 A.M. Pulling on her robe, she went to stand beside him. Below the shelter and the Pamillon ruins, a pool of light shone across Voletta's yard, a wider circle than the porch light could ever make.

The wide, weedy yard was full of cars. Three darkly clad figures were pulling cars out of the old barn, lining them up facing the road. Most of them were new or late models, shining in the floodlights.

Only a few days ago the barn had been empty, she had seen Lena open it to get a length of hose. Just a few bales of hay in there, some farm tools and ladders. A couple of dusty trailers pulled in, at the far corner. Now, watching with disbelief, she looked up at Scotty. "Not the *stolen* cars! Here in Voletta's yard! This *can't* be part of the car ring!"

"I've already called the department." Scotty, feeling her shiver, pulled her closer, his arm warm around her. "Where else would those cars come from?"

"But that gang isn't working the village now. That night when the wind was so bad was the last night. The paper said they've moved on, that they're somewhere up the coast. Eureka, I think. And Voletta—how could that frail old woman be mixed up in a crime ring? That's ludicrous."

Scotty hugged her closer. "Looks like they're using her place as a storage stop. They might bring cars from anywhere. Or these could be the Molena Point cars, they steal the cars in the village and hide them here. Move them later, during the time the gang has gone on up the coast, drawing more of the highway patrol with them. That means they have more crew than we thought." He looked down at Kate. "How long has this been going on? Have you seen this before? Seen lights down there?"

"No. But I haven't been staying up here long, just since we moved the cats in. And I don't usually wake at three in the morning—not until the storm hit, and you were knocking on my door," she said, coloring slightly. "I'm up at midnight to check on the kennel cats, then fall back asleep until about six."

He stood thinking, his red hair and beard caught in the light from below. "How often did Lena visit her aunt, before Voletta was hurt and Lena moved in?"

"Every few weeks, I guess. I didn't make a point to go down and visit with her," she said coolly.

Scotty laughed. "No girly chats over a cup of tea?"

She made a face at him.

It was then that Ryan called to tell them about Joe and Dulcie and Courtney. "There may be a car headed to Voletta's. We . . . Kate, if a dark SUV pulls in, it's Wilma's stalker and that heavyset man. We don't *know* where they're going, but Kit says the scent on the tires could lead there, to Voletta's place. Joe and Dulcie and Courtney are trapped in that car."

"Oh my God."

"The cats dove in behind the driver's seat. When it stops, see if you can delay the car, give them a chance to get out . . ."

Kate said, "Voletta's yard is full of cars, men we've never seen are moving cars out of the old barn. These have to be the stolen cars. Scotty's already called the department."

When they'd hung up, Scotty, moving into the bedroom, pulled on his boots and a jacket over his sweats and hurried outside. "I'm going over to the mansion," he said, "where I can see better."

She watched him cross her freshly mown yard and then the tall grass of the berm that separated the shelter from the mansion. He stood just inside the missing wall of the living room, keeping to the shadows. She dressed quickly in a sweatshirt and jeans, strapped on her shoulder holster feeling slightly foolish, and pulled on a vest to conceal it. *Better foolish than unprepared.* Max had insisted she be armed when she moved up here alone. "You have your permit, Kate. Use it." He didn't know, then, nor had she, that she wouldn't be alone. She was watching Scotty again when something pale moved beside him. One of the feral cats? Surprised, she watched him crouch and reach out to it.

The ferals never came that near strangers. Even when they watched Scotty working on that part of the house, they were shy and wary. Scotty wasn't one of the inner circle, those few who knew the speaking cats' secret. She stood frowning and puzzled.

Yesterday morning when she woke at five, Scotty had already eaten and left; the apartment smelled of coffee and fried eggs and bacon. In the tiny kitchen she'd found his dishes neatly washed, resting in the drainer. Looking out at the frost-pale lawn she had seen where his dark footprints had crushed the frost from the mowed grass; had seen the taller, wild grass of the verge falling aside where he had walked through. Maybe, she'd thought, he'd had some new thoughts about the work on the living room, maybe he had gone over to the worksite to consider some change?

But his footprints did not lead to the front of the house, they went toward the back of the old mansion. Dressing quickly, she had gone into the biggest shelter, down at the end, petting cats as she went and talking to them. Standing on a log that was part of a tall cat tree, she could see Scotty behind the old house at the edge of the small, sheltered patio that joined a large bedroom— the private little garden where, not long ago, Ryan and Wilma had found the Bewick book buried.

She had watched him kneel down. She had frozen with surprise when three of the feral cats came out of the bushes and fairly near to him, stood watching him, unafraid: pale Willow and Tansy, and dark tabby Coyote.

She could swear he was talking to them, trying to entice them closer to be petted, these wild cats who would have nothing to do with most humans.

Did the feral cats sense something in Scotty that

made them trust him? Did they see a quality in him that drew them, maybe sense the old Scots-Irish traits that might be sympathetic to their own heritage? The cats did not move closer, they were still for a few moments, listening to him, studying him with interest—but then they turned away, almost as if something he'd said had startled them. They drifted back into the shadows and were gone—and within Kate something joyful had exploded, a hope that bubbled up fiercely and made her smile.

All that day she had found it nearly impossible not to wonder if Scotty had guessed the cats' secret or was on the verge of guessing. Might he have thought he heard them talking and, though he really couldn't believe that, he was curious?

Or was it the cats alone who were making the advances? But why? Even if they were drawn to him, why would they want him to know their secret, these cats who were so shy and careful? The secret that no one who knew, could ever tell?

This solemn confidence was the reason she wouldn't marry him. How could they be one when she was bridled with deception, with a lie by omission that she must forever hide?

All yesterday she had thought of little else. She was

so excited that he might know the truth, it was hard to act normal. But now, tonight, with the serious activity below, she put aside her own questions.

Scotty still stood unmoving against the open living room wall, the pale cat companionably beside him, both of them watching the men busy below, moving cars—and was that Lena down there, helping them? Lena dressed in dark sweats, dark boots, dark cap pulled over her hair, stepping out of a pale convertible that she had just pulled into the line of cars? Kate studied the three men, and didn't recognize them. And where was the dark SUV that Ryan had called about? The car carrying the three terrified cats?

It was hard to think of Joe Grey frightened, but this time he had to be—terrified for little Courtney and for Dulcie, the three of them trapped in a strange car, traveling through the night with men who might be killers. Kate pressed against the office window. Where was the SUV? *Was* it coming here or headed somewhere else? Where were Ryan and Clyde, where were the cops?

In Clyde's Jaguar, Kit stood on Wilma's lap, her front paws on the back of the front seat, looking up the dark freeway, watching the SUV they followed. There was not much traffic at this hour—until they heard sirens behind them and saw flashing lights and Clyde pulled over into the right lane, out of the way. Two police cars passed them fast, rounding a curve where, ahead, emergency lights flashed from a fire engine and from rescue units. Two trucks were turned over, blocking both lanes. An officer was putting up barriers and red lanterns as a cop with a flashlight flagged Clyde down; he parked on the shoulder.

A bright yellow pickup was rolled over, a blue and white bakery van half on top of it, one wheel still spinning. On the side of the road just ahead, the dark brown SUV stood parked, with a long dent down the left side. The left front door had been pried open or maybe sprung open at what appeared to be a sideswipe. The black-haired, muscled driver was leaning halfway out, trying to pull himself free. A CHP officer stood with a gun on the man. At last the big man, grabbing the roof, hoisted himself up and out. As he tried to stand erect, leaning on the door, the three cats exploded out behind him—they fled under the car away from the freeway, across the dirt shoulder and up the grassy hill to vanish among the oaks.

While two sheriff's deputies shackled Randall, Ryan was out of the Jaguar chasing Joe and Dulcie and Courtney, Kit beside her, Rock and Pan racing ahead. Climbing the rough ground in the dark, trying to avoid protruding roots, Ryan called to the cats, "It's all right, you can come down! Come down, kitties. Come down, Joe! Come here to me!" She knelt, waiting for them.

Slowly the three cats came out from among the trees. Even Joe Grey looked haggard, staying close to little Courtney, who was still shivering. Clyde and Wilma climbed up to kneel in the tall grass beside Ryan. Wilma picked up Dulcie and Courtney and held them close in her arms. Clyde hid his frown as Joe Grey clung to his shoulder, the tomcat's face pressed against Clyde's morning stubble, Joe's sudden need for him bringing tears to Clyde's eyes. Kit leaped to Wilma's lap and began to wash Courtney. Rock, rearing up, licked the three escapees and sniffed them all over, picking up the scents of their journey in a strange car. No one scolded them for their wild expedition and for getting themselves trapped—but Wilma looked accusingly into Joe Grey's yellow eyes.

Joe had gotten Dulcie and Courtney into this mess. She was thankful that at least the boy kittens were away at the Firettis' and safe. *But Joe,* she thought, smiling just a little, *he was only being his macho self; he was only trying to catch a killer.* "Did they get the Bewick book?" she asked him.

"In the back," Joe said, looking down the hill toward the SUV, where an MPPD officer was handcuffing Egan. "Maybe I can slip in and get it . . . It's heavy as hell. If you . . ."

"Leave it there," Wilma said. "It could be evidence, proof that Egan stole, as well as broke in."

"But you paid a lot for that book."

"It's more secure at the PD. If he knows where it is, and if he's released, he'd have a hard time trying to break into the department's evidence room."

Two MPPD vehicles were pulled up behind the brown Toyota. The cats went silent as McFarland and Crowley left the other officers, came across the road, and started up the hill to them. The humans rose, holding cats, wondering how they were going to explain having the five cats out here in the small hours of the morning during a car chase.

Rock, delighted to see his cop friends, trotted up to lick their hands, distracting Jimmie long enough for Clyde to say, "We're headed for the shelter. Kate called, she's been staying up there until she gets a live-in caretaker. She sounded scared, and that's not like Kate. Sounded like she desperately wanted some backup, she said something was going on down at the Nestor place—men she'd never seen before, moving expensive cars out of that old barn. What would Voletta Nestor be doing with a bunch of fancy cars?" Clyde knew he was talking too much. "Kate said she called you?"

"She did," Jimmie said. "We're headed up there, backup behind us and roadblocks ahead. But what are you doing with your cats out here in the middle of the night? That *is* Joe Grey? Why . . . ?"

"The damn-fool tomcat," Clyde said. "They leaped out of the SUV. I don't know what happened, the driver must have left the window down, somewhere in town; maybe there's food in there."

McFarland just looked at him.

"I don't know where they are half the time—but to see them jump out of that car . . . One of these is Joe's kitten. Wilma was worried sick." Clyde started down the hill. The cats watched young Jimmie McFarland, wishing he weren't so nosy. And, walking down the hill, McFarland watched Clyde. He was silent for a long while, keeping pace with Clyde. "I guess," he said at last, "unless something more turns up, we don't need to bother the chief with the cat story. I don't see how it affects the case."

Down on the road, Officer Crowley was helping Randall, in leg irons and handcuffs, into the back of an MPPD squad car, pressing his head down so he wouldn't crack his skull. Crowley's big, bony hands handled Randall like a rag doll. On the other side of the seat, Egan was already confined. He looked across at Wilma so sadly that she approached the car. He said, through the cracked-open window, "I wanted to talk to you. When I was watching you? It was because I wanted to ask you something."

She looked at him and said nothing.

"About my father," he said. "You knew my father."

"What's your name—your real name?"

"Egan. Egan Borden. Randall, here, he's my stepfather. I took his name, Borden." He looked over at Randall. "You hurtin' pretty bad?"

"Nah," Randall growled. "Hitch in my side is all."

Wilma looked at Egan. "What was your family name, who was your father?"

"My father was Calvin Alderson. He got the chair for murder, you helped send him there. I know he was executed for murder but that's about all I know. A social worker told me that much, when I was older. They think he killed my mother, too."

"What was your mother's name?"

"Um . . . Marie. Marie Alderson." Wilma watched him, knowing he was lying, and, again, she was silent. If this young man was *Rick* Alderson, he was seven years old when his father went to prison, he'd remember quite a bit about Calvin. And why lie about his mother's name? But how *could* he be Rick when the fingerprints didn't match? She was filled with questions—questions she couldn't ask here, with officers listening. She wanted a proper interview with this man, maybe a recording—and so would Max.

She was convinced Randall was Barbara's and Langston's killer, but was his stepson—Rick or whoever this was—a part of that murder? "You'll be in Molena Point jail," she said. "We can talk there." She turned away, walked over to the Jaguar, slid into the back between the cats and Rock. In the front seat, Ryan and Clyde were quietly talking.

McFarland, stepping over to the driver's window, put a hand on Clyde's shoulder. "CHP has cleared a path around the wreck, there against the hill. Wait until our units are through." He scowled at Clyde. "Though I'd rather you turned around and went home. We don't know what we have, up at Voletta's."

"Kate sounded pretty worked up," Clyde said. "Sounded scared." He didn't mention that Scotty was there; their personal life was their business. He guessed Kate *was* frightened, if even tall, capable Scott Flannery wasn't enough backup. "Whatever's happening," he told McFarland, "Kate asked us to come, and that's where we're headed."

McFarland sighed. "Take the main road to the shelter, up above Voletta's road. Stay off her place, and keep out of sight. Stay at the shelter with Kate, stay out of the way, Clyde." No more was said about the two prisoners who were headed for jail. And McFarland said not another word about hitchhiking felines.

20

The five cats sat on the desk in the shelter office, their noses pressed to the window, watching the spotlighted farmyard below. The old place *had* once been a farm. The house, and the barn half hidden by eucalyptus woods, showed little change from their distant past except for the absence of crops and useful livestock. A once productive piece of land now dry and sour. Overhead the night sky had turned from black to the color of wet ashes. The cats' tails were splayed out on the desk behind them, Dulcie's striped tabby tail very still; Courtney's orange, black, and white appendage twitching with interest; tortoiseshell Kit's broad, fluffy flag flipping with her usual excitement. Pan's orange-striped tail was curled around him, Pan himself rigid and predatory—as was Joe Grey as he joined them.

Across the way, Clyde and Ryan, Kate and Scotty, and Wilma stood in the shadows of the mansion's open walls watching the cars lined up on the weedy gravel yard, the men and Lena milling around as if waiting for someone, perhaps waiting for more drivers.

Beside the desk Rock reared up, paws on the windowsill, wanting badly to bark; Dulcie had already silenced him twice, receiving that reluctant, *I'm bigger than you* look. Now Joe shut him up—Rock knew to mind Joe Grey.

"Where's the PD?" Kit said. "Where's McFarland? Where's Dallas, and the chief?" They had thought the law would be there by now, would already have these men surrounded, would be shackling them, locking them in squad cars. There wasn't a cop in sight. "If they get those cars away, if they head up the coast . . ."

"Not to worry," Joe said, twitching a whisker. "Dallas just called Clyde. There won't be any cops, they're letting them go."

"Letting them go?" They all stared at him. "They can't let them go," Dulcie said. "With all those cars . . . They can't just . . ."

Kit's yellow eyes blazed. "Why would . . . What is Dallas thinking, what did he say?"

"They're not coming *here*," Joe said. "They'll tail the cars as they turn onto the freeway. He has eight men following for backup, in four unmarked cars, those older, used cars with police radios. They'll follow them, with two sheriff's backups way behind and three CHP units up ahead. They'll see where they take the cars—chop shop, dealer, who knows? They'll let them pull in and get on with their business, then nail them. Maybe I could just slip into one of the—"

"No you don't," Dulcie said, her ears back, her dagger paw lifted. "I've had enough scares for tonight."

"I didn't say *you'd* be . . ."

She just looked at him, her green eyes blazing.

Joe didn't like that she was scared for *him*. But then he thought, maybe he did like it, maybe he liked that fierce female caring—maybe she was thinking about the kittens, about the safety of their father. Below them, the entourage, apparently deciding Egan and Randall weren't going to show, began pulling out. Two of the five men who had arrived earlier were pulling the trailers with clamped-on hitches behind their stolen cars, the trailers loaded up with a Lexus and a Porsche, both nearly new. Leading the entourage was a short, fat man in a black Audi. Eight cars, and each would bring a nice piece of cash—and two more cars that should be following, left behind in the barn. Bringing up the rear, Lena drove her old white Ford station wagon. This would be their return vehicle, once they'd dumped the stolen cars. "I'm surprised," Pan said caustically, "that Voletta isn't driving."

"I'm surprised," Joe said, "that old woman allows this. She has to be part of it. From what Ryan and Kate say, she's cranky as hell, but no one thought of her as a crook."

"And sweet little Lena," Dulcie said, "with her little-girl voice. Was she using this place, or letting them use it, before she ever moved in with her aunt? That Randall Borden is her husband, then? The dark-haired man headed for jail? You heard Egan." She looked at him, scowling. "*This* is where Egan and Randall were headed, they're the two missing drivers."

"Just a cozy family business," Joe said, smiling.

Lena had shut the barn door where the two cars remained, had left them in a dark corner next to the tired-looking stack of baled hay. There wasn't much else now in the big, hollow building. A few hanging tools, shovels, two ladders propped against a blank wall, a cardboard box on the floor, pushed back into the empty space where the trailers had stood. As the cars left Voletta's property, one could follow their parade by the faint reflections of lights up the trees, and the fine layer of dust rising against the slowly lightening sky.

The cats watched from the window as their human

friends left the mansion, heading back for the shelter, Scotty and Kate lagging behind. When Scotty leaned over and kissed Kate on the forehead, the cats smiled. Courtney cocked her head with interest.

"I wouldn't speak of kisses," Dulcie told her. "They're very shy about this new relationship. New," she said, "but maybe thinking of marriage? We'll know in time." *Oh my*, Dulcie thought, *how much I have to teach our kittens*. Courtney didn't ask questions, she only grew more thoughtful; behind that solemn little face, was she seeing fleeting visions of weddings from lives past, was she putting incidents together?

The entourage of stolen cars was gone a long time, but Scotty's phone didn't buzz, there was no word from Dallas. Kate and Wilma made breakfast in the tiny kitchen, scrambled eggs, bacon, and toast—just about the last scrap of food in the apartment, and the last of the coffee. No one wanted the remainder of the store-bought cookies. "When the shelter volunteers get here," Kate said, "I'll make a grocery run." They sat crowded around the tiny table, the five humans comfortable on the two kitchen chairs, the desk chair, and two wooden boxes. The cats had the desk to themselves, their plates laid out on newspapers. Rock lay in the doorway sighing because he never got human food, because he hadn't been allowed to bark and protect the property, because he felt ignored. When they'd finished breakfast and Wilma had done up the dishes, still there was no word from Dallas; Dulcie fell soundly asleep on Kate's bed, tired from a long night. Kit and Pan went off up the hills to hunt. Joe Grey, waiting for the call, began restlessly to pace, passing back and forth where Courtney lay deeply asleep on the desk. Before the call finally came, three unlikely events stirred the morning.

Young Courtney pretended to nap until everyone was off on their own business, Clyde walking Rock, Wilma helping Kate and the volunteers, her mama sound asleep in the bedroom. When Joe Grey quit pacing and left the shelter to be near Scotty and his phone, Courtney opened her eyes, leaped to the floor, and eased the outer door open with stubborn paws. Slipping out, pulling the door closed behind her, she was off on her own adventure. She could hear Scotty and Ryan and their two carpenters at work, could see Joe sitting atop Scotty's truck. She could see Clyde far up the hills taking Rock for a run. Quietly she headed through the tall grass behind the Pamillon mansion, into its tangled gardens, fallen stone walls, its vine-invaded rooms, into the magical places where the feral cats lived.

Crossing the grassy berm she kept glancing back, but she was quite alone. She prowled the little courtyard where, Kit had said, Wilma and Charlie had dug up that valuable book, the book that Wilma had later burned. She knew nothing of the exact location and circumstances of that amazing find. It was the courtyard with its shadowy, overgrown bushes, walled on three sides by the old house, that drew her, a tangled garden mysterious and appealing, that smelled of the feral cats.

Leaping onto a boulder facing the patio, she sat as tall and straight as a small princess, looking into the old garden with its masses of roses and vines. In that fairy-tale world she watched for the feral, speaking cats, praying they would come out, praying they would be curious and acknowledge her.

She had waited a long time when a pale tabby appeared quite suddenly from the bushes beside the house. He leaped to a windowsill, his cream coat blending with the light stone. That was Sage, she knew from Kit's description. Kit and Sage had almost been lovers, had almost become a pair—until Kit rejected him. *Oh my*, she thought, *such a handsome cat*. Farther along the wall Willow appeared, her bleached calico fur, too, matching the colors of the rock-walled house. Both cats watched Courtney, not with hissing confrontation, but with a look of amazement; both gave her ear gestures of greeting and a flicking of tails.

Should she come down off the boulder and approach

them, or would they come to her? She felt shy and then bold. She was filled with awe at these cats who must know so much more than she of the history of their own race, more than Kit or her parents had ever told her. Willow approached first.

Willow knew, watching her, that this kitten had a secret. Whether the kitten herself knew, was another matter. A secret larger, even, than her heritage of speech. *She is the image of the young queen,* Willow thought, *the once queen.* And Sage was thinking the same.

The two cats came close through the grass, approaching the stone where she sat. She shivered at their look of intensity. They reared up and sniffed noses with her, they purred for her. They looked carefully at her markings of orange and black laid artfully across her white patches, they looked a long time at her three black bracelets.

"Joe Grey and Dulcie's child," Willow said. She said no more. Whatever she was thinking, Courtney was silenced by the wonder she saw in Willow's eyes.

Willow was thinking of the Netherworld where she and Sage had traveled with the band of ferals, the hidden land that was part of the speaking cats' past—and that was part of this kitten's heritage. Though Willow would never tell her—that was for her parents to reveal, if they even knew. Much more of the speaking cats' history, and thus Courtney's history, lay in times and countries far more distant than the caves below this coast, lay in medieval lands in ancient times.

But, Willow thought, *Kit and Pan know about the lower world, they have seen the old, old pictures there of a cat who looks like Courtney—pictures, Kit says, the same as the paintings and tapestries in books in the village library. Has Courtney seen those pictures? As young as she is, does she remember anything of those long-ago lives?*

Sitting on the rock with Courtney, Willow licked the kitten's ears, as she had mothered so many of the feral clowder. Then she and Sage led the young cat among the ruins, showed her secret dens and hiding places. But at last when they heard someone shout from below and heard a car take off, Courtney, frightened and expecting a scolding, streaked for Kate's apartment, where she was supposed to be asleep.

21

The morning was growing bright and warm as Joe Grey slipped into the cavernous barn, but inside it was cool and dim. The vast space was high ceilinged and hollow, its distant rafters festooned with cobwebs as dirty gray as rotting lace curtains. The noise from within intrigued and puzzled him: a clawing, tearing sound.

Slipping into the shadows, he froze in place.

Across the barn was the giant of all rats. A monster rat chewing and clawing at a cardboard box, making so much noise it didn't hear him, so preoccupied it didn't see him in the darkness beside the door.

The box stood near the pile of baled hay, some of the bales so blackened with age they were unfit to feed any animal. But what matter, when Voletta let her donkey and goats graze on the neighbors' gardens? The two stolen cars that remained were parked beside the hay, half hidden against the barn wall—a big gray Lincoln Town Car and a tiny black Mini Cooper left over from last night when Egan and Randall hadn't shown up to drive. Beside the cardboard box, bubble wrap and white Styrofoam packing spilled out, littering the floor.

Was this the box from the BMW? Had the men tossed it aside thinking it was worthless? Joe could see where it had been slit open then taped closed again by human hands. Now the rat had opened it once more and was at it tooth and claw.

The rat himself looked almost as big as the Lincoln, Joe had never seen such a beast—bigger and heavier than Joe's nearly grown kittens and looked a thousand times tougher. Where it had torn away one side of the box, scattering the wrappings, tiny white flecks shone on the dirt all around, like fallen stars, and led in a path under the Lincoln. What was in its simple mind? Nest making? Was it making a nest in the Lincoln? With its back to Joe, busily clawing and chewing, it still didn't know it was watched—didn't know it was stalked until Joe Grey, slipping up behind him, leaped on his back, dug all his claws in, and bit hard into his throat, expecting the beast to gurgle and fight for breath.

Lightning fast the rat flipped Joe over. Now it was

on top and somehow, despite Joe's teeth in its throat, it managed to grab Joe's face. Its teeth were like razors. Joe bit deeper. The rat choked and tried to squeal. Joe raked him in the belly, and bit harder. They flipped again, now Joe was on top and then on the bottom— blood was flying when something grabbed the rat. It screamed once and went still and limp.

Someone pulled the rat's teeth gently from Joe's face, pulled the rat away. *Clyde.* Clyde knelt beside him, his handkerchief stanching the blood, his own face white with shock. Rock, his mouth bloody, picked the rat up again where Clyde had dropped it, stood with it in his mouth once more like any good retriever, his ears up, his short tail wagging. How can a dog smile with a dead rat in its mouth? Shakily Joe stood up, put his face up so Clyde could clean it more easily. How could he let a rat get the best of him? He was ashamed and embarrassed and mad. "How bad is it?" Would he be marred for life? Or maybe infected with some horrifying and incurable disease? Joe and Dulcie never listened when Clyde warned them about the foolishness of hunting rats.

"It's not bad," Clyde lied. "Just bloody, must have hit a vein." Reaching in his pocket for his phone, he called Ryan. "Bring the Jag down to the barn. Can you leave your work? We need to go to the vet. It's not serious, but . . . Bring soap and water and towels from the shelter. And a heavy plastic bag."

Ryan didn't ask questions. "On my way," she said, feeling shaky. Quickly she collected what he wanted from the little dispensary by the office and jumped in the Jaguar. Within minutes she was pulling the barn door wider to brighten the dim space.

They cleaned Joe up as best they could. Ryan dampened a washcloth from the water bottle she'd brought, squeezed on soap from a dispenser and washed Joe's torn face, then bound the wound with gauze. "Thank God they've had their rabies shots." She scowled up at Rock. The big dog still held his prize, wanting her to praise him. Instead she said, "Give." She had to say it twice before he dropped it on the ground. She wet a clean towel, soaped it, washed Rock's face then opened his mouth and washed it out, the poor dog backing away, gagging.

When they were finished, Ryan dropped the towels in the bag. She laid one towel over the rat, lifted it into the bag, tied the bag shut and handed it to Clyde. She started to pick Joe up but, "Now that I'm bundled up like a mummy," the tomcat mumbled, hardly able to speak, "take a look in that box."

Carefully Ryan pulled the wrappings back, revealing

a delicate saucer and cup. There was a whole set, each piece secured separately in bubble wrap and packed among Styrofoam crumbles. One cup was broken, where the rat had knocked it from the box. When she held a piece up, it was so thin that light shone through around the hand-painted decorations: acanthus leaves, flowers, and in the center a little fox laughing at her. She held several pieces for Joe to see. "It's not china," she said, "it's porcelain, worth ever so much more." Gently she turned over a saucer. "Worcester, 1770." She studied the delicate tea set, then unholstered her phone and called Kate.

"Could you and Wilma come down, and bring a big, strong box, like a big cat food carton? Better drive down, this will be cumbersome to carry. We think Joe found the box from the stolen BMW.

"It contains old, delicate porcelain. I'd like to leave it packed, but put its box into the larger box. I think we'll leave the torn wrappings, and the little white flecks of Styrofoam, for Max or Dallas to deal with. The box will be safe in the house until he picks it up."

While they talked, Clyde had wrapped a towel around Joe's head where he was bleeding through the gauze, had gotten the tomcat settled in the car. Ryan grabbed the bag with the rat in it, signaled Rock to get in the back. They took off for Dr. Firetti's just as Kate and Wilma pulled up; Ryan held Joe close as she phoned ahead to the clinic.

Kneeling by the box, Kate looked at the broken cup, then unwrapped an equally delicate saucer with three hunting dogs spaced around the circle among the floral design. She unwrapped a cup, then another. She looked at each then secured it again in its bubble wrap. One cup showed a long-legged bird, maybe an egret. The next, a prancing horse. The third cup featured a cat. Kate drew her breath, her green eyes widening. The cat was a calico. A perfect image of Courtney, the exact same markings, three soft calico ovals saddling her back above a white belly. The white and calico patterns on her face were the same—as were the three dark bracelets around her right front leg. She held the cup for a long moment, wishing Dulcie were there to see—but maybe not so good for Courtney to see? How much self-glorification did the kitten need, to play on her ego?

Yet the delicate painting was there, as were the paintings and tapestries they had found in the library's reference books and that Kit had already shown to Courtney. Kate rewrapped the frail cups and saucers, including the broken cup, and packed it all back in the ripped-open box—a handmade treasure nearly three hundred years old, and, apparently, the thieves hadn't a clue.

The way Clyde was driving, it didn't take long and they were pulling up before the two-cottage complex with its high glass dome. A tech met them, hurried them through the reception room past waiting clients into a large convalescent area where most patrons were not allowed.

Their entry brought two yowls from an open cage. The first yowl sounded suspiciously like "*Pa . . .*" but quickly turned into "*Pa . . . meoowww.*" No one noticed Striker's slip in language but John Firetti. As the kittens dropped from their open cage, Striker landing deftly on three paws, John took Joe from Ryan and settled him on the examining table; Buffin and Striker leaped up wanting to be all over Joe until John pulled them away.

"Wait until I examine him," he scolded. "This isn't for kittens. Look how patient Rock is, lying in the corner. What's gotten into this family? A torn paw. And now this," he said, removing Joe's bloody bandage, seeing the misery in Joe's eyes—misery not only because he hurt, but for letting a stupid rat nearly do him in.

Ryan had given the bagged rat to the technician; the

middle-aged blonde already had instructions to pack it on ice, call a courier, and get it to the county lab at once.

"Usually the lab doesn't test a rat for rabies," John said. "Rats don't get rabies." This made Joe, and Ryan and Clyde, go limp with relief. "They *can* get it," John added, "but their bodies kill the virus almost at once. This rat would have had to be in a fight directly before Rock killed him."

"I only saw the one rat," Joe said, "and he was busy tearing up papers, looked like he'd been at it a long time, dragging them under a big car. Not another animal in sight."

"Making a nest," John said. "Likely inside the engine. Some driver will suffer for that. Bats and skunks are the real danger for rabies." He looked seriously at Joe. "You and Rock have your shots regularly. But even so, you'll have to be confined for two days, until the report comes back. If it's negative, you're free to go home."

At the word "confinement," Joe stiffened.

"State law," John said.

Joe knew that. It wasn't John Firetti's fault. Even so, he was rigid with anger as the good doctor worked on his wounds. John gave him a mild shot for the pain, cleaned out the deep bites, and put in three stitches, smearing the area with something that stunk. Joe watched John swab out Rock's mouth and examine it for wounds. He gave them both antibiotic shots. The needles stung, Joe could feel it as much for Rock as for himself. John gave them each a loving pat, and the ordeal was over—this part of the ordeal.

But now, the cages. He and Rock would be in cages. Joe couldn't even touch his two kittens who crouched at the end of the table, he couldn't properly greet them, couldn't even lick their faces, and how fair was that? Now Joe and Rock were the jailbirds, and Buffin and Striker could go home.

John hugged both Joe and Rock before he shut them in their cages—but he spent more time holding the kittens. Looking sad, he picked up the phone and called Mary. "The kittens are going home."

Almost at once they heard the cottage door slam. She must have run across the garden; she burst into the room still in her apron, her shoulder-length brown hair in a tangle. She took the two kittens from John, cuddling them in her arms.

"They've been sleeping with us every night," she said. "The kittens and little Lolly. She didn't do so well at home, they brought her back for a while. I didn't tell them I thought Buffin was helping to heal her." Mary glanced toward the cage the kittens had occupied; the tiny brown poodle lay there shivering, watching Buffin longingly.

"Pancreatitis," Mary said. "We're flushing her with more liquids and giving her all she will drink, and of course an IV. But Buffin has been the real wonder.

"We don't know how he does it, he just lies close to her when she looks like she's hurting, and almost at once she grows more comfortable. You can see it in her eyes, in the way she relaxes. At night, in bed with us, Buffin wakes us when she's about to throw up so we can put a towel under her and then give her more liquids. But now," Mary said, "look at her. She knows Buffin's leaving."

"Can't I stay?" Buffin said, looking up at Ryan and Clyde. "Just a few days? She hurts so bad. I don't know how, I just know I help her. I can feel the change in her."

"Could the kittens both stay?" Ryan said. "We could quarantine Joe and Rock at home, keep them away from Snowball, that would be easy."

John said, "Snowball is due for her yearly exam and boosters. You could bring her in. If only Joe and Rock are at home, can you keep them away from other people, keep them confined in the house? It's such a slim chance that the test will be positive." He gave Joe Grey a hard look. "Would you promise to stay inside, away from other animals, away from Dulcie and Courtney?"

"I promise," Joe said hastily, but with mixed feelings. Shut in the house for two days, hardly knowing what was going on in the world around him? Well hell, what choice did he have? Better that than a kennel.

Striker was just as dismayed. He *wanted* to be home, he wanted to run free, he wanted to wrestle with Courtney and, big tomcat that he was, he missed his mama—but he guessed he'd miss Buffin more, leaving him alone with just little Lolly. And he knew he'd miss the Firettis.

"I'll stay," Striker said. And as Joe Grey and Rock left the clinic, Rock prancing beside Clyde like a thief released from jail, and Joe resting in Ryan's arms, Striker settled down in the big cage beside his brother and Lolly. *And,* Striker thought, *I can run in the Firettis' house at night, Mary and John don't care. I can climb the furniture, leap on the bed—if I'm careful of my paw.*

Riding home in the Jaguar, Joe Grey, warm in Ryan's arms, was unusually silent. She frowned down at him. "It's only two days. If we leave you alone in the house, Joe, you *will* do as the doctor told you?" He looked up at her innocently. They were just approaching home when Clyde's phone buzzed. He clicked on the speaker so Joe could hear.

Dallas said, "We got our car thieves, all but one. It was some dustup. Two of their men were shot, but none of ours. Those two are in the infirmary in Salinas, the others in county jail. We lost Lena Borden—you *did* see her leave there with the cars?"

"We all saw her," Clyde said. "Dark clothes, dark cap, but definitely Lena. Driving her old white Ford."

"The Ford was there in the wreckers' lot," Dallas said, "with the other cars. She either ran from the scene when we showed, or had someone pick her up. We're keeping Egan here, on charges of break and enter and theft. We'll interrogate Randall, see what we can get out of him, then send him on over to county.

"We drove and hauled the stolen cars back here," Dallas said. "They're in our lockup." This was a fenced, securely roofed compound behind the station next to where the police cars parked. Its gate was kept locked and the area furnished with surveillance cameras.

"It'll take a while," the detective said, "to collect evidence from the vehicles, and for the insurance adjusters to look them over, before their owners claim them."

Joe could tell Dallas wasn't in a good mood. Maybe because Lena had evaded them. Maybe, Joe wondered,

Lena was more involved than anyone thought. How could she have escaped among all those cops? Who had picked her up? Clyde didn't have time to ask anything more before the phone went dead.

At home, Joe and Rock were shut in the house. Ryan put Snowball in her carrier, to go to Dr. Firetti. Giving Joe a stern look, she phoned her father to come and check on the animals while she dropped the little white cat at the clinic, so Clyde could go on to work and she could return to her crew. This enraged Joe, that she had to call her dad to babysit, that she didn't trust him. But luck was with him. When she couldn't get her dad, she tried Lindsey. "We're in Bodega Bay," Lindsey said. "We . . ."

"It's all right," Ryan said. "I'll work it out." They talked a moment and Ryan hung up, looking deep into Joe's eyes, "Rock can get out into his yard and so can you. But *you* can get over the wall. He can't. You can also get out through your tower. I love you, Joe, and usually I trust you—though there have been times. If I leave you in the house, will you promise to do as I say, as John Firetti says? It could save a lot of trouble later. Rabies is a scary thing to deal with."

Joe gave her as innocent a look as he could muster. He didn't point out that his tower and the roof itself were both integral parts of their house. He promised himself that he'd stay to the physical body of their residence, the structural entity. And didn't that include the roof?

What he'd really like to do was slip into her truck, ride back to the Pamillon estate, and have another look at the contents of that box. Courtney's picture on the porcelain cup had shaken him considerably, combined with the pictures like her in so many library books. Those ancient tapestries and paintings and porcelain relics did not sit well with Joe Grey.

22

Kate approached Voletta's house feeling silly with her little plate of store-bought cookies. But manners were manners. Voletta was a Pamillon, who knew what the old woman had once been used to in the way of neighborly visits?

Though the kitchen and living room were around at the back, facing the big yard, Kate chose the more formal front door, which was seldom used. She had started across the wide porch when she paused.

It was late morning but the blinds in all three bedrooms were drawn tight. If Voletta had company, besides Lena, were they still asleep after a busy night? Who would have slept here but someone connected to the thefts? She shivered, hoping they were all in jail.

There were no cars in the front yard, Lena and Voletta parked in back. Turning, she headed around to the kitchen. Yes, the lights were on in those windows, and she could smell coffee. Of course the big yard was empty, only Voletta's old truck—and a blue Ford hatchback parked close to the back door. She knocked, hoping the lame little gift of stale cookies would give her an excuse to be invited in, not just stand awkwardly in the door and be sent rudely away.

She waited, then knocked again. She wanted to know how long those men had been using Voletta's barn to store their hoard, concealing the stolen cars and, when the cops eased off in their search, moving them out again, at night. And how long had Voletta's niece been involved? Lena visited Voletta every few weeks but Kate couldn't remember whether those times coincided with the Molena Point car thefts. She hadn't been staying up here at night, then, not until the shelter was finished and she moved the cats in. No one but Voletta had been here at night to know what went on. Even the feral cats, in the small hours, would have been up the hills hunting.

As Kate rounded the house she didn't see Dulcie and Pan and Kit slip along behind her through the tall grass, didn't see them pad silently up to the front porch. Kate was already at the back of the house when tortoiseshell

Kit swung hopefully on the front latch, was thrilled to find the door unlocked and, kicking softly, swung it open. The three cats disappeared inside, pushing it not quite closed behind them. Already Dulcie missed Joe, off at home, in quarantine. She'd had the whole story from Kate.

The cats crouched in a small entry beneath a narrow table against one wall. A hall led left and right to the bedrooms and bath. All three bedroom doors were cracked open, the doors of the two end rooms at right angles to the hall. Kit and Pan watched Dulcie slip ahead into the living room and behind the couch where she could see into the kitchen.

At the back of the house Kate had to knock a third time before she heard footsteps. When Voletta opened the door Kate tried, awkwardly, to hand her the cookies. "I came to see how you're feeling, after your trip to the hospital. To see if there's anything I can do, any errands?"

"Lena's here now," Voletta said sourly, blocking the slightly open door. "We don't eat cookies." Kate could smell cinnamon rolls as well as coffee, could see three cups on the kitchen table. "Whatever you want," Voletta said, "I'm busy."

Kate slipped her foot against the door. "I thought

maybe Ryan's carpenters might help with the broken window, or anything else that was damaged. That was a terrible storm."

"Ryan. That's that woman carpenter?"

Kate nodded.

"Pretty nice truck she drives. Must be full of all kinds of tools, those locked cabinets along the sides, that locked lid on the truck bed. Well, a carpenter makes good money. We'll do the repairs ourselves." She yawned, and pushed the door forward in Kate's face.

Kate shoved the door in gently with her foot as she faked a matching yawn. "You didn't get much sleep, either?" she said, smiling kindly. "With all those lights down in the yard?"

"What lights?"

"I don't know," Kate said. "I woke around three, I saw lights reflected from down here. I thought your porch lights were on, but they seemed very bright. I thought about getting up to look but I guess I fell back asleep."

"Lena turned the lights on when she got home. Their car was acting up, they were trying to fix it. Her son's car, he's visiting." Voletta looked at her for a long moment, kicked Kate's foot out of the way, and slammed the door.

Her son? Kate turned away and headed home with her plate of cookies. She didn't know Lena had a son.

Dulcie, behind the couch, crept to the end where she could see better into the kitchen, could see the old woman more clearly. She, too, was surprised to hear of a son. She retreated a few steps when she heard voices from the living room, Lena's voice, and a man. They moved to the kitchen, sat down at the table, Lena reaching for the coffeepot, filling their half-empty cups. But when the man appeared, a chill gripped Dulcie.

Egan! Egan Borden! . . . Egan Alderson, he'd said.

But Egan was arrested late last night. He should be in jail, not here in Voletta's kitchen. Why had Max Harper let him go? Or had he broken out?

He was freshly shaved, his blond hair slicked back, and had changed clothes, a cream shirt and tan chinos. Watching him, she had to willfully stop her tail from lashing. *Why had Harper released him?*

Lena had driven off with those men last night, but when the rest were rounded up, she had disappeared. Had Egan somehow talked his way out of jail and raced north, to pick her up?

Or, Dulcie thought, startled, *could this be Rick Alderson? In and out of prison, evading police inquiries, and now suddenly appearing out of nowhere? Oh, but that isn't possible.*

Last night Dulcie had had plenty of time to study Egan. No other man could look so exactly like him. Long, slim face, long thin nose, blond hair. Egan's square shoulders thrust forward on his thin frame. Of course this was Egan but why was he out of jail? She wished Joe were there. Sometimes Joe Grey, fierce and predatory, was keener in what he observed than she was. *Is this Rick Alderson, out of prison in Texas and secretly making his way here? But how can that be? Egan said Calvin Alderson was his father. The police think his mother is dead—but Voletta said this man, Egan, was Lena's son.*

Behind Dulcie, Kit and Pan had tunneled along under the couch to crowd against her peering into the kitchen. Lena and Egan sat guzzling coffee while Voletta laid bacon on a grill, broke eggs into a bowl. The two cats were as shocked as Dulcie, they had all seen Egan locked in a squad car, handcuffs, leg irons, the works, along with his stepfather—Randall mad as a stuck pig.

Now, before the bacon began to cook, Egan rose to open a loaf of bread. As he passed close to the living room they got a good scent of him. They looked at each other, ears back, tails twitching. This man wasn't Egan, he didn't smell like Egan though he looked more like him than a twin. Soon they crept away to the far end of the couch where they could talk softly.

"This," Kit whispered so faintly they could hardly hear her, "this has to be Rick Alderson. He was waiting for Lena last night and gave her a ride away from the cops? And Egan *is* still in jail? Rick's been here, been part of the gang all along? And what do we do now?"

Pan's yellow eyes glowed. "What would Joe Grey do?"

Kit and Dulcie looked at him.

The red tom smiled. "Joe would go straight for the connection, for why those two look alike. Calvin Alderson had only one son when he was sent to prison, and the cops think he'd killed the wife as well as her lover."

Pan turned away; Kit followed him up the hall to prowl the bedrooms. This man had to have some identification, maybe a billfold left on the dresser. Dulcie returned to watching the thieves.

In the corner bedroom Pan made a flehmen face; the clothes tossed about stunk of Randall Borden and Lena.

The middle room smelled of the young man they were sure was Rick Alderson. The room was painted tan, furnished with twin beds, old mahogany headboards, and a dresser that might have been there fifty years. And, again, decorated with strewn-about clothes, jeans, shirts, shorts, and smelly socks. When they heard a cell phone ring from the kitchen, heard Rick answer then chair legs scrape and his footsteps coming, they slipped under the bed.

Rick sat down on the bed, his cell phone to his ear. "Okay, I'm alone." He listened, then, "What the hell, Randall!" Silence, then, "They'll be after you like fleas on a dog. Where are you?" The cats could hear only one side of the conversation until he said, "We're breaking up, my battery's about dead, I'll call you back on the house phone."

Rising, he listened to the voices from the kitchen then sat down again, dialing the phone on the night-stand. When his back was to them, Kit and Pan slipped out of the room and past the bathroom into the farthest bedroom. This was Voletta's room, her scent, the austere furnishings old and dark but the room neat and tidy, only a pink robe lying across a chair. Leaping to the nightstand, Kit slipped the phone's headpiece off, lowered it silently to the tabletop. They crowded side by side, listening.

". . . walked right out of that small-town jail," Randall was saying, a smile in his gruff voice. "I told you my stomach hurt. I made it seem worse, like maybe appendicitis. That shook up the rookie on guard, he came right on in, the dummy. I knocked him out, took his keys and gun, locked him in and beat it out of there, out the back gate to the street. Tourists everywhere, I just fell in among them—they hadn't made me change clothes because I was headed for county jail as soon as they interrogated me. They'd took my belt, though. And my phone and billfold."

"Where are you calling from?"

"Woman working in her yard, back among some cottages. She left the front door unlocked. Don't worry, I can see her from the window, she didn't hear the phone ring, I put a pillow over it. I saw her husband leave, there's not another sound in the house."

"Oh hell, Randall. Get out of there."

"Can you come get me?"

"Where? You can't stay there."

"It'll take me a while through these fenced backyards—they're bound to have patrols out. I can hide safe in that . . ." Footsteps were coming, Lena's steps. Quickly they slipped the phone back on its cradle and dove under Voletta's bed. At the other end of the hall, Rick was saying, "Hell, you can't go there. That's the first . . ." A pause, then, "That's a *damned* stupid idea. But all right—though it could put us in a hell of a mess."

He listened again, then, "I *said*, all right. Now get the hell out of that house before someone comes in."

Above the cats, Lena was searching the drawers of Voletta's nightstand. She rummaged until she found a bottle of pills, maybe Voletta's pain medication. Turning to the mirror, she fussed with her hair, using Voletta's brush before she returned to the kitchen.

In the other room, Rick had apparently hung up the phone. When the cats could hear him changing clothes, Kit beat it to the living room, leaving Pan slipping down the hall and under the hall table to watch him. *Was* Egan still in jail, had Randall just left him there?

Kit, crowded under the couch against Dulcie, wondered if, the next time someone cleaned house—and it could sure use it—they would puzzle over cat hairs mixed with the dust bunnies.

Rick came into the kitchen jangling his keys, Lena following him. "Going to pick up Randall."

"Pick him up?" Voletta said. "He's out of jail? How come they let him out?"

"He broke out," Rick said, laughing. "Knocked out the guard. He left Egan locked up."

Rick laid his keys on the table, picked up his cup to swallow down the last sip of coffee. Fast as a viper Lena grabbed the keys. "I'm going with you." She spun around, headed for the bedroom, perhaps for her purse.

He snatched at her, hit her a glancing blow. "You're staying here." She hit him, pulled away, and raced to their corner bedroom.

In the hall, Pan crept out from beneath the table far enough to see her pull on a leather jacket and open the dresser drawer. She found a clean handkerchief, used it to lift out a revolver. She used a corner of the cloth to open the cylinder and check the load then wrapped the gun and slipped it in her jacket pocket. She fished through a lower drawer beneath silk undergarments, dropped some small item in her left pocket, stuffed her cell phone in on top. She raced for the kitchen, flung out the door leaving it open behind her, jumped in the car just as Rick put it in gear. Voletta watched them, not interfering, sour and expressionless.

When Lena ran for the kitchen, passing the couch a few feet from Dulcie's and Kit's noses, Dulcie lay quietly watching her. She didn't want to follow and get tangled in this, she'd had enough of being trapped in cars. But Kit and Pan, their heads filled with Rick's phone conversation, sped for the front door they'd left cracked open, leaped up the vine beside the porch, were across the roof to the back just as Lena raced out. All the car windows were open against the warm morning.

Kit crouched to leap through behind Rick's head into the backseat. There in the shadows they'd never be noticed, they could find where Randall was hiding, they could find a phone and call in, they could—

Sharp teeth in the nape of her neck jerked her away from the roof's edge, Pan's growl low and angry. Shouldering her down, he pressed her so firmly to the shingles that she couldn't move, even when he let go his bite.

"What were you thinking?" he growled. "There've been enough wild car rides. What did you mean to do? You have no idea where they're going."

"I . . . but I . . ." She scowled at him, her yellow eyes blazing—and she exploded out of his grip, attacking him, biting him; they were into an angry scuffle, snarling and kicking. Kit had never dreamed they'd fight like this, she loved Pan. But now, raking him with her hind paws, she broke away and headed again for the edge of the roof—just as the blue Ford took off speeding across the big yard and onto the narrow road.

They were gone.

Neither Kit nor Pan knew where, they had no idea where the killer would be hiding.

Rick drove, scowling. "Your aunt—could she guess where we're headed? Sure as hell she'll call the cops."

"Why would she call the cops? She's as guilty as we

are. And how could she guess? She didn't hear anything, you never said where he is."

"She calls the cops, it'll be the last thing she does."

She stared at him. "Don't be such an ass. You're in a
vicious mood."

He looked at her with surprise. "What the hell's
with you?"

"Tired, Rick. You're getting as mean and rude as
your father was—or as mean as Randall. Why did I
marry someone so like Cal Alderson? I'm tired of Randall's sarcasm. I'm tired of his cheap womanizing, of
his coming home with another woman's stink on him.
I'm tired of him making me a part of this heist business. I'm tired of having to get up in the middle of the
night and drive hot cars all over hell, my belly twisting
for fear the cops will tail us. Tell the truth, I'm tired of
Randall! I *told* him it was better to move the cars one
at a time, not head out of there with a whole line of cars
lit up like some damned parade. Now look at the mess
he's in—that we're all in."

"*I* think the cops were tipped," Rick said. "Someone ratted on us." He gave her a look cold as ice.

She said nothing.

"You tip the cops, Ma?"

"No, I didn't tip the cops. Go to hell." Then, smiling, "But I thought about it."

"Maybe it *was* your aunt. After I came out from Texas and joined up with Randall . . . Well, hell, she never did like me. And why does she think Egan hung the moon, for crissake?"

Lena was silent, sudden tears running down. Her brown hair was mussed, her face pale but blotched with red. She felt carefully in her purse for a tissue but didn't find one.

"As mad as you are at Randall," Rick said, "I'm surprised you *didn't* try to call the law."

"How could I have? You wouldn't wait for me, you didn't say where he was. And Voletta *wouldn't,* even if she knew where he's going."

But there *was* someone to call the law. As the blue Ford headed for the village, Kit and Pan streaked up to the ruins where Ryan's truck was parked. Digging out the old cell phone that Ryan kept there—the phone with no GPS and no ID—they called the department. They had no destination, but they had the car's description and part of the license number.

23

Joe's quarantine grew boring pretty fast, he felt like a parolee under home confinement. It was a wonder he didn't have an electronic leg bracelet to keep track of where he was, to make sure he didn't stray. As for Rock, even with Joe for company he never liked being left for long without humans. Now, with his little white cat gone too, his little napping buddy, he was miserable and brooding, morosely pacing the house. If Joe started up to his tower, Rock would bark up a storm. The tomcat, dropping down again to the bedroom, pounced on Rock and teased him until at last the big dog gave chase: they ran up and down stairs, leaped over chairs, played tag until both were panting and the living room furnishings and rug were awry. Only then, when Joe had worn Rock out, when the silver dog climbed into

Joe's chair for a nap, did Joe Grey head for his rooftop aerie.

Clyde had agreed that the tower was part of the house, so was also quarantine territory. He wouldn't agree to the roof itself, but Joe reasoned that of course roof and house were all one structure. Padding on through his tower into the sunshine that warmed the shingles, he stretched and yawned. He rolled on his back, he snoozed for a few moments in the sun; but then he sat up, and considered.

No one had ever said exactly where the roof ended. With the line of roofs on their block all so close, and joined by tree branches reaching across lacing them together, no one had ever drawn a line to show where that vast, shingled territory ceased to be a single entity. If one could move so easily from one patch of shingles to the next over heavy, tangled branches, then in sensible feline logic the roof ended at the next cross street.

Off he trotted, filled with his virtuous decision that he was still in the quarantine area. At the side street where the roofs ended he crouched, looking down. Of course he would go no farther.

Two blocks away stood Barbara Conley's house, yellow crime tape still surrounding the property. He was watching it idly when he saw, in the high attic window, a shadow move, a figure looking out.

There was no police car parked nearby, no car in front or in the drive—and no one should be there but the cops, the house was off-limits. Curious, he abandoned all thoughts of his quarantine in favor of expediency. Whatever was going on was more important than the unlikely danger that he'd bite someone and give them rabies.

Crossing the streets on overhanging branches, soon he crouched in the rain gutter just across the street from Barbara's house. Directly below, only scattered cars were parked, though usually the curb was bumper to bumper. A blue Ford cruised slowly by, heading west toward the seashore, the driver slowing to gawk at the crime tape. The driver . . . Joe came to full attention.

Egan Borden. Long thin face, pale blond hair, a thrust of his broad slanted shoulders against the side window—but Egan was in jail. Joe had *seen* him shackled and shoved into a squad car. The man drove on to the next intersection, made a U-turn, came back and parked just below Joe, headed in the direction of the freeway. Now Joe could see his passenger, a thin middle-aged woman with medium-length brown hair. Lena? He had seen her around Voletta Nestor's place when he rode up to the ruins with Ryan; he had heard Ryan describe her, not flatteringly. Their voices were sharp with argument. Straining to hear, he almost lost his footing, almost fell off the gutter.

Backing away, forgetting about quarantine promises, he slipped down a stone pine that grew against the end of the house. There he crouched in the bushes beside the car not three feet from Lena's open window. When Egan started to get out, she reached a hand to stop him.

"Stay here, Rick. For once, will you do it my way!"

Rick? This was *Rick* Alderson? The executed guy's kid who might be in jail or might not, who might have warrants out for him or might not? Rearing up to get a better look, still Joe couldn't see much of him. Where had he come from? What was he doing in Molena Point? And who the hell was Egan?

"I told him I'd park around the corner," Rick said. "He can see out the side window. What do you mean to do?"

"Just stay in the car and watch for Randall, we don't know if he's even here yet. How dumb can he get, breaking out of jail? What a stupid place to hide, right under the cops' noses. Stay here and watch for street patrol. I'll see if he's in there."

"When he sees the car, he'll come out. What's taking him so long? If someone sees you go in there, if you blow his cover, he'll be mad as hell."

"I told you, the way Randall's treated me, I don't

give a damn. I don't feel the same about him anymore, I hate his guts. It's you who wanted to rescue him."

"He's my father—my stepfather! He didn't always treat you this way. And he always treated me decent. Why were you so hot to come along, when you hate him?"

She leaned over, looked through the windshield at the upper story of the frame house, up at the attic window high in the peak. Did she see the faint movement there, a disappearing shadow beyond the dirty glass? She had her hand on the door handle.

"How you going to get in? If he has the key from under the back porch . . ."

"I have the front-door key—I *think* that's what this is. Randall took it off his key ring, the morning after the murder. Took it off and hid it. What else could it be but Barbara Conley's key? He wanted to get rid of it before the cops found it on him."

"What else do you have in your purse? Is that Randall's gun, wrapped in that handkerchief?"

"You're a nosy bastard. Yes, it's Randall's gun. I know enough about you, Rick, that the cops don't know, you'd better mind your own business."

He raised his hand to slap her; he seemed to have no more love for his mother than she for him, had no compunction against hitting her. But then, what kind of mother was she? She had run off and left him there that night, a seven-year-old kid in the midst of a grisly murder. She had run away and never tried to help him.

Lena got out, slid the wrapped gun into her right pocket. The tomcat followed her among the tree shadows as she headed across the street. She stepped up on the narrow porch, tried the key, and unlocked the door. She stood in the open door listening, looking around the living room. In that instant Joe Grey was behind her and inside, slipping beyond a wicker chest. The house had that empty, musty, unoccupied smell.

"Randall?" she whispered softly and moved on in, leaving the door on the latch. Again, a louder whisper. *"Randall?"*

No answer.

She began to prowl the rooms, her footsteps echoing faintly, her hand in her pocket on the gun. Joe could see into the kitchen, and into the hall where there would be bedrooms. If she found Randall, what did she mean to do? Hadn't they come to rescue him, to get him away from the cops? Then why the gun? Would she shoot a cop, would she put herself in that jeopardy to save a husband she'd grown to hate?

Having covered all the rooms, she opened the door of the hall closet. There wasn't much there, a few coats thrown to the floor. She knelt, examined the floor, brushed at something that looked like dirt or sawdust, then looked up.

A string hung from the ceiling, with a metal washer knotted at the end. She used both hands to pull open the trapdoor, its mechanism lowering a folding wooden ladder.

"Randall?"

A moan echoed from the hollow attic. Quickly she climbed—as Joe Grey slipped into the closet behind the pile of coats.

"Randall? Come on, the car's waiting."

A long silence, then another moan. Joe heard her move across the attic, imagined her ducking under its beams. He could see enough of its low ceiling to wonder how much head room Randall had, up there. When he heard another groan, Joe abandoned common sense, scrambled up the ladder and crouched among the shadows. The long dim space was lighted only by a tiny window at each end.

Randall lay on the dusty wooden floor, his knees pulled up, his arms wrapped around himself, his face, even in shadow, pale and twisted. It was strange to see the heavy, muscled man huddled on the floor, helpless. Lena knelt beside him, her expression unreadable. "What is it? What's wrong? Were you shot?" She leaned down, looking for blood, her expression half of concern and half of cold satisfaction.

"Not shot," he mumbled. "The pain . . . Can you get me down the steps? Something's bad wrong. I think I need a doctor . . . someone that won't call the cops."

She reached in the pocket where she'd had the key. Joe saw her phone light up, saw her press a single button. When Randall realized she was calling 911 he tried to get up, tried to grab the phone. "I said a doctor, not the cops!" He fell back clutching his belly, letting out an animal-like cry. She stood looking down at him, dropped the phone in her pocket, and removed the wrapped revolver. Cradling it, she looked steadily at Randall, her expression ice-cold.

"Where's the book, Randall?"

"Cops have it," he groaned.

"Well, that was smart. That's a one-of-a-kind edition. When a collector sees what's in it, it's worth more than a few hundred thousand. That information, if it's true . . ."

From a few blocks away, a medics' siren screamed—and from the street below they heard a car take off, moving fast. Lena, ducking under the rafters, raced to the little window to peer out.

"Gone! The damned bastard took off on me!" Spinning around she paused again over Randall, the revolver pointed directly at him. "You sure the cops have the book?"

"They have the whole damn car. Book was . . . right there in the back." Again a groan, and he pulled up his legs to ease his belly. Outside, the sirens screamed to a halt. Joe watched Lena unwrap the revolver not touching the metal, keeping only the grip wrapped. She stood a moment, the gun pointed at him, a hungry look on her face.

At last she knelt, moved his hands from his belly, rolled him on his side making him cry out with pain, and slipped the gun in his pocket. She eased the handkerchief out and stuffed it in her own pocket, and she fled down the ladder into the shadowed closet. Left the ladder down for the cops to see, and ran out the back door. Joe could hear her outside crashing through the bushes. Would she vanish, to lose herself in the village? Or did she think Rick would wait for her, farther up the block? *Fat chance*, the tomcat thought.

But he was wrong. As the cop cars and medics pulled in, Joe was out the back door behind Lena, chasing her through the neighbors' yards to the next street where he heard a horn toot softly.

There stood the blue Ford, its passenger door open. Lena swung in, they took off fast onto a narrow side street to disappear among the crowded cottages. She hadn't, in her rage, shot Randall as Joe had guessed she would. Maybe she thought, whatever his pain was, it would do him in. And if he didn't die, she had left the gun to entrap him, certain proof he'd shot Barbara and Langston.

Was part of her hatred, her disgust for Randall, a mirror reflection of twenty years gone, when her first husband shot her own lover? Frowning over her mixed signals of hatred and maybe regret, Joe sped up a pine to the roofs trying to see which way they were headed, but they were already long gone. Spinning around he raced for home, for a phone, to get the cops on the Ford's tail. Both passengers were wanted: Lena for helping highjack cars, Rick with at least one warrant out on him, and both of them for helping a killer escape. Fleeing across to his own line of roofs, Joe looked back once to see Max Harper and Detective Garza arrive in a squad car, parking beside the medical van. He didn't wait to see the medics ease Randall down the attic steps on a stretcher, to see Dallas, wearing gloves, frisk Randall, bag the revolver and hand it to Max— but he could imagine the scene. Racing across the roofs for home, Joe didn't see Clyde's truck coming down the street behind him.

24

Clyde, heading home to check on the quarantined animals—not that they would get into trouble, he thought wryly—found patrol cars and the medics' van blocking the street at Barbara Conley's corner house. Turning, he went around the block and swung onto his own street again—as a flash of movement across the roofs made him slow, a streak of gray racing for home, white paws flashing, and a hot anger struck Clyde. *This* was Joe's idea of quarantine? Not only his tower but a whole block of rooftops and how much farther? What happened to the tomcat's solemn promise? Whatever was going on at Barbara's house, that's where he'd been. Damn cat heard a siren, he took off across the village like a fire horse to a three-alarm blaze. Had he been inside that house, as well, watching, hiding from the cops? What was going on?

Joe had never before broken a promise, that Clyde knew of. He wanted to honk the horn and shout at the racing little liar. Instead, as Joe swerved into his tower, Clyde pulled quietly into the drive. Getting out, he didn't click the car door shut, he made no sound. Quick and silent, he unlocked the front door, slipped in, pulled off his shoes, and in stocking feet, headed for the stairs. He paused at the bottom, listening. There was silence for a moment, then—who was he talking to? Had he dialed the dispatcher? But why? The cops were already there.

". . . Yes," Joe was saying, "in the attic with him. She called you from there, then she ran out the back." . . . Silence, then, "Blue Ford hatchback, Rick Alderson driving. Yes, *Rick* Alderson. Don't you have Egan in the lockup? You *do* have a warrant for Rick?" Another silence, Joe gave the license number, then he must have hung up, Clyde heard him drop to the floor.

By the time Clyde reached the top of the stairs the gray tomcat was curled up on the love seat with Rock, lying against Rock's chest appearing to be sound asleep, the gray dog's paws wrapped around him. Clyde stood looking down at them. Rock *was* asleep, snoring slightly, maybe worn out with playing, because the living room was a shambles. The Weimaraner probably hadn't stirred when Joe Grey slipped in between his big paws.

Clyde pulled the desk chair around, sat down facing the two animals, fixing his gaze on Joe, staring at him intently.

Joe, feigning sleep, could feel Clyde's gaze sharp as a laser beam. He daren't even slit an eye open; the minute he stirred a whisker he'd get a dressing-down that would be the grandfather of all lectures.

But what had he done wrong? His promise was that he'd stay in the house, not go through Rock's door in the patio; they'd agreed that he could go into his tower. So he had pushed a little in his own mind, for purposes of clarification, reasoning that the roof was part of the house. So what was the big deal? And, where had Clyde seen him? Not racing across the neighbors' roofs, he hoped. Or worse, coming out of Barbara's house.

Could he help it if, when one thing led to another, he found himself past his own block and into the extended crime scene? Joe ignored the word "deception." This was simply good detecting.

When Clyde, admiring the faking ability of the gray tomcat, could stand it no longer he picked Joe up from Rock's protecting forearms and held him dangling, scowling angrily into Joe's startled yellow eyes.

"What happened to the quarantine promise?"

"We agreed that the tower was part of our house, so I figured the roof was, too. I *said* I'd keep away from other cats."

"How did *our* roof, Joe, turn into three full blocks of rooftops? You want to explain how that could happen?"

"You are *so picky*. They're all laced together with tree branches. Where do you draw the line? And that rat . . . You know there's little chance that rat had rabies. A rabid rat would have been nervous and probably would have attacked us all, it wouldn't have been busy tearing up boxes. It was only a female rat making a nest."

He looked intently at Clyde. "This was urgent. This was . . . if I hadn't called the department they wouldn't know what kind of car they were driving. Those two are wanted . . . Rick Alderson for grand theft auto, and Lena . . . I don't know what that charge will be."

Clyde was silent a long moment. "*Rick* Alderson?"

"Would you mind not dangling me?"

Clyde, despite his anger, gathered Joe over his shoulder, cradling him in a more comfortable position. "So you sneaked into the crime scene. But where did *Rick* come from? And who called the medics? Who was hurt? What happened in there?"

"Randall Borden. He was in the attic. He apparently escaped from jail. He's sick, I don't know what's wrong. Lena found him, called the meds then she got the hell out. Rick was waiting, in a blue Ford. Bear in mind, Clyde, the police have warrants for both Rick and Lena."

"You said that. *But where did Rick come from?*"

"I haven't a clue. He was just there. Lena *called* him Rick. When I looked closely I could see a little difference between him and Egan, a tiny difference to the shape of their noses and ears. I think they're headed for Voletta's place. We need to get Courtney and Dulcie, and Kit and Pan away from there. At least the boys are safe with the Firettis. We need to get Wilma and Kate out, I don't feel good about this. Those people are . . . I thought Lena was going to shoot Randall, going to shoot her own husband."

The tomcat scratched his ear. "I don't know why they'd bother the cats, but . . . their interest in the Bewick book with pages about speaking cats . . . and Voletta's interest in the feral cats . . . I want my family away from there. I want them home, and Kit and Pan, too."

Clyde picked up the phone and called Ryan. Briefly he gave her the picture. "You have time to bring the cats down, or shall I come up?"

"I'll bring them now—as soon as we round them up,

as soon as we find Courtney." Joe imagined Ryan on the jobsite, pulling off her cap from her dark, mussed hair, hastily putting her tools away. How long would it take to round up the cats? They'd all come to her . . . all but Courtney, who, at times, had surprisingly selective hearing.

But the cats were all together, crouched on a bed of boulders high above the ruins. Courtney sat straight and wide-eyed among the circle of ferals, joined by Dulcie and Kit and Pan. A little breeze stirred their whiskers and stirred the tall grass. They sat fascinated as the ferals took turns telling tales. The ancient Celtic and Irish and Scottish myths, the Welsh legends. Kit had told Courtney a few of these but they both liked hearing them again, they liked best the way pale-calico Willow told them. Nine ferals were there, some of them having returned only recently from the under-earth lands of the Netherworld.

It was the tales of the Netherworld that Dulcie really didn't want Courtney to hear just yet, but that was hard to prevent. Already Kit had told the kitten enough about that land where Kit and Pan had ventured, that realm of mythical beasts, and of powers that had destroyed many parts of its kingdoms. One could hardly stop Kit from telling the stories around the fire at Kit's own house, or at Wilma's house, with Courtney ever demanding to hear more. (Striker and Buffin preferred sagas of the Irish wars.) Dulcie didn't want Courtney's head filled, yet, with the Netherworld, to which the strong-minded calico might decide to slip away alone and wander down into its deep tunnels, to see its marvels for herself.

But before the tales began, Dulcie had asked Willow about the lights at Voletta's and the gathered cars.

"It's the first time we've seen them," Willow said, "we watched them pull out, but we didn't see them come in. That must have been the night of the terrible wind, we were deep in a cellar, out of the blow, sleeping warm and cozy. We couldn't have seen the cars drive in, and in that storm we couldn't have heard them."

"But had you seen them before?" Dulcie said. "Maybe weeks ago?"

"No. We'd see a car or two pull into the woods behind the barn, but never a whole fleet of them. Not going into the barn or coming out. Those few we saw parked back in the woods were lovers, the way young people do."

"They could have put a lot of cars back in the trees," Sage said. "That night maybe they put them in the barn to keep them from being dented and scratched with falling branches, there were trees down all over."

Kate found them there, the cats so immersed in the stories they had ignored her searching calls, ignored Ryan's calls farther up the hills. They were gathered among the boulders, and for a few moments she crouched nearby, enjoying the stories, too. But there was another event tangled in that moment, a glimpse that shocked and thrilled Kate. Watching Courtney, Kate started suddenly when she saw movement in the deep shadows of a crumbled doorway, a tall shape that disappeared at once beyond the door's darkness, a tall figure, as she had seen that night standing at the office window looking out.

Had *Scotty* been standing there listening to the cats' stories? Listening to them speak, and had slipped away when she saw him? A thrill of amazement filled Kate, a joy that brought tears—or had she not seen him at all, was it only the breeze stirring the vines that grew up the side of the house?

If Scotty knew about the cats, why hadn't he told her? She almost ran to find him. But no, it couldn't have been Scotty. Why would he not tell her? Shivering, she remained crouched in the grass not looking in that direction, pretending to have seen nothing.

It was here that Ryan found Kate and the cats. She

waited for a tale to end, then told the Molena Point cats that Clyde wanted them at home, that he felt Rick Alderson might be a danger to them—and that the ferals should stay away from him, too. She bundled up Kit and Pan, Pan shining golden against her dark hair. Kate settled Dulcie and Courtney on her shoulders, and they returned to the shelter to find Wilma.

When Wilma and the four cats had headed home in Ryan's king cab, Kate turned back to the rocky meadow. She approached the back of the mansion where she thought Scotty had stood.

She paused and stepped back.

Scotty sat on a boulder, his back to her but in plain sight, talking with Willow, the faded calico comfortable on the smooth rock next to him, one paw on Scotty's knee. Willow was saying, "Kate has known for ever so long, for many years. But how could she agree to marry you, when she thought *you* didn't know? When she would, for all your lives, have to keep the secret?"

"But—" Scotty began.

"But what?" said Willow. "*You* only found out by accident, when you were moving those boards. When we weren't careful, and you heard us talking." The matronly cat looked hard at him. She had the look of the leader she was, queen of the feral band, a cat who had reprimanded and coddled generations of kittens and perhaps a human or two. "I think," Willow said, "it's time you two had a talk." She patted Scotty's knee with a soft paw, sprang from the boulder lithe and quick, and bounded away, losing herself among the walls of the old house, leaving Scotty and Kate alone.

Scotty looked at her, and took her hand, and for some time, neither spoke. A little breeze blew the tall, wild grass against the rocks. Scotty took her in his arms. If a feral cat or two watched from among the fallen walls, neither Kate nor Scotty minded.

"So now," Scotty said, "so now that you know *my* secret—was this your secret, all along?"

"It was," she said shakily.

"And now," he said, "now that all is clear between us, will you marry me?"

She couldn't answer, she could only nod against him, and try to wipe away her tears.

25

The four cats rode crowded on Wilma's lap, spilling across the front seat as Ryan's king cab headed for the highway. Dulcie and Kit dreaming of the old tales, Courtney with lingering visions of the Netherworld. Pan stretched out between the girl cats and Ryan, and who knew what he was dreaming?

"You can take us to my house," Wilma said. "Egan's in jail, and Randall's in the hospital, there's no one to bother us." She smiled. "No reason to toss my place again, anyway. They got the book, or think they did. They know the police have it."

"Rick and Lena aren't in jail," Ryan said.

Wilma was silent.

"Lena isn't stable," Ryan said, "but she's clever. She might guess there was another volume, might wonder if that one was a substitute, if you still have the valuable copy. Who knows, at auction, what the original would have been worth? And if she knows the *whole* story, she might come after . . ." She glanced down at the tangle of cats. Dulcie and Kit stared up at her, wary and silent.

"No one knows if *she'll* break in," Ryan said "no one knows what she'll do—she knows she could never catch the feral cats. And Rick, he has a long, ugly record—while they're both still free, you're coming home with us."

"But what about your quarantine?" Kit said.

"Joe and Rock can stay in my studio, it's nice and light and there's a soft couch to share. The isolation will be over by tomorrow night, the two of them will be free. Striker and Buffin can come home, Joe and Dulcie can cuddle their kittens. Maybe, by that time, Lena and Rick will be locked up, instead of our poor animals."

With Wilma and the cats settled in, Ryan didn't go back up the hills to work. She thawed a pot of bean soup for dinner and made corn bread—while the four cats galloped upstairs to rub against the glass door of her study. And Joe Grey, inside, did the same, his nose and whiskers pressed against the cold door, as close as he could get to Dulcie and Courtney, to his calico child and his lady. Rock paced the length of the studio restlessly, more interested in getting out than in the cats' familial concerns. When Clyde got home Rock barked up a storm until Clyde put a leash and muzzle on the Weimaraner and took him for a long run.

When Lucinda and Pedric Greenlaw came down to get Kit and Pan, of course they stayed for supper, for Ryan's good comfort food and to catch up on the tangle of events. They were sitting at the kitchen table with a cup of tea as Clyde and Rock came storming in the back gate to the patio. Clyde brushed sand from the silver dog and wiped the sand from his feet. He fed Rock in the patio then took him upstairs to his prison. He sent the four cats down to the kitchen, knowing very well the two inmates didn't have rabies, but obedient to John's instructions. Pan, leaping to the table with the lady cats, had started to tell about Kate's visit to Voletta when Kit jumped in with her usual monologue. ". . . and that wasn't Egan, it was *Rick* Alderson with the long record and Voletta pretended she never heard them moving all those cars that night and didn't see lights but how could she *not*, she's a mean woman, I don't like her even if she was hurt when the window broke, I don't even like the way she smells and—"

"Slow down!" Dulcie and Pan hissed.

"And then Lena's husband Randall called Rick and said he broke out of jail and we couldn't hear all the conversation because Lena came in and we had to hang up the phone and hide and when they drove off to get him I wanted to jump in the car but they were too fast and Pan grabbed me and bit me hard and they were gone before I could leap off the roof and then we couldn't call the cops because we didn't know where they were going and . . ."

"Kit . . ." Ryan said, scooping up the tortoiseshell, snuggling Kit against her. Kit looked up at Ryan innocently, yellow eyes wide.

"They're gone now," Ryan said, holding Kit tight. "Long gone. Joe found them and he did call 911. Maybe the cops have them by now. Oh, Kit, do settle down."

Clyde was silent, taking it all in, putting the pieces together from Joe's story and Kit's. Only when Ryan put supper on the table, steaming bowls of bean soup, cooler bowls for the cats, big slices of corn bread all around, was Kit wordless, settling greedily in to her feast.

It was after supper, when they'd gathered around a warm fire, that Ryan thought again about Kate and Scotty up at the mansion—about Scotty standing in the shadows listening to the cats' ancient tales. She wondered what had happened after she left. Surely all the cats had seen him, but no one said a word, not even talkative Kit. Ryan started to say, "I wonder if —" when Kit interrupted.

"Now Scotty knows about us," she said as if she had read Ryan's thoughts, "and *Kate* knows that he knows and there won't be any secrets between them now and *I* think they'll get married."

They all looked at her. She had to tell that tale, too, about sitting among the boulders with the ferals hearing the old stories—she ran on until Dulcie hushed her. Courtney wished her daddy were there with them so he could hear all Kit had to tell—but then, maybe it was better that he didn't hear. She didn't look at her mother, she knew Dulcie didn't like her listening to tales of the Netherworld that so thrilled her. Dulcie didn't like hearing that Courtney's own pictures were there in that underground world, as Willow had told, antique paintings of a long-ago cat who looked exactly like Courtney—those visions too sharply stirred Courtney's dreams of that magical land.

When the living room fire had burned nearly to coals, the Greenlaws rose to leave, Pan happy to be going home with Kit. As much as he loved the Firettis, he hadn't meant to move in with them forever, only long enough to comfort them in their loss over Misto. But how could he tell when that was? John and Mary would grieve for Misto forever, they all would. But now, at least for a few days, the Firettis had Buffin and Striker to ease them, while Pan himself hunted with Kit and lounged in the tree house.

It wasn't long until the Damens' lights went out, until they were all asleep, Rock and Joe in the upstairs studio, Wilma tucked up in the guest room with Dulcie and Courtney. The cats slept lightly, their ears at alert. There was no attempt at a break-in with Egan in jail and with Randall under guard in a hospital bed, probably hooked up to plastic tubes and with a uniformed guard at his door. And, hopefully, Lena and Rick on their way to jail, though they had had no word from Dallas or Max Harper.

At three that afternoon, the call came. Not from Max, but from John Firetti.

Clyde was just home from work. When he answered the phone, John nearly shouted in his ear, "Negative, Clyde! The test was negative! No rabies! Joe and Rock are free, you can let them run. My God, this waiting has been hell. Shall I bring the boys and Snowball home?" he asked hesitantly.

"I'll come," Clyde said. "I'm on my way."

But the conversation, when Clyde arrived at the clinic, was not at all what he'd expected. They stood in the recovery room, Striker, freed from his cage, racing the length of the room round and round on three legs, working off an endless burst of energy—while Buffin remained curled up close to the fluffy little dog. Watching Buffin and Lolly, Clyde felt a hollowness in the pit of his stomach at separating them.

John seemed to have trouble putting his words together. This was the first time Clyde had ever seen John Firetti shy and uncertain. They were both watching Lolly and the buff kitten pressed lovingly together.

"I think our little dog is going to make it," John said. "We've done everything we can for her. It's Buffin who has kept her comfortable without heavy drugs. The minute he hops in her cage and curls up beside her she sighs, you can see her muscles ease as the pain subsides, as she relaxes against him.

"I don't know how he does it," John said. "It's a quite amazing talent, it's the kind of healing that scientists have argued about for centuries. And here it is, in this young, half-grown kitten."

Clyde moved closer to the cage, looking in at Buffin then glancing at John. "Would you like him to stay for a while longer?"

"I would indeed . . ." John began. "Until she's completely healed."

"Yes," Buffin told Clyde, his blue eyes pleading. "I want to do that. She's better but there's still some pain, she still needs comforting." The big kitten looked up intently at Clyde. "Is this what I was born for? To help other animals, to help them heal?"

"To help heal," John said, nodding. "To give solace. Everyone is born for some special reason, some special good." He sighed. "But so many never find it."

Clyde smiled. "Wilma told me once, everyone is born *about* something, some passion or talent that will guide his or her life. If he doesn't have such a longing, or never discovers and uses it, he is only a shell, empty, to be filled with something ugly instead."

Buffin looked from John to Clyde. "May I stay, then? For a little while? Maybe . . ." he said, looking up at the doctor, "maybe John and Mary need me, too?"

"We need you very much," John said, reaching into the open cage to stroke Buffin.

"And maybe they need me," Striker said, jumping up into the cage, rearing up to touch his nose to Clyde's, then placing a paw on John Firetti's shoulder. "And Pan can be home with Kit, in the tree house."

So it was that only Snowball went home to Rock and Joe, the little white cat kittenish with delight to be back with her big dog to snuggle and protect her. So it was that Wilma and Dulcie and Courtney were at home— without Courtney's brothers—and Dulcie's heart was heavy. Her two boys had left the nest, had left so much sooner than she had ever imagined.

Wilma said, "It won't be long and they'll be home again. It's no different than human children off to camp."

Dulcie wasn't sure it was the same. Buffin and Striker might be home again for a while. But this sudden parting was the first of many, of a long voyage for her children as they started out on their own. They would be back, might be in and out of the house, but they would never again be homebound kittens needing only this one shelter, needing only her and Joe, needing only this one safe place in their lives. Now, already, they were heading out into the bigger world.

Though maybe, she thought, maybe Striker with his predatory nature might decide to join her and Joe in their own pursuits, might hunger for secret investigation, hunger to stalk the bad guys who preyed on the world. That would comfort her, and would make Joe Grey more than happy.

And Courtney? Dulcie nuzzled her calico kitten. She knew where Courtney's dreams lay, where perhaps an ancient fate waited. Courtney's longings frightened Dulcie, but she knew she couldn't change them. This young lady had been born knowing images of distant times, and of times perhaps yet to come. Dulcie and Joe could only love her and keep her close when she was willing—or could only love her from a distance when she was far away.

But that day hadn't come yet. Now, Dulcie would treasure the time they had with their kittens and not dwell needlessly on the future.

26

When Ryan opened the studio door and released Joe and Rock from their glass-walled prison they burst through Clyde's study and raced down the stairs, Rock leaping over Joe, dog and cat circling through the house upsetting furniture again, then pounding into the kitchen looking pitifully up at Ryan as if they had been on starvation rations for weeks. Trying not to laugh, she gave Rock a big hug, as Joe Grey leaped to the table.

"So where's supper?" said the tomcat. There was no food in sight, nothing but scattered sections of the morning paper.

"It's a little early. It's not like you haven't been eating, I've waited on you hand and foot, treats from the deli, the works."

Joe stared at her unblinking, his yellow eyes intent,

one white paw lifted, whether in supplication or threat wasn't clear. Ryan turned away, amused, and fixed a plate for him of cold steak and sardines. She fed Rock his usual homemade vegetable and chicken stew with slices of steak on top. Joe ate standing on the open paper reading the latest details of the local car heists; eight cars had been examined and photographed for evidence and returned to their owners. All the thieves were behind bars, either in the village jail or in county lockup. All except Randall Borden, in the surgery wing of the village hospital. One woman was on her own recognizance as a person of interest. That could be Voletta. The paper was tight as hell with its information. He wasn't going to learn anything more until he hit the station.

Quickly swallowing the last sardine, he dropped from the table and took off for MPPD, not even waiting for Clyde and the kittens to get home. He was up the stairs, up on his rafter, and out through his tower racing across the rooftops.

He entered the department on the heels of tall, thin Officer Blake and Detective Juana Davis, both in uniform, holstered weapons, radios, phones, nightsticks, Tasers, the works. When Blake turned into the conference room, Joe stepped up to walk beside Juana as casually as would another officer. She looked down at him, her black eyes laughing.

They got a laugh, as well, when Joe marched into Max Harper's office beside her. "You two working the streets together?" Max said; then, "How was San Francisco?"

"Foggy," Juana said. "The three days did me good, nice hotel, breakfast in bed, shopping." She sat down at the other end of the leather couch from Detective Garza. As Joe strolled in, Dallas gave him that look that always made the tomcat uneasy. That *what are you up to?* gaze that Joe could never quite decipher, that he didn't want to decipher. The detective was dressed in a tweed sport coat and jeans. His half of the couch was scattered with files and an electronic notebook.

Ignoring the softer furniture, Joe leaped to the chief's desk and past him into the bookcase, purring at Max's familiar scent of fresh hay and clean horses, at his comfortable jeans and frontier shirt. Only a police chief with Harper's reputation, and maybe in a small town like Molena Point, could get away with the casual clothes and western boots that he preferred.

Making himself comfortable between two piles of reports, Joe scanned the papers on the chief's desk and the notes on his clipboard. A list of the stolen cars, check marks as to whether they had been recovered (including the two that had been left behind in the old barn). There were check marks indicating whether each car had yet been gone over for prints and other evidence and whether it had been returned to its owners.

Max was saying, "Barbara Conley dated Robert Teague, too. My guess is, Randall saw them together. When, maybe weeks ago, they left Teague's BMW parked on the street, Randall had the equipment to hack into the electronic security, including the garage door opener. Then, the night that Teague got back from the city, the night of the heists, Randall opened the garage door, cranked the car, and drove off neat as you please."

"With that box of porcelain in the back," Davis said. "You think Randall even knew it was there? Think he knew what was in it? Didn't Teague say the porcelain was worth over thirty thousand?" She was quiet a moment, then, "You're not looking at Teague in connection with Barbara's murder?"

Max shook his head. "We've got the gun that killed her and Prince, got the report from ballistics. It was in Randall's pocket when they brought him out of the attic. Question is, between the time he was arrested, then escaped to Barbara's house and crawled up in the attic, where did he have the gun stashed? It wasn't on him or on Egan when we hauled them out of Randall's car and locked them up."

Dallas said, "Possible he hid it in the attic after the murder, before we knew that house was connected to the car heists. The fingerprints were smeared like there'd been a cloth wrapped around it, but we got some clear ones. What makes me mad is losing the young girl who called that the BMW was there. She wasn't one of our snitches, I know their voices too well."

She was my daughter, Joe Grey thought smugly, hiding his smile.

"But the guy who called later, after Randall escaped from jail," Max said, "we know him all right. Randall didn't have a phone but he contacted Lena somehow. She's there to pick him up, then finds he's too sick to move, even with a partner to help her—sure as hell Rick was in the car, waiting. *She* calls the medics.

"Then we get our snitch's call about the Ford, driver, and a passenger. Less than three minutes we have five cars on the street and freeway, plus a couple of sheriff's units, but not a sign of them."

Dallas said, "How does the snitch do that? He had to be there in the house with them. Did he follow Lena there? Or follow Randall?" The detective shook his head. "Pretty quick moves. This stuff gives me the creeps. And," he said, "he knew who Rick Alderson was, he knew both Rick and Egan."

Dallas was silent, looking at the chief and Juana, knowing they didn't have any more answers than he did. No one glanced at the tomcat snoring on the shelf behind Max, no one had a notion that their snitch was listening right there beside them.

"*Then,*" Dallas said, "we get that call from the woman who works over at the drama center."

"I haven't heard this part," Juana said. "Only what McFarland told me on the phone, then my phone cut out. Borden escaped, to the embarrassment of Officer Bonner," she said, grinning. "You got a call on Randall, the medics haul him out of the attic, and he's in surgery for appendicitis. Very nice. He goes to emergency and the state pays for it. But what's with the woman from the drama center?"

"She was parked in that big lot behind the classrooms," Dallas said. "Came back to get a sweater from her car, saw this guy crouched down between two parked cars removing a license plate. She drew back, watched him replace it with another. Removed California plates, bolted on plates from Washington State, the front plate dented."

"So," Max said, "our men are already out on the highway while they're still in the village changing plates. The traffic was heavy, a lot of trucks—somehow the Ford slipped in between the big rigs. Even our patrol unit parked by the high school missed them, and that sure as hell made me feel lame.

"But then," Max said, "you'll like this part. Two CHP units are still patrolling up Highway One along near the Pamillon land, near Voletta Nestor's place. They knew, from Randall, that he and Lena had been staying there. They turn on up the narrow road, pull around behind that dense eucalyptus stand—and there's the Ford jammed in among the trees, almost invisible. Dented Washington plates. Lena and the driver were gone.

"Well, our guys ease around behind the barn; the barn doors are open and here comes barreling out a gray Lincoln Town Car. They radio ahead for the units on the freeway and they take off after it. That road, dirt and gravel, is rough as hell. Lincoln is scorching toward the freeway as two more of our units pull in, damn near hit the Lincoln. Our guys swerve into the dirt embankment—at the same moment, the Lincoln coughs a couple of times, bucks to a stop, and just sits there. Stalled on that narrow dirt road. Brennan said the driver looked like Egan Borden. He's cranking and grinding, but can't get a rumble out of the Lincoln. Lena's crouched down in the front seat, and now they're surrounded by cops. Officers pull them out, secure him in a squad car, lock Lena in another unit, leg irons, the works. Called a tow truck to haul the two cars in."

"How could it be Egan?" Juana said. "He's already locked . . . Oh! *Rick* Alderson!"

Max nodded. "Both Egan Borden and Rick Alderson are in the jail. No release, no bail. Lena's in the women's cell. She can go on home if she can make bail, so she can take care of her aunt—but only with the condition of home confinement for both her and Voletta."

Juana rose to make fresh coffee. "So what made the car stop?"

"The box of porcelain you were wondering about? Thieves had put it in the barn with the missing Lincoln and Mini Cooper, just dumped it on the floor like they thought it was worth nothing."

Max leaned back, smiling. "While it was in the barn a mouse or rat got into it, pulled out the stuffing and dragged that under the Lincoln. It was building a nest under the hood. I'd say a rat, the way it had chewed the car's electrical wires. So bad that, coming down that rough road, the last bit of wire broke and that's all it took, the car stopped cold and we had them."

Juana doubled over laughing. Dallas and the chief sat smiling. As the coffee started to gurgle, Joe Grey curled up tighter to hide his own grin. *That rat,* he thought, *even if she is dead now, even if she did get me and Rock locked up, she ought to get some of the credit for rounding up the last of those no-goods.*

27

Kate and Scotty's small, casual wedding was held at the Damens' house late Sunday afternoon. But hours before the ceremony, the happy couple was honored with a secret gathering behind the Pamillon mansion. The time was early dawn, the sun's first orange glow edging the eastern hills, shining into the ancient courtyard where Courtney had first met the feral band. Where Kate had discovered Scotty watching the speaking cats, listening to their tales and in that moment the restraint between the two lovers vanished.

Sunrise glowed on the big boulder where pale Willow sat, the bleached calico leader of the feral band. Feral cats and the little group of four village cats and two kittens gathered before her. Only young Buffin was absent, he would not leave his small patient even for such an important event. Ryan and Clyde, Wilma and Charlie, the Firettis, and the Greenlaws stood close behind the feline celebrants.

Kate and Scotty knelt at the foot of the boulder, so as to be face-to-face with Willow. For a long moment she looked silently at the quiet couple, gentle and thoughtful. She touched her nose to their cheeks in a simple feline benediction, a rare endearment of friendship for humans to receive from the cat community. She put a paw on Scotty's shoulder, placed her other paw on Kate's hand. The words she spoke seemed to join their two spirits more closely and to join them securely to the cat family.

May the stars shine bright above you,
May the sun warm you,
And the world hold you softly.
May your thoughts and needs be as one,
For all time,
Your joys and conquests as one,
In this world and forever.

Then all the cats gathered around closer, clowder cats and village cats leaping up on the boulder, purring and caressing and nosing at the couple, rubbing their faces against them. So the Pamillon cats celebrated their acceptance of two people they had come to love, these feral cats who, for long generations, had feared and avoided humans. Now they and their human friends shared a long moment of joyful bonding. But then as the sun rose higher and the golden light spread, the ferals slipped away. They purred a good-bye, offered a last nuzzle, and they were gone. Suddenly the glade was empty, not a clowder cat to be seen.

Kate and Scotty stood a moment, holding hands, then the little party of humans and village cats headed back across the grassy berm to the shelter, the warmth of the ceremony a part of them now as it always would be.

They were in the apartment, the four cats and two kittens on the desk, Kate and Ryan and Wilma making breakfast, when Dulcie said, "Look, where's Voletta going? How can she drive with her leg all bound up and her stitches still healing?"

In the yard below, Voletta's dirt-covered pickup was heading across the big yard for the road, Voletta's tangle of white hair blowing where the window was down. They all watched, cats and humans, until, at a turn in the road the truck disappeared, hidden by eucalyptus trees.

"She's going to bail Lena out," Joe said.

Everyone looked at him.

"I guess she made bail, after they arrested her with Rick."

"Where," Dulcie said, "would Voletta get enough money for bail?"

"Bail bondsman," Joe said. "He can meet Voletta at the station, she gives him ten percent of whatever the bail is, and Lena walks. You can bet that old woman isn't destitute."

"No, she isn't," Kate said. "When I kept raising the offer on the house and land, she didn't blink an eye. Refused it cool as you please. She's a Pamillon. As little as the family thinks of her, I'll bet there's a trust fund, a nice yearly income."

"That may be," Wilma said, "but I've seen her in the village carrying that old shopping bag, moving among the aisles of some small shop in a way that made me wonder."

"Rich people shoplift, too," Dulcie said. She and Joe had seen Voletta in the village, slipping along between the counters with her shopping bag. They had never pursued the matter, maybe because Voletta looked so alone and poor—though it was not in their predatory nature to be that forgiving.

Whatever the case, long before the volunteers had arrived at the shelter for duty, Voletta's dirt-encrusted truck came lumbering home, Lena driving. A white Prius followed them, a shiny, new model. It pulled up in front of the house, to park beside Voletta's truck. A small, bespectacled driver stepped out. He was neat as a pin, dressed in a pale gray suit and gray tie; he stood waiting for Lena and Voletta. The older woman was slow and stiff getting out of the passenger's seat and into the walker that Lena pulled out of the truck bed.

"Probation officer," Scotty said, "come to check out where she lives, to look at the living conditions."

"How do you . . .?" Kate began.

"I talked with Max, when he called about that box of porcelain. Lena will be on probation, under home confinement. He said Voletta needs someone to care for her until her leg heals."

"That means Lena can't go anywhere," Kate said.

"She can if she calls in—grocery, drugstore, essential trips. I guess, for a while, she'll be driving Voletta where she needs to go, like to the doctor. Max said he let her out, in part, to take care of the old woman." Scotty looked at Joe, wondering how much Joe Grey already knew, hanging around MPPD.

Kate said, "She was well enough to drive to the station to bail Lena out."

Scotty smiled. "Maybe she was embarrassed to ask us, or didn't want us into her business. You can tell it didn't do her any good, the way she's limping, going up the steps." Scotty sipped his coffee. "I don't think the department knows, yet, exactly how involved Lena was in the car heists. But Randall *is* her husband. Max thinks Randall may have run the show."

Kate looked again at the little, neat man entering the front door behind Voletta and Lena. "Will he be nosing around up here, too, getting in our way?"

Scotty laughed. "He's not an out-for-blood building inspector, just a county PO doing his job. I guess we'll see him around every few weeks—until we find a caretaker and move into a place of our own."

"Well, at least we have the Wilsons to stay for a couple of nights," Kate said. "They're a nice couple. I called Ryan's dad, hoping he and Lindsey would volunteer." She shook her head. "They're off on another fishing trip, up in Oregon. Took Rock with them again. I think they mean to kidnap that good dog."

"I wouldn't blame them," Scotty said.

"They were sorry to miss the wedding. They sent their love to us both. But poor Rock will miss a good party, he'll miss snatching treats. A party does set him off, trying to greet everyone at once and to work them for handouts."

Scotty put his arm around her. "Just a two-night honeymoon. But we'll take a longer trip later. The

Bahamas? Alaska? And," he said softly, "our whole life will be a honeymoon." Kate had never guessed, the years she'd known Scotty as a quiet, no-nonsense friend, a rough-hewn kind of guy, how romantic he could be.

The Damens' driveway and the street were solid with cars. Clyde's Jaguar and Ryan's red king cab were trapped in the carport, three rows of cars behind them. Joe, looking down from the roof, thought the scene resembled another gathering of stolen vehicles—except that he knew most of these cars and, cozied in among them, a number of friendly black-and-whites lent a different interpretation. As did the open front door with talk and laughter spilling out and the good smells of the buffet supper. It was the aroma of food that drew Joe from the roof through his tower and onto the rafter, down to Clyde's desk, scattering papers, and down the stairs—where Dulcie and Kit and Pan were already working the room. Striker and Courtney sat obediently on the mantel, sniffing at the good smells.

Casually Joe finessed a hand-offered snack here, then crab salad on a paper plate, a slice of chicken. A stack of small paper plates stood on the coffee table. The Greenlaws were there, and Wilma, and Max and Charlie; the four senior ladies had arrived, and a dozen officers including detectives Davis and Ray, both with cameras to take wedding pictures. John and Mary Firetti came in, Mary carrying Buffin on her shoulder.

"We won't stay too long," she told Ryan, "but Buffin's little dog is better." She watched John pick up Striker from the mantel, to have a look at his paw. Striker and Courtney had been restricted there to avoid being stepped on, and to stay away from human food. John insisted on a limited diet until, as the kittens grew older, he was sure that human treats were as agreeable to them as to the older cats.

Now, taking Striker into the guest room, John removed the weed-covered, damp wrappings from his paw, examined the stitches, applied a salve and a clean white bandage. That was better, Striker thought. His paw *had* felt damp and grainy. When they returned to the living room, everyone was headed for the patio. The minister had arrived. Tall, bent Reverend Samuel, in his dark suit, stood before the barbecue, which was covered with a fresh white sheet and pots of white daisies. The walled brick terrace was crowded with folding chairs. When John and Mary, carrying the three kittens, took seats beneath the young maple tree, immediately the kittens climbed up its branches to join Dulcie and Kit and Pan for a fine view down on the wedding party. One could hardly see Joe Grey on the roof above, peering over the edge, beneath the maple's foliage.

The music was the same collection of folk tunes that Charlie had selected for Ryan and Clyde's wedding, happy Irish music. Quietly the bride and groom took their places before the reverend. Scotty's brother-in-law, Dallas, stood next to the groom, as best man. Ryan, as matron of honor, did not lead Kate to her place but stood beside her, her pale brown shift setting off Kate's rich cream suit that shone softly with her blond hair. Scotty wore a pale tweed sport coat and light slacks. Clyde, who would give the bride away, wore tan slacks and a light linen sport coat. *Yes,* Joe thought, *Clyde* should *give the bride away when, at one time, he came near to marrying Kate himself.* And it had been the same with Charlie. Joe had been sure that she and Clyde were headed for wedding bells—until Max stepped in, until he and Charlie were suddenly head-over-heels, had set the wedding date, and before you could shake a paw, the deed was done. Joe had been sorry about that, he loved Charlie. But Max and Charlie *were* a better match—and now he was mighty glad that Clyde had waited for Ryan.

In the years Joe had known Clyde, he'd had more women than a stray tomcat. It was luck when he met Ryan Flannery, when she remodeled their house and they started dating. Clyde didn't know that Joe had used every wile he knew, to charm Ryan. Maybe Clyde and Ryan's romance would have happened without his help, maybe not.

Ryan *had* been clever enough to discover, on her own, that Joe could talk. She had been wise not to go to Clyde with her discovery, but to discuss the matter directly with Joe. None of your "*kitty, kitty, can you speak to me*" foolishness. She just came right out with it, person to person—though Joe had remained shy and startled for some time. But Ryan was a true gem. She could not only cook, she could fix the roof and the plumbing, she had rebuilt their poky cottage into a handsome home. She had built Joe's tower and, best of all, she knew how to handle Clyde.

The minister had begun his short reading. He was blessing this union that was for all time, then soon was asking Scotty if he took this woman to love, to honor and cherish. He was asking Kate the same when Joe, from up on the roof, heard the sound of metal scraping on metal, a harsh grating that came from the carport below him.

He couldn't see under the carport from this angle. Trotting across the shingles to the front of the house, he looked beneath the shelter that jutted out in front of the garage. A person with tangled white hair was at work on the far side of Ryan's red king cab, she was at the lockboxes that ran along the side of the truck. *Voletta!* What was she *doing?* He watched, unbelieving, as she worked away at one of the compartments. When he looked up for an instant, looked down the block to the side street, there was Voletta's muddy blue pickup parked along the curb.

Moving across the carport roof, where he could see her better, he watched her remove Ryan's newest, most expensive Skilsaw from a lockbox and slip it into a canvas carryall. She had all the locker doors on her side open, she had hauled out all kinds of tools, the two other carryalls were already full.

Stealthily Joe slipped into the neighbors' pepper tree. Mad as hell, he eased down above the truck, leaped to its roof just inches from Voletta's face snarling and growling and raising threatening claws. Voletta yipped and flew backward against the carport wall, her cry choking her, Joe slashing out at her, keening and yowling, his gray coat standing stiff, his yellow eyes fierce with rage. He slashed out again with a roaring scream but he daren't bloody her, he didn't want quarantine again. He struck so close that her hands flew up to protect her face; and suddenly behind Joe, Pan came racing.

The red tom sailed onto the truck growling like a

tiger. Joe could see now that Voletta had wrenched and bent most of the cabinet doors open rather than trying to unlock them. The old woman, white hair flying, slapped at them with a leather carpenter's apron, trying to drive them away—and over the roof came the other cats, all in attack mode. Kit, in the lead, crouched to leap. Behind them, the wedding party streamed out.

Joe hissed at Kit to stop her, thinking of the trouble a wound would cause. Dulcie was slashing hard at the woman, but then, thinking the same, she drew back. The three kittens crowded the roof behind them, all wanting to jump Voletta. It was then that Ryan came running, grabbed Voletta, grabbed a box of drills from her hand—it was then that Joe saw the bride and groom. They stood a little apart on the sidewalk, Scotty's arm around Kate. He was grinning, but Kate was laughing so hard, leaning against him, that Joe wondered if she could *stop* laughing. He did see, looking carefully, that the ring was on her finger, that the ceremony had not been interrupted, that among all the furor and cat screams, Kate Osborne had become, officially, Mrs. Scott Flannery. He envisioned Scotty placing the ring on her finger and kissing her while, from the carport, bloodcurdling feline challenges cut through the soft Irish music; and Joe Grey, himself, had a hard time trying not to laugh.

But stern Reverend Samuel? Tall and bent, he stood a little way from the bride and groom, solemn faced and grim. This was not how weddings were supposed to proceed. Weddings were courteous, proper affairs. Yet was there, Joe wondered, was there the shine of a smile in the reverend's dark eyes?

Joe daren't look at Clyde. He knew the look he'd see on Clyde's face, as if this were all Joe's fault. When again he looked at Ryan, she had backed away from Voletta, letting Max and Dallas handle her, but Ryan's green eyes still blazed. Joe watched Max take Voletta gently by her arm, lead her to a squad car, carefully help her in, locking her in the back. Already Juana Davis and Kathleen Ray were taking pictures of the stolen items jumbled in the bags, and of the jimmied lockers.

Why had Voletta done this? Why had she come here? Now she was in as much trouble as her thieving niece. *If Voletta wanted the expensive tools to sell, why didn't she sneak them from the truck up at the job?* Joe thought. *Too risky, with Ryan, and Scotty and the other men working there in broad daylight?*

Or did Voletta create this disturbance to purposely put an ugly note on the wedding, to turn Kate's happy day sour? A crazy, vindictive old woman with no love for Kate, who had tried hard to buy her land. No love for Kate and Scotty, who had surely reported the move-

ment of the cars that night. What could be better than an ugly burglary right in the middle of their wedding?

And what better victim to steal from than Ryan Flannery, who was tearing up the old mansion of the family estate, and who had put that big cat shelter on the open land so near to Voletta, spoiling her privacy? Voletta might have little to do with the rest of the Pamillons, Joe thought, but she still looked upon the abandoned estate as her land, as her heritage. She might easily hate anyone who moved onto it with, in her mind, no right at all to be there.

28

The wedding party resumed as congenially as if there had never been an ugly disturbance, as if Voletta's wicked destruction and the cats' screaming confrontation had never occurred—as if Ryan's beautiful king cab did not sit in the carport cruelly battered and forlorn. While the old woman was escorted to MPPD and booked by officers Wrigley and Brown, the wedding guests crowded into the Damens' big family kitchen, where the bride and groom cut the cake, exchanged bites and, laughing, smeared each other's faces with white icing. The only folks who had missed the excitement were Ryan's dad, his lovely wife, Lindsey, and Rock, who, trying to keep his balance in the small outboard, watched his companions reel in their catch, reaching a paw now and then to pat at the long string of trout already dragging beside the boat.

The half-demolished wedding cake sat on the decorated kitchen table; guests carried plates of cake and canapés to the patio where the chairs had been rearranged, small tables were unfolded, and Ryan and Charlie poured coffee. The three kittens roamed the top of the patio wall, leaping down to the white-covered barbecue to bat at the pots of daisies. The four older cats settled in friendly laps near to Max and Dallas. Max had just taken a call: Randall Borden was out of surgery, his appendix removed with no complications. He would remain in the hospital, then be sent to a recovery unit until he was well enough to be transported to county jail, facing arraignment for two counts of murder and for car theft.

The cats knew that Egan Borden would soon be arraigned for car theft and on breaking and entering, which, though it was only a misdemeanor, carried a jail sentence. His brother, Rick, would board a flight for Texas accompanied by two U.S. marshals, his hefty list of charges enough to keep him locked away for some long time. Life, it seemed to Joe Grey, had a way of rolling over just as pleasantly as he rolled over now on Ryan's lap. *Life,* the tomcat thought with uncommon sentiment, *is not only challenging, wild sometimes, it can be tender, too. Warm and tender and good.*

When Ryan looked down at him, her green eyes amused, he again had that feeling that she could almost read his thoughts. Across the table, Clyde grinned at them, and reached to take Ryan's hand—but soon Ryan picked Joe up and wandered across the patio holding him against her face, whispering to him. "They didn't see Courtney's picture, no one saw the teacup. Max and Dallas must have examined that box before Robert Teague picked it up, but maybe none of them noticed the painted cat or that she looked like Courtney."

Joe Grey smiled. It was enough that the cats' attack on Voletta Nestor had alarmed everyone present—and had more than alerted the cops, the cats were still getting thoughtful glances from them. *We don't need that,* Joe thought, *and we don't need the chief and detectives thinking about our attack or about the teacup, either. About Courtney's likeness on a centuries-old porcelain treasure. We don't need any more questions.*

Ryan returned to the table, tucked Joe back on her lap and took Clyde's hand again. As Joe watched the two of them, and watched the happy newlyweds across the patio, he was filled with pleasant thoughts—but when he glanced up at the three kittens playing, suddenly his spirit dropped like a heavy weight. Suddenly he realized how lonely life would be now, how very empty with Striker and Buffin leaving home, leaving their mother and Wilma, leaving the nest where they were born. Joe watched the two buff kittens batting at Courtney through the potted daisies, he watched them look up as if laughing, to where the Firettis sat, and the sad feeling filled him, the cold knowledge that tonight their two boy kittens would have a new home.

Buffin and Striker had made their own decision. Not Joe nor Dulcie nor Wilma meant to forbid them. The boys had bonded with the Firettis, with these two loving humans; they had bonded with the life of the hospital. They would not be going home with Dulcie and Wilma when the party was over. Even when he looked up at Courtney playing happily with her brothers, he saw a lonely sadness touch the little calico's face, he knew she'd miss Buffin and Striker, and his own dismay nearly choked him. Dulcie reached out to him from where she lay in Wilma's lap, her soft paw covered his paw and he saw the same loneliness on both Dulcie's and Wilma's faces.

But it was the kittens' right to step out into the first chapter in their new lives. He looked around the patio at the rest of the party, so happy, talking, laughing, congratulating bride and groom. He didn't want Kate and Scotty to see his sour mood, to put a painful note on the wedding—Voletta had done enough of that. Though her destructive temper tantrum had caused as much amusement as anger.

Clyde rose to change the music to the old forties hits that they all loved, and as a CD belted out Artie Shaw, half a dozen couples were soon dancing. Max danced the first dance with the bride. At the next number he handed her over to Scotty. After several dances, Kate returned to the kitchen to cut small slices of what was left of the wedding cake. She wrapped each in foil, and handed them around to all the single officers, gleaning laughs and a few startled looks. "This is not to eat, it's to sleep on. It might not be traditional," she said, "for men to get the wedding cake and dream of their brides. But who knows, stranger things have happened." That gained more laughter and rude teasing, enough to make her blush. When she gave the two female detectives their cake, Juana Davis said it was a bit late in her life, when she was already expecting a grandchild. But beautiful young Detective Ray smiled and tucked the cake safely in her pocket.

The bride and groom stayed for a half-dozen more dances before they departed. They were there for the sad moment when Mary and John Firetti cuddled the two boy kittens and headed home—the kittens receiving many kisses from Dulcie and Courtney and Wilma, and nose nudges from Kit and Joe and Pan. It wasn't as if they were leaving Molena Point, they were only a few rooftops away. Joe thought of Buffin's future, of the many animals he might help, and maybe humans, too. As for Striker, that kitten knew the number of roofs from the clinic to MPPD as well as to his father's house, and of course he knew the way back to his mother.

"I'm not leaving for good," he told Joe. "But right now Buffin needs me, and the Firettis need both of us. And," the big kitten said, "the first time *you* need a partner, I'm right there with you."

Wilma and Dulcie and Courtney left shortly afterward, Wilma carrying them both, Dulcie wiping tears with her paw. Heading home, Wilma was satisfied that the threat of housebreakers was past. Those who had wanted the Bewick book knew well enough it was locked in MPPD's evidence room—or, they *thought* the rare volume was there. They had no idea the real book was only ashes. Now the thieves' minds would be on other matters, on lawyers, on the county attorney, and on their imminent indictments.

Party-cleanup time was plate-licking time for Joe and Pan and Kit. Trash was bagged and taken out, the kitchen given a quick wipe-down, the chairs and tables folded and stacked, then Ryan collapsed on the couch. Upstairs, Snowball woke at the silence and came padding down from her retreat to be hugged and petted and loved; the little cat might not like crowds and parties but she loved the attention afterward that centered on her, alone.

Ryan went out once to look at her poor truck, but soon came in again. They had already brought the bags of tools and power tools inside. Now, Clyde held her close. "I'll take it to the shop in the morning. We'll have it right in a day or two if we can get all the parts. You'll look mighty grand, taking the Jaguar to work among lumber and torn-out walls."

"I'll look mighty grand to Lena," she said coldly. "I wonder if Max will keep Voletta in jail or set bail and send her home. They can't care for her wounds very well in a jail cell, and he did release Lena to take care of her. At least Lena's good for something. And," she said, smiling, "will Voletta get bail under the same conditions? Home confinement and a PO?"

"And a leg bracelet?" Clyde said. That set them laughing, until Snowball, with too much noise again or maybe feeling left out, went back upstairs. But soon they were all in bed, doors locked, lights out, Snowball and Joe Grey snuggled close to Ryan and Clyde.

At the Firetti cottage, Buffin cuddled with his little dog, Lolly, who felt well enough to caper around the bedroom before she settled on the bed, the three animals and Mary and John cozy together.

At the Greenlaw house, Kit and Pan started out in the big bed with Lucinda and Pedric as they usually did. Maybe later, in the small hours, they would head for the tree house and, if the moon grew brighter, maybe for a short hunt.

The clouds did clear, and up the coast where the moon gleamed over the sea, at a small, exclusive inn, embers burned in the fireplace and the terrace doors stood open. The bride and groom, having risen from bed, sat on the wide deck, a quilt wrapped around them, listening to the breakers crashing below. "It wasn't the usual wedding," Scotty said, "thanks to Voletta and to our wild little cats."

"It was the *best* wedding," Kate said. "I hope Juana and Kathleen got some pictures of the cats going after that woman and all of us crowding to help them, what a wedding album that will make."

"That, and the picture of you with icing all over your face."

"Pictures of both of us with icing," she said, leaning close against him. "This is a marriage of sharing."

And it would be. They both knew that, just as the cats knew. At Wilma's house, where Dulcie and

Wilma and Courtney were tucked up in bed, Dulcie said, "They will be happy. Happy because they love each other and because now they don't need to keep secrets, because they can talk together honestly. And because, knowing those two, they won't fight but will talk things over, come to a sensible understanding, the way two cats would do."

"Always?" said Wilma, turning to look wryly at her.

"Almost always," Dulcie said; and she smiled and rolled over and in seconds she was asleep. Wilma slept, too.

But Courtney pawed under the pillow for the tiny foil package of wedding cake that Kate had given Wilma to save for her. She lay holding it in her paws, sniffing it, at first dreaming wide-awake memories: but soon dreaming visions of times long past, pictures of lands far away, of handsome tomcats suddenly remembered. Yawning, she drifted into sleep clutching her little cake against her whiskers, wondering if the wedding cake would tell her where her future lay, tell her where this new life in which she had landed might take her. Tell her what grand dreams this new world would unfold for her.

About the Author

In addition to her popular Joe Grey mystery series for adults, for which she has received eleven national Cat Writers' Association Awards for best novel of the year, Shirley Rousseau Murphy is a noted children's book author who has received five Council of Authors and Journalists Awards. She lives in Carmel, California, where she serves as full-time household help to two demanding feline ladies.

HARPER LUXE

THE NEW LUXURY IN READING

We hope you enjoyed reading
our new, comfortable print size and found it
an experience you would like to repeat.

Well — you're in luck!

HarperLuxe offers the finest in fiction and
nonfiction books in this same larger print size and
paperback format. Light and easy to read, HarperLuxe
paperbacks are for book lovers who want to see
what they are reading without the strain.

For a full listing of titles and
new releases to come, please visit our website:

www.HarperLuxe.com